WHAT HAPPENED ON BOX HILL

Book One of the Austen University Mysteries

ELIZABETH GILLILAND

Paperback ISBN: 978-1-7377525-3-0

E-book ISBN: 978-1-7377525-2-3

Printed in the United States by Bayou Wolf Press, Mobile, Alabama

Bayou Wolf Press

Mobile, Alabama

USA

www.bayouwolfpress.com

❀ Created with Vellum

VOLUME ONE

"A WOMAN ESPECIALLY, IF SHE HAVE THE MISFORTUNE OF KNOWING
ANY THING, SHOULD CONCEAL IT AS WELL AS SHE CAN."

JANE AUSTEN, *NORTHANGER ABBEY*

PROLOGUE

After weeks of rushing, pledging, bonding, and participating in mandatory fun, at long last came the night of the Kappa Initiation. The night that everything would change, though not for the reason most of the hopeful young pledges believed. Most anticipated they would be entering a lifelong sisterhood, a bond that would only end when they went to the grave.

True enough, though for some of them, this eventuality would prove to be much sooner than for others.

But now the night was still young, bright with nubile, unwrinkled promise. For Pi Kappa Sigma president Emma Woodhouse (resplendent in a powder-blue sheath dress) the night signaled a silent victory—that somehow, against all the odds, she'd managed to keep the Kappa ship afloat. Vice-president Karoline Bingley (still deciding between the black and red cocktail dresses just arrived from Milan) was celebrating a different kind of triumph, a thorn in her side that would soon be removed. Graduate Resident Advisor Anne Elías (in the same dress she'd worn for last year's ceremony) was just relieved that all the activities would settle down so she could get back to her dissertation. Pledge Jane Fairfax (also in a repeat white dress, which she hoped no one would notice) prayed that tonight's ceremony would put an end to so much forced sisterhood, freeing up her time for other, more pleasant activities. Pledge Caty Morland (wearing an A-line dress that her parents saved up to buy and surprised her with at dinner the night before) couldn't wait to be a Kappa, and to put all the weirdness with Isabella behind her now that they were sisters.

And Pledge Isabella Thorpe (who hadn't yet changed out of her robe, not after that last text) was deciding she wouldn't go down, not without a fight.

In one of the many shared bathrooms of the Kappa house, Caty finished curling the last strand of her hair, brushing it into the style that Emma had informed her was the most flattering to her face shape. Her roommate Isabella appeared in the mirror next to her, applying a dark red shade of lipstick.

Caty had thought the whole point of the night was to look innocent and (for lack of a less creepy term) bride-like, but Isabella had chosen a different aesthetic. Her slip dress looked more like an actual slip, tight and low-cut and sheer enough that it was obvious she wasn't wearing a bra. Her makeup was thick and intense, more of a mask than the "natural, fresh" look they'd been advised to adopt for the evening. In short, it looked like Isabella was going to war, not Initiation.

It was a bold move, considering how tense everything had been in the days following the Talent Show That They Weren't Supposed to Talk About, rumors swirling throughout the house—about the intense meetings of the Kappa leadership, with Karoline Bingley screaming herself hoarse about the stain on the Kappas' reputation. The Kappa House Mother, Mrs. Norris, pushing to get rid of "trouble" before it took them all down. Anne suggesting mercy, that they all give Isabella another chance. Emma an uncharacteristically quiet wild card.

Throughout it all, Caty waited for Isabella to open up to her. But there was only nervous, cagey silence from her friend, even after it was ruled that Isabella could continue to pledge, but on probation. Caty thought this would bring an end to Isabella's odd behavior, but if anything, her moodiness increased in the days that followed.

"What?" Isabella snapped at Caty now, glaring at her roommate through her reflection.

Caty turned to her friend, waiting until at last, reluctantly, Isabella faced her. "I don't know what's going on, but I miss you. I'm worried about you. You've been acting so strange lately. I don't know if it's something to do with James, or something else that you feel like you can't tell me. But I love you, Bella. You can talk to me. I'll help you; I promise." And she embraced her, holding on until the tension in Isabella's shoulders at last melted away, and the two of them were hugging for real, for the first time in so long.

At least, this was what Caty wished she'd done later, when it was no longer an option. In the moment, all she felt was resentment, that Isabella was shutting her out yet again, trying to ruin what was no doubt going to be one of the best nights of her life.

"Nothing," she said, and walked away.

$$\pi \kappa \Sigma$$

The Kappas gathered in the ceremonial room in the basement, the pledges in their white dresses, the others in their ceremonial robes. Each held a candle, the only light in the otherwise darkened room, and as Caty looked around, she felt an overwhelming sense of awe, that this was happening to *her*.

The ceremony itself is a secret, sacred (albeit, slightly boring) thing, and some vows of sisterhood should not be broken. Suffice it to say, the girls began the night as separate pledges, from different backgrounds and families, with disparate hopes and dreams; but by the end of it, they were sisters.

As the rites reached their conclusion, Emma motioned behind her to a stack of thin jewelry boxes. "Each girl will now receive her Kappa pearls. By accepting these pearls, y'all are agreeing to join this sisterhood, and to become a Pi Kappa Sigma sister for life."

They formed a line, each girl accepting her necklace. Caty took her pearls and promptly burst into tears, which made Emma and the other older sisters laugh and circle her in an embrace.

Isabella accepted hers with almost giddy relief, her nervous energy palpable. It was clear that despite her bravado, Isabella—like everyone else—hadn't been quite certain that the vote would pass in her favor.

Afterward, there was a vegetable tray and sparkling cider in the foyer. The girls chattered, complimented each other on the dresses that were now visible without their thick ceremonial robes, and sipped at their sparkling cider as Vivaldi played over the speakers.

Then, when Mrs. Norris excused herself to go to bed, and Anne went up to her room to study (giving the girls a knowing look as she left), the undergraduates slipped out of the house, making their way to Box Hill, where the *real* afterparty would be.

Other sororities and fraternities who'd finished their ceremonies were already there, the music blaring through the thick, rolling fog, and the booze flowing freely. They weren't on school property, so no single house could get into too much trouble, and it was something of a well-known understanding in the small campus town that tonight everyone would look the other way.

The last time that Caty saw Isabella, alive, she was dancing with a group of Kappa girls, her spirits too high to be entirely produced by nature alone. "This is the best day of my life!" Isabella shouted over the beat of the music, and a chorus of resounding cheers echoed after her.

In a few hours, Isabella would be dead, but she didn't know it then. For a brief moment, she was able to forget about the father who left them without looking back, and the mother more concerned with trying to recapture her youth than helping her daughter through hers. For a brief moment, she didn't have to think about how sad she felt when boys didn't text back after they promised they would, how small she felt when she heard other girls whispering about her behind her back.

Later, Caty would think back on this moment with fondness, relieved that Isabella had found at least a small window of happiness before what happened to her. At the time, though, she felt consumed with bitterness, watching Isabella laugh and toss her head. Thinking of James sitting at home alone, brokenhearted and feeling like he wasn't enough, Caty hated the callous, cruel-hearted girl who had done this to her brother.

Determined to enjoy herself that night, Caty celebrated with other acquaintances, soon made fast friends in the giddy exhilaration of the night. At some point, Caty's crush Tilney found her in the crowd, and the two of them danced badly but enthusiastically and drank in much the same spirit until she couldn't quite believe it was already two in the morning.

It was only then that Caty realized she hadn't seen Isabella for hours—not since that earlier spotting. Some people were already calling it a night, heading to the designated drivers waiting near the bottom of the footpath, but Caty doubted Isabella would be one of them. She always saw a party through to the very end.

"She's probably just finding someone to make out with for attention," Tilney snarked at first, but when he saw that Caty was really concerned, he offered to help her look. "Have you seen Isabella?" the two of them asked as they made the rounds, and the more people who hadn't, the stranger it started to seem. A girl who was always the life of the party was nowhere to be found, and no one seemed to be able to remember having seen her slip away.

Was it foreboding that made Caty enlist some of the Theta boys, and ask them to spread out through the forest? Was it intuition that prompted her to follow the running path she'd taken with Emma a few weeks before, to search the base of the hill, just in case Isabella had somehow gotten lost?

The fog was even thicker down at ground level than it was up at the peak, and Caty soon found herself wishing she'd brought somebody else along with her. But Tilney was asking the D.D.s if they'd seen anything, and Emma was overseeing the search through the woods, and Caty was just being silly. Most mysteries had a reasonable explanation. Most missing girls eventually found their way home again, no harm done. There was nothing lurking in the fog, waiting to reach out and grasp her.

This last thought happened to be spectacularly ill-timed, as Caty stumbled over something that very much felt as though it were reaching and grasping. It was only a branch, Caty told herself as she rose, shaking, to her feet once more.

But it wasn't a branch, Caty saw with no little horror as the fog parted enough to reveal the ground beneath her. It was an arm.

And there was Isabella, lying on her back, hair matted with dark blood, eyes frozen open, with her Pi Kappa Sigma pearls scattered around her on the forest floor.

FROM THE FILES OF CATY MORLAND:

[*OFFICIAL INFORMATION FROM THE* PI KAPPA SIGMA *HANDBOOK*]

MOTTO: *QUI AUDIT ADISPISCITUR* [SHE WHO DARES, WINS]

FLOWER: HOLLYHOCK [*SYMBOLIZING AMBITION*]

CREED: [*EXCERPT*]

MY SISTER IS MY FAMILY; MY SISTER IS MY FRIEND.
MY SISTER IS MY DUTY I'LL SEE THROUGH TO THE END.
MY SISTER GIVES ME AID, A MUCH-NEEDED LIFELINE,
AND WHEN MY SISTER STUMBLES, HER TROUBLES BECOME MINE.

I

Before her body had even begun to decompose, Isabella Thorpe had been branded by the press, the public, and her peers as a slut. Had young Isabella lived to see her newfound fame, she would have been tickled pink, instead of the grayish-bluish tint of her current color palette. She might have been delighted by the sight of her photographs plastered across the media, even if her carefully applied makeup and the outfit she'd spent hours choosing proved to be ultimately less than durable. Seeing her name pop up on multiple threads and comments—some sympathetic, but others making her the punchline of a slew of wincingly morbid jokes—might have made her giggle, because the Internet was forever and she was, like, totally famous now.

Even the word "slut" itself might not have given her much pause, because wasn't she always yelling that at her sorority sisters as they laughed and danced and put on a show? It didn't mean what it used to. It was a term of endearment now, empowerment.

But not, as it turned out, when it was being whispered behind her back—or, to be more accurate, over her dead body. Not when armchair detectives were discussing, in detail, the number of people she'd hooked up with during her brief time as a freshman at Austen

University; and boys were coming out of the woodwork to testify she'd been the aggressive one, pursuing them; and the same girls who'd laughingly grinded with her only weeks before were giving "special interviews" about how out of control she'd been. Anything for those fifteen minutes of fame.

It all started out innocently enough, this frenzied piranha-feeding of Isabella's reputation. Before the school issued a formal warning to the students about commenting to the press, Isabella's roommate, Catherine Morland, was ambushed as she left the sorority house. Petite, wide-eyed Caty looked terrified in the video clip that eventually went viral, and the wolves circled in on her, expecting her to be easy prey. Indeed, when asked about her relationship to Isabella, Caty was barely able to stammer out she was her "best friend" and that "Bella" had been girlfriend to her brother James. (Both claims were later torn to shreds in online forums, in which people speculated why a girl like Isabella who had a "boyfriend" also had an active Tinder profile, and why Caty would claim to be her best friend when she appeared in hardly any of her social media.)

But the moment that pushed the video into viral fame was when one of the reporters asked Caty if she had any idea what happened to Isabella. Suddenly small, trembling Caty went still, looking straight into the camera. "Of course I do. She was murdered."

That was when the president of Pi Kappa Sigma, Emma Wood-house—tall, blonde, and with a formidable Southern-belle glare—swooped in to wrap a protective arm around Caty. "No more comment, y'all," she insisted before guiding the younger girl to the safety of her waiting Mercedes. Online, however, no one could protect Caty or Isabella from the ensuing media circus.

Perhaps in the end, even Isabella would have shied away from this kind of attention—regardless that her name briefly became the top "Isabella" in search engines in North America and trended in hashtags, too. The kind of fame she daydreamed about in her life-time came through merit or achievement: Miss Louisiana, for example, or winner of a televised singing competition, or top Pharma rep in the Southeast U.S. Division.

This kind of fame? It was not earned—it was taken, and turned against you. Voyeurs, gobbling up every gory, illicit detail, just so they could teeter to the edge of danger, then pull back at the last minute. All the while reassuring themselves they were okay, this could never happen to *them*.

Isabella could have told them differently, of course. This couldn't have happened to her, either, until it did.

FROM THE FILES OF CATY MORLAND:

[ISABELLA THORPE'S LAST INSTAGRAM POST, PUBLISHED ROUGHLY THREE AND A HALF HOURS BEFORE HER DEATH.]

POST: SECRETS, SECRETS ARE NO FUN. SECRETS, SECRETS HURT SOMEONE.

❧ 2 ❧
(MARCH - ABOUT 1 WEEK AFTER ISABELLA'S DEATH)

Caty Morland was not one of those gawking spectators who believed the unbelievable could never happen to her. She had, in fact, been planning for something like this for most of her life. Her interest in crime had developed as a young girl, when her father allowed her to stay up later than usual on Sunday evenings to watch the latest British crime show on *Masterpiece Theatre*. This had led to an interest in mystery novels from the local library—starting with Nancy Drew and evolving to Mary Higgins Clark, Agatha Christie, and eventually some of the meatier fare like Tana French and Laura Lippman. When true crime took on steam in the world of podcasts and docuseries, Caty was already primed to be its target audience, raised on a diet of death and deception.

Surrounded by murder as a constant source of entertainment, Caty perhaps cannot be faulted for anticipating it would make its presence in her day-to-day life. As such, Caty was constantly on the lookout for murderers. She would not be carrying textbooks for any affable young men with conveniently broken arms, thank you very much, nor would she dismiss the death of any heads of wealthy families without first inspecting the possibility of foul play. Caty knew, as certainly as that she was a Hufflepuff and that yellow was her favorite color, that murder would someday play a role in her life.

What she hadn't quite anticipated was just how unpleasant murder would prove to be. That seemed like something that should probably have been a given—that, as an experience, the death of a person within one's social circle at the hands of another probably wouldn't be getting a slew of positive Yelp reviews. But in her imagined reality (all right, let's call it by its name, *fantasy*) of coming face-to-face with an honest-to-goodness murder, Caty had always supposed it would happen to someone on the periphery of her acquaintance. A distant relative, preferably one with a sizable inheritance up for dispute, whose death she could investigate with detached interest.

Isabella was… Isabella was young, vibrant, alive, not someone who could fathomably be past-tense. She was, despite Internet conjecture to the contrary, Caty's best friend, even if there had been that fight and the weird distance between them that Caty had assumed they'd resolve before the end of the term. And now she was just … gone.

There was no time to process it; no time, really, to grieve. First there had been the uproar with the viral news interview, then Emma's lawyer warning Caty not to speak to any more members of the media. Then the university shut down, and a hundred or so Kappas suddenly had too much time on their hands (and *oh my God, do you think she was really murdered* and everyone talking about it as if Caty couldn't hear them, as if just a few nights ago Isabella hadn't been one of them).

And then the police arrived.

Detectives Wentworth and Lucas, to be more precise. The parish was too small to have its own homicide division, but despite being kind of low-budget, the detectives looked appropriately grim and businesslike as they asked to have a private word with Caty, three days after Isabella's death.

Their entrance turned commotion into chaos, partly because there were actual police detectives in the sorority house, investigating a potential murder; and partly because Wentworth—it was universally acknowledged—was so incredibly good-looking.

"I want to faint straight into his arms," Louisa Musgrove gushed. "Scarlett O'Hara style."

"You should choose a better role model," retorted Caty.

There would have been a time, not too long ago, when she would have been the giddiest of all at the prospect of two real-life detectives, coming to pay *her* a visit, but a lot had changed in the last week. The Caty of yesterday might have daydreamed about solving mysteries, the thrill of something dangerous touching her life. But the Caty of today had seen the true face of danger, of death, and now she couldn't stop.

(Hair matted with dark blood, eyes frozen open, Pi Kappa Sigma pearls scattered around her on the forest floor.)

Anne Elías insisted on coming with Caty to meet with the two detectives. She was the graduate-student RA for the Kappa house, and unlike the other occupants of the house, who seemed intent on ogling the true-crime show playing out in their parlor, she simply wanted to be there for Caty.

"It's my job to look after you girls," Anne said resolutely, taking her arm.

Caty heard the unspoken self-recrimination in that statement. Anne had looked even more tired and pale than usual the last few days, which was weirdly gratifying. To find someone genuinely moved by Isabella's death—not just gobbling up every piece of gossip, or producing teary eyes to garner extensions on papers—meant more than she could say.

Downstairs they found the two detectives waiting. Caty's gaze landed first on Detective Lucas, who was plain and dressed sort of like she could be a bank teller, though the intelligent look in her eyes told Caty she'd be foolish to sell her short. The other one, Wentworth, was handsome in a no-nonsense way, with his buzzed head and clean-shaven face. Something about his athletic frame and rigid posture suggested a military background.

Beside her, Anne stopped, one hand going up to her throat. "Freddy."

"Anne." Detective Wentworth's tone was polite but revealed no other emotion. Beside him, Detective Lucas gave him a wry, searching look, but said nothing.

Anne straightened, composing herself. "We can talk in the study. We should have some privacy there…"

They secured themselves from the prying eyes of the Kappas—including the House Mother, Mrs. Norris, who would have kept entering with sweet tea and cookies every five minutes if Anne hadn't finally locked the door.

"Shouldn't I have a lawyer present?" Caty spoke up. "You know, in case y'all decide to coerce me into a confession."

"Sounds like somebody watches too much TV," said Wentworth in his vaguely Cajun accent.

Caty resented the tone, like she was some dumb, hysterical kid. "Sounds like somebody doesn't watch enough."

Detective Lucas interrupted the standoff with a disarming smile. "You can certainly have legal counsel present if you'd like, but this isn't an interrogation. We just have a few questions about Isabella."

And with that, they began. The questions echoed those from when Caty had first been interviewed by the police. *Was she the one to find Isabella?* Yes. *When was the last time she'd spoken to Isabella?* In the shared bathroom at the Kappa house. Etcetera. Even if Caty hadn't been plagued with sleeplessness since the night of the party, she would have still yawned out of sheer boredom over the mundanity of it all.

At last, Detective Lucas got to the point. "You told the media that you believed Isabella was murdered. Why is that?"

"Because I do believe she was murdered," Caty returned with a defensive shrug. "Why else would I say it?"

Wentworth shrugged back at her, exaggerated. "Some people like the attention."

"If I wanted attention, I'd enter a wet t-shirt contest. Not brag about my dead best friend."

"People have done stranger things for fifteen minutes of fame."

Infuriatingly, Caty felt tears rush to her eyes. She sat in stony silence, hoping to pass it off as anger. "I don't want to be famous," she said as soon as she was able. "I never should have said anything that day."

The detectives exchanged a glance, not as subtly as they thought. "Why not?"

There it was—that surge of rage, the only thing carrying Caty through the past few days. "Because blurting it out tipped my hand, to whoever did it. Let them know I was onto them. But it won't matter, because I'm gonna find whoever killed her, if it's the last thing I do—"

Anne's warning hand on her arm was overshadowed by the sound of a key turning in the locked door, and Emma Wood-house breezing into the room. "I'm sorry, Detectives, but I'm going to have to ask you to leave." This said in a drawl that was just the right shade of charming but not provincial. "We've just received word from President de Bourgh's office that the Kappa house is shutting down until further notice. I'm afraid Miss Morland won't be able to answer any more questions until you formally summon her to the police station, with counsel present."

Realizing they were being dismissed, Detectives Lucas and Wentworth said their goodbyes and left their card with Caty, in case she "changed her mind." At the door, Wentworth paused, but didn't look back. As soon as they were gone and Anne checked that Caty was all right, she excused herself to her room.

"Was that true, about the Kappa house?" Caty asked Emma once they were alone.

"It will be as of tomorrow morning. President de Bourgh's office put out a bulletin that the Kappa house needs to be emptied by 9 a.m. Supposedly to help with the investigation, but I think it's because the parents are going BALLISTIC. I'd mock, but I'm pretty sure my own father would be calling nonstop, if he weren't on a health retreat in Sedona where they don't allow cell phones. Thank God."

The Kappa house was closing. Caty tried to find some deep well of emotion, but realized she just felt inconvenienced, that she would have to pack up her things and find a place to stay. Though it *would* be a relief to get away from the room she once shared with Isabella, now conspicuously empty.

"I guess the Allens might let me stay with them?" she mused aloud. Her parents had been calling incessantly, trying to get her to come home, but she knew their fretting would drive her crazy. And she had no idea how she was supposed to face James.

"You'll be staying with me, of course," Emma interjected. "My father's house has plenty of empty rooms, and you'll keep me from losing my mind during the break."

Caty doubted Emma's mental health was the actual source of her concern, but honestly, it was a relief that even in all the chaos of the past few days, Emma still wanted to tell her what to do.

$\pi\kappa\Sigma$

By dinner that night, Caty was installed in the Woodhouse home. "Home" was maybe something of an understatement, considering that the place was bigger than the Kappa house, and complete with a cook and household staff; but it was decorated with Emma's usual knack for bridging style with warmth, and the old Caty might have died from excitement at the size of the entertainment room.

She and Emma retired there after dinner, as Emma browsed through Netflix. "What are you in the mood to watch? Maybe something action-y?"

A sudden memory struck Caty, unbidden: That first semester at Austen University, when she'd been lonely and far from home and so homesick she thought she might just quietly drop out at the end of the semester and make the move back to Baton Rouge. Her only comfort had been sneaking to the common room to watch *The Cases of Otranto*, a true-crime-television series investigating a cluster of strange disappearances in a small town in the Midwest.

To her surprise, one night another girl joined her: Isabella, who turned out to also be a massive *Otranto* fan. For hours after the show was over, they speculated about who the killer might be. Isabella thought it was the weird coroner: "No one in his right mind would think he was pulling off that combover."

But Caty was convinced it was the father of one of the missing boys. "It's always the father in these kinds of stories," she'd said sagely, and Isabella looked duly impressed by her insight.

It was the beginning of a beautiful, macabre friendship, founded on murder. Maybe the only way it could have ended, truly, was like this.

Caty flinched from the thought. "Nothing with any death."

Emma paused, just for the briefest of moments, but otherwise gave no indication of having noticed anything amiss. Her voice came out bright and cheerful. "A romantic comedy then. My fav."

They settled in to watch something with two impossibly beautiful people facing the usual obstacles to falling in love. It was nice, and mindless, and Caty thought she was doing all right for the first time in a long time, until Emma paused the movie. "Are you okay, hon?"

"Yeah. Why?"

"You're crying."

"Am I?" Caty reached up to find her face wet with tears.

Emma put an arm around her shoulders. "It's okay to be sad about Isabella's death. You know what might help? Some guided meditation—"

"I'm not sad." Caty realized she was shaking, finding it difficult to even breathe. "I'm . . . enraged. It isn't right that this happened to her. It's not right. And they don't care. They're treating her like a joke, and whoever did it—they're just gonna get away with it."

Silence. Then Emma took her hand, squeezing it. "No, they're not. The police and TikTok may not be taking this seriously, but we will." She gave a short, determined nod. "We're going to fix this."

FROM THE FILES OF CATY MORLAND:

FROM: EWOODHOUSE@AU.EDU

SUBJECT: YOU ARE CORDIALLY INVITED...

You are Cordially Invited to a Dinner Party
Hosted by Catherine Morland and Emma Woodhouse
Friday - 7:00 (prompt, please!)
The Pi Kappa Sigma House - 1815 Greek Row
Semi-Formal Dress Required
(Please refer to the attached Pinterest link for outfit
inspiration)
RSVP by Tuesday with any dietary requirements

❦   3   ❦

I s there anything that causes a wider ripple effect than the death of the young and beautiful? Had Isabella Thorpe been old or haggard, her plummet from the top of Box Hill may have caused a mild sensation in local news, but nothing that would not have been forgotten with the next cycle of stories, the latest celebrity gossip or political scandal.

Much to the consternation of Austen University, however, their young, attractive, freshly dead co-ed was proving to be a far more durable media sensation. Due to the continued aftermath of Isabella Thorpe's death and the attention being paid to it, the school's annual Mardi Gras break (usually a Monday and Tuesday to allow students to attend celebrations around the state) was extended the full week, or pending further updates.

Most of the students, only peripherally connected to Isabella, could not help but rejoice at such a development. Many tried their best to couch their euphoria with platitudes ("such a tragedy," "bless her soul") but this did little to dampen their enthusiasm for the lengthened vacation. Trips to New Orleans were arranged. Parties were planned. Even the most studious of students, who might have otherwise used the break to catch up on schoolwork, found they were suddenly in the spirit for parades and beads and day drinking.

Those closer to the perhaps-murdered girl opted to steer clear of such festivities, some out of genuine respect to Isabella's memory, others to show their solidarity with a mourning Caty, and others to avoid any appearance of being callous. Regardless of which camp an individual fell into, it must have been a great surprise to the ten who received an invitation to the Kappa house the weekend after Isabella's so-called murder, for a dinner party to be hosted by Emma Woodhouse and Caty Morland.

The invitation was odd for any number of reasons: Because it would be held at the Kappa house, meant to be closed to any students until the university officially reopened. Because it would be co-hosted by Caty Morland, who was meant to be solving the murder of her dead best friend. And, to any who had previously been to an Emma Woodhouse dinner party, because it had not been announced months in advance, everyone's dietary preferences thoroughly vetted, and an RSVP required at least three weeks prior.

Strange, strange, and stranger still.

With abnormalities such as these, how could all ten invitees do anything but accept? Even still, most did so with wary curiosity, some with trepidation, and at least one with no little amount of nervous dread.

I DON'T KNOW WHAT YOU'RE UP TO, V.M., BUT COUNT ME IN, texted Tilney once he received his invitation, and Caty smiled to herself, pleased.

"Tilney just confirmed," Caty told Emma. "That's everyone now, right?"

"All ten," Emma agreed, giving a fretting sort of sigh as she looked over her list.

John Thorpe, George Knightley, Fo-hian Darcy, Jay Rushworth, Frank Churchill, Henry Tilney, Karoline Bingley, Jane Fairfax, Elizabeth Bennet, Marianne Dashwood. Plus Caty and herself, of course.

An odd combination of personalities, and very difficult to seat around a table, but Caty had insisted it had to be done this way. Emma was not accustomed to taking orders from anyone, but she was trying to be accommodating, because Caty was grieving. So Emma was trying, really trying, not to make this about *her*. Even though yet another scandal had happened in Kappa House under her watch, and rumors circulated that Karoline Bingley was trying to instigate a re-vote for Kappa president, bless her manipulative little heart...

But this, Emma reminded herself yet again, taking in a deep breath, was about Caty. "Are you sure you want to do this?"

Caty had seemed so sweet to her when they first met, so innocent, such a perfect antidote to all that Marla Bertram nonsense. How gratefully Emma had swept Caty up under her wing, adoring her big Bambi eyes and her endearing Dorothy-Gale naivete.

Looking at Caty now, Emma realized with a start that this previous version of Caty was nowhere to be seen in the Caty-of-now's flat, determined gaze, the hard set of her jaw. She had died, just as certainly as Isabella Thorpe, that night at Box Hill. Murdered by the very same hand.

It was probably, Emma reflected, not going to be her most pleasant dinner party. But perhaps her most scintillating, if everything went according to plan.

"I'm ready," Caty told her. "But they won't be."

$$\pi\kappa\Sigma$$

On the evening of the party, the weather proved to be exceptionally accommodating, with blustering winds and the ominous rumble of thunder in the distance. It was just the sort of ambience one might have ordered for a murder-themed dinner party, though it was one of the few aspects of the evening that Emma had not carefully cultivated. Not even a Woodhouse could control the weather, though she would gladly take credit for the atmosphere it so helpfully created.

The first to arrive was Tilney, uncharacteristically early, and bearing a bottle of rum. For someone attending a dinner party that could at best be described as "suspiciously timed," he seemed remarkably cheerful, in a way that might have even been deemed "ghoulish" in someone less charming. As it was, he gave Emma his most winsome smile as he handed over the beverage, looking over her shoulder to wink at Caty. "Ladies. I thought a dark liquor might set the tone."

Emma looked less affronted by the callous treatment of Isabella's death as some great adventure, than by the alcohol extended in her direction. "Kappa is a dry house," she reminded him.

"Emma, darling, we're breaking into Sorority Row during a university-wide shutdown to investigate our peers for murder. I think we've crossed that line."

There was little arguing with that. Tilney swept past Emma, pausing in front of Caty. He lowered his voice a little, the enjoyment in his eyes diluted for a moment by real concern. "You doing all right, Veronica Mars?"

She managed a smile. "Holding up."

He reached out, squeezing her forearm. "Go get 'em, tiger." Over his shoulder to Emma, "I'll see myself into the dining room, shall I?"

When he was gone, Emma looked to Caty with a frown. "So, Tilney. He's the one you——?"

Caty, quite unexpectedly, blushed. Even hardened murder detectives got a bit embarrassed about their crushes, it seemed. "Yeah."

"He's very . . . colorful for a Sigma Rho."

No response was forthcoming, as the next guests had arrived: Marianne Dashwood, Elizabeth Bennet, and Jane Fairfax. Strange, the three of them coming together, since Jane had received bids from both the Kappas and the Deltas, the self-professed "alternative" sorority created by Elizabeth and Marianne's sister Nora. Jane had ultimately chosen to bid Kappa, even though she seemed to spend most of her free time with the Delta girls. Which begged the question, just why had she bid with the Kappas in the first place?

Case in point, Emma had seemed perplexed when Caty insisted

that Jane's name be included on the invitation list. "Why Jane Fairfax? She's not…" But Emma stopped herself short of uttering anything that might come across as un-sisterly. " . . . very social."

"It's important," Caty replied, "trust me." And that had been that.

Now, in person, Jane Fairfax looked as perplexed as Emma as to why she had been invited, though she offered Caty a smile, along with a small rectangular Tupperware. "Rugelach. My aunt insisted I bring something along. That's the Southern way, right?"

A recent transfer from New York, Jane Fairfax was about as Southern as Rugelach, and her discomfort at being part of the Greek system in a small Louisiana school was the only thing about her that Caty had really been able to glean for certain. The girl was an enigma.

She started to reach for the Tupperware, but Emma intercepted her, wrinkling her nose a little as she inspected its contents. "How exotic. Are these homemade?"

Her overly bright tone was not as convincing as she thought it was, and Caty saw this register in Jane's eyes. Her response was a stilted, guarded, "Yes."

"Your aunt is always *so* thoughtful. Please do give her my very best. She was one of my most memorable teachers at AU." This said with a quivering lip, suggesting that Emma was only barely managing to contain her laughter.

Oh, Emma, thought Caty, wincing a little for her friend. Fortunately the moment was interrupted by Marianne Dashwood abruptly stepping forward to envelop Caty in a fierce hug. "I'm so sorry for your loss, Catherine. The Deltas stand behind you in sisterly solidarity."

The hug was uncomfortable for many reasons, not in the least because Marianne was almost a foot taller than Caty, and—as the use of Caty's full name indicated—they were at best acquaintances. Caty managed to extract herself, trying her best to meet the full intensity of Marianne's Rosetti-esque features without flinching. "Thanks, Marianne."

"The way Isabella has been treated online is a travesty," Marianne continued heatedly. "That an adult woman should be berated for her sexual activities in the 21st century shows that we're all still pawns of the patriarchy, no matter how progressive we might pretend to be."

Unbidden, a memory from a few days before returned to Caty. She had been mindlessly scrolling through an online article about Isabella and made the always-a-mistake of clicking on the comments section. While there had been many, like Marianne, who ferociously defended Isabella, Caty had not quite prepared herself for those spectators who had picked at Isabella—her looks, her sexual activity, her online profiles, it was all fair game—like wild dogs scavenging a carcass down to the bone.

Closing her eyes against the unexpected resurgence of hatefulness, Caty reopened them again a moment later to find Emma and Jane looking at her with concern. An oblivious Marianne continued on with religious fervor: "The change has to start with us. A young, vibrant woman was murdered at this school, without her consent, and the most we get is an extended Mardi Gras break? There should be protests, candlelight vigils, organized walkouts—"

"Borscht," said Lizzy Bennet out of the blue.

President and co-founder of the Delta house, Lizzy was a bit of an anomaly on Greek Row. For starters, she wasn't blonde, and her hair was neither long nor straightened. The extent of her makeup was some mascara and a little chapstick, and though she wore a dress—as any sorority girl would know to do to a semi-formal dinner party—it was a comfy dress-shirt style, and it had pockets.

At Lizzy's sudden, strange outburst, Marianne gaped at her, and the others turned to stare. Completely unperturbed, Lizzy continued, "I just wanted to make sure you aren't serving that tonight. Borscht, that is. I'm allergic to beets, and I forgot to mention that in my RSVP."

Emma blinked. "We aren't serving borscht. Or beets, for that matter."

"Color me relieved." Lizzy linked her arm through Marianne's, all but dragging her through the door. "Let's check out the appetizers. I'm starving!" They disappeared into the house, Jane slipping silently after them.

Frowning, Emma followed them with her gaze. "I have never understood that Bennet girl."

As if summoned by the insult against Elizabeth Bennet, Karoline Bingley—Kappa vice-president—tottered up the front walk on some very high heels. She carefully held down her dress to keep it from being blown upward by the wind, though the girl herself looked just as liable to be knocked over by a particularly strong gust. She was tall, lean, and angular, the sort who took it as a compliment when someone thought she might have an eating disorder.

Following a pace behind her was John Thorpe, Isabella's brother, carrying a motorcycle helmet under one arm.

Karoline squealed at the sight of Emma—as though it had been weeks, rather than days—since the last time they'd seen one another. She leaned in for an air-kiss with the blonde. "Emma, thank God you're hosting something. I was dying of boredom." Her bright green contact lenses—a stark contrast to her dark skin—cast a swift, pointed look over her shoulder at John. "We aren't here together. Obviously."

John didn't even register the insult, too busy scowling at Caty. "Well, well, well, if it isn't the tease."

If Caty had been anticipating a tearful, broken John, in mourning for Isabella, he had just made very clear she would not be getting it tonight. Still, she decided to treat him as someone whose sister had just met an untimely death, whether that affected him in any discernible way or not. "Hi, John. How are you holding up?"

"Been dating lots, if that's what you mean. Can barely fight the girls off with a stick."

Caty frowned. "I meant about Isabella."

John's scowl deepened. "If that's what I'm here for tonight, I might as well drive straight back to Baton Rouge. I already told you, I'm not getting involved with this Isabella-was-murdered nonsense." He took a step in, lowering his voice. "There were other ways to get my attention, Caty."

He was, thankfully, interrupted by the arrival of the Thetas: Rushworth, Frank Churchill, Darcy, and Knightley. The former three were dressed in nearly identical uniforms of khakis, loafers, pastel-colored dress shirts, and navy blazers—the essential (though unofficial) uniform of the rich fraternity bro.

Knightley, the graduate RA of the house, had interpreted the "semi-formal" mandate on the invitation loosely, with his jeans and scuffed sneakers, though even something about his attempt to dress down still suggested a casual prestige that John Thorpe could never replicate no matter how closely he patterned his outfit.

Seeming to recognize this, John fell into a sort of deferential silence in the face of such easy privilege.

Emma gave her first genuine smile of the night, relieved to once again be in the presence of equals. "Thanks for coming, y'all. Just straight into the dining room."

Frank, Rushworth, and Darcy passed by with little more than cursory, curious glances in Caty's direction, with Karoline trotting after their heels. "Darcy! Wait up...!"

"I need to find somewhere to put my motorcycle helmet down," John said loudly as he followed after, in the hopes that someone might overhear and be impressed. "Because I rode here. On my motorcycle..."

Only Emma, Caty, and Knightley now stood in the entryway. Knightley looked back and forth between the two girls before giving a long, resigned sigh. "For the record, I think this is a spectacularly bad idea."

His eyes began on Emma, though by the time he had concluded speaking, he was looking meaningfully at Caty.

She stared back at him a moment before her chin rose a fraction in quiet defiance.

"Duly noted," Emma said cheerfully, linking her arm through Knightley's. "Let's mingle!"

FROM THE FILES OF CATY MORLAND:

27

[TEXT EXCHANGE BETWEEN KNIGHTLEY AND EMMA, 3 HOURS BEFORE THE DINNER PARTY]

KNIGHTLEY: I HOPE YOU KNOW WHAT YOU'RE DOING.

EMMA: DON'T I ALWAYS?

KNIGHTLEY: DO YOU REALLY WANT ME TO ANSWER THAT?

❧ 4 ❧

As the first course was served (a creamy lobster bisque, homemade by Emma's very own cook) Caty let her gaze run over the assembled party. She knew she was prone to being a little over-sensitive as of late, but she didn't think it was just her imagination that the conversation seemed stilted, strained. Everyone was trying so hard to act like nothing was wrong. Like Isabella's death had been nothing but an inconvenient footnote to their Mardi Gras break.

It was only natural, she supposed, for people to want to go back to normal. Normal was comforting, normal was safe. That was why Caty knew tonight needed to happen exactly like this. Because one of these people was having to try even harder than she was to pretend that nothing had changed, that normal was still achievable, when really that possibility had disappeared the moment Isabella fell from Box Hill.

At last, Caty clinked her glass, drawing all the eyes in the room to her position at the head of the table. She cleared her throat. The game was afoot.

"As many of you may know from the interview that went viral, I believe that Isabella Thorpe's death was no accident. I've called everyone here tonight because you're in some way connected to Isabella's murder—whether as a key witness, or as the murderer himself."

"Or herself," said Marianne, ruining the suspense that Caty had been trying so carefully to curate with such a tantalizing statement. "Or *theirself*."

"Yes, thanks, Marianne. Regardless of gender, it could be any one of you here tonight. And in fact, I now know for certain that it is."

The wind outside rattled against the windowpanes, and the lights in the chandelier overhead flickered. Caty did her best not to smile in triumph. There—*there* was the ambience she'd been striving to create. How convenient for the weather to be so unexpectedly compliant.

On the other end of the table, Darcy frowned. He and Caty were not well acquainted; she really only knew him as one of the other Asians on campus, often brought up to her in conversation during bid week—*"Oh, you must know Darcy!"*—as if all the Asians had some secret club and were on a first-name basis. (No matter that Darcy was half-Chinese, while Caty was Vietnamese; or that his father's side of the family came from a long line of rich old white dudes while technically, Caty was the first person from her birth family to live in the United States. That he had been privately educated and that his aunt was the president of the university, while Caty had gone to public school and had an uncle who drove an ice-cream truck. Small, petty details.)

But even knowing him as little as she did, Caty could still imagine from the easy furrow of his features that his face was more accustomed to frowning than smiling. "This doesn't sound very safe. Assuming that Isabella was murdered and you really did figure out who the murderer is—both pretty big leaps, frankly—putting all of us into the room with that person seems like a recipe for disaster."

Clearly the boy was not a Poirot fan. Before Caty could explain to Darcy that this was how it was done, Frank Churchill spoke up. "Don't get me wrong—normally I love a murder mystery dinner party as much as any other red-blooded male." He gave Caty one of his trademark, easy, slightly-crooked-but-somehow-all-the-more-charming-for-it smiles; and even though Caty had seen him give the same smile to countless other Kappas, under the bright intensity of its direct focus she found herself melting a little, and half-wondering if maybe Frank had been secretly in love with her this whole time…? before she managed to snap herself out of it and pay attention to what he was saying. "But with an actual potential murderer on the loose, isn't this usually the point where one of us gets poisoned by the soup?"

"The soup isn't poisonous," said Emma sharply, affronted by the mere suggestion. "It's locally sourced."

Already halfway through his own bowl, with a healthy smearing around his mouth to show it, Rushworth offered his enthusiastic endorsement. "It better not be poisoned—it's delicious!"

A sliver of a moment passed in which it was possible everyone was waiting to see whether Rushworth suddenly pitched forward into the bowl. As that did not happen, everyone else began to tentatively dig into their own dishes. It was soon widely agreed that the soup was, indeed, delicious, and that it seemed unlikely to cause imminent death. Emma sighed, relaxing back against her chair.

"I doubt the murderer will strike again tonight," Caty said once dinner had resumed. "Whoever it was believes he/she/they have gotten away with it. But their cockiness will be their undoing."

John made a derisive noise. "Hogwash." With the attention of the room now upon him, he waved his spoon around to punctuate his point. "We all know Caty's desperate for attention, but it's all a bunch of hooey. Isabella wasn't murdered. She *fell*. The only reason I came tonight was to make sure this nonsense didn't get even more out of hand."

Across the table from him, Marianne visibly bristled, her voluminous red curls aquiver.

"How dare you silence a woman's truth?"

"Uh-oh. Snowflake alert." John elbowed Frank, who looked very much like he wished he'd been seated elsewhere at the table. "Someone's been brainwashed by the media."

"Of course. Any woman who has an opinion that makes men

uncomfortable must have been brainwashed. I bet that's a comforting lie to tell yourself when girls won't give you the time of day."

Marianne had managed, once again, to steer the night off course. Was she really that passionate about feminism, Caty mused, or was there a reason she was trying so hard to draw attention away from Isabella's murder?

It was time to get everything back on track. Caty cleared her throat again, louder than necessary, drawing it out until it bordered on uncomfortable, until she was certain she had made her point. With the attention of the room reclaimed, she continued.

"You're probably wondering why each of you was called here tonight. I'm happy to explain. The best mysteries are the democratic ones, where everyone gets to have the same information as the detective, so they can all draw their own conclusions."

Knightley tilted his head a little. "So you're a detective now?"

Caty ignored him, starting with the guest seated to her left. "Henry Tilney. Sophomore in Sigma Rho. You weren't well-acquainted with Isabella, but you did know her, and found her annoying."

Tilney looked positively tickled by the entire proceeding, and he nodded along enthusiastically. "I did."

"You also know more about crime than anyone else at this table, excepting yours truly. Is it possible that you decided to see if you could concoct the perfect murder and get away with it? And why not start with Isabella, only peripherally tied to you, not well-liked or well-connected enough to cause too much of a fuss?"

"It sounds like something I might do. If I were a murderer, that is."

Caty didn't know whether she was fighting a scowl or a smile; he really wasn't taking this seriously at all. Rather than encourage Tilney with more attention, she moved next to Jane Fairfax, who winced, as if she'd hoped Caty might just skip right over her. "Jane Fairfax. A junior in Pi Kappa Sigma, and a recent transfer to Austen University. You didn't know Isabella well, but she thought you were exciting and glamorous, because you've lived in New York City and Europe."

Jane looked taken aback by this. "She did?"

"Is it possible you confided something in Isabella—something about your mysterious past, that you regretted afterward? Isabella was notoriously loose-lipped, after all, and you're just as infamously secretive. What is it that Jane Fairfax has to hide?"

Jane gave no reply, so Caty moved on to Lizzy Bennet, who was trying to look very solemn and serious about the entire thing, though her bright eyes sparkled with amusement. "Elizabeth Bennet. President of Delta Lambda Epsilon. Known enemy of the Pi Kappa Sigmas."

"Enemy's a *little* strong. I don't exactly lose sleep over you people."

"You should," Karoline retorted from across the table, but she obediently closed her mouth after a warning look from Caty.

Caty redirected her focus back to Lizzy. "You and Karoline have had more than one public altercation about the Kappas and the Deltas, and it's well-known that you have a tumultuous history. Might you have decided to exact your revenge on the Kappas by shoving one of their recent pledges off Box Hill?"

"Seems like a stretch," Lizzy returned, though she no longer looked quite so amused.

"Marianne Dashwood," Caty continued down the row. "Treasurer of Delta Lambda Epsilon. A passionate defender of women's rights, as we've all witnessed here tonight. Could you have taken umbrage with Isabella's antiquated, attention-seeking behavior with boys and decided to make an example of her?"

Marianne looked positively outraged at the accusation. "I would *never* contribute to the systemic problem of violence against women—"

Caty moved on before she could get herself too worked up. "Emma Woodhouse, president of Pi Kappa Sigma."

Emma smiled back at her, the only person at the table who didn't look unduly nervous, irritated, or amused by the proceedings —until Caty continued on: "After the scandal that happened last semester with Marla Bertram, the pressure was on to get the Kappas back on track. Did Isabella ruin those plans, by proving to be more of a handful than you'd anticipated?"

Emma's jaw dropped. "I'm a suspect? I helped you plan a three-course meal. With hors d'oeuvres."

Caty offered a guilty smile. "And I really, really appreciate it. Isn't the soup delicious, everyone?"

After it was yet again agreed upon that the bisque was exceptional, Caty let her gaze flicker briefly to Knightley, directly across the table from her, before moving on to Karoline, seated to his left. "Karoline Bingley, vice-president of Pi Kappa Sigma, and one of its most fanatic supporters."

"Thank you." Karoline had somehow interpreted this as a compliment.

"You have a well-documented obsession with keeping the Kappas untainted. So did it push you over the edge when Isabella was voted into the sorority after that fiasco at the talent show— enough that you decided to push Isabella over the edge, too?"

Karoline just frowned at this, though Emma—perhaps a little salty over being tricked into believing she was a hostess instead of a suspect—spoke up in her defense. "Karoline doesn't even do her own homework—do you really think she would commit her own homicide?"

"Not likely," agreed Karoline.

Caty moved on to John. "John Thorpe, Isabella's brother. Also not a fan of Isabella's talent show performance, to put it mildly."

John snorted. "What God-fearing man wants to watch his sister slut it up onstage for a bunch of horny frat bros?"

"Was it just too much of an insult to your family's reputation, John? Did you need to kill Isabella to restore the Thorpe honor?"

He rolled his eyes. "How stupid do you think I am?"

"I very much doubt you want me to answer that, John." Caty moved on before John could fully process what she'd said, looking to Frank, Darcy, and Rushworth. "Frank Churchill, Fo-Hian Darcy, and Jay Rushworth. All upperclassmen in Theta house. All from prominent Southern families."

The three exchanged confused glances. "How does this connect to Isabella Thorpe, exactly?" asked Darcy.

"Because you were all on Isabella's Hit-It List." Caty tried to maintain the right level of gravity necessary for a murder investigation, but found it difficult to stave off the blush that threatened to overtake her features.

A moment of silence followed, which Frank was the one to break. "I'm sorry—Hit-It List?"

As if it were all very commonplace, Caty explained the tipsy night where she and Isabella had gone through the online roster of Theta upperclassmen, deciding who was most (and she was strictly sticking to the terminology used on the evening in question) bangable. Isabella had decided that her top three were Frank, Darcy, and Rushworth, because they were all three (quote) hot and super loaded and from old-school Southern families (close quote).

Not making eye contact with any of the boys in question, Caty concluded with a mumbled, "Louisa Musgrove can verify the conversation." She reconsidered, remembering how drunk Louisa had been that night. "I think."

Frank, for one, seemed pleased by the distinction. "I'm flattered. But what does 'old-school Southern' mean?"

Grateful for the distraction, Caty latched on to the question. "She didn't really say, but presumably, prestigious, having a long, illustrious history. That narrows it down to the three of you—who, I think you'll have to agree, all have a distinguished Southern pedigree."

"On my mother's side, sure. But my father's family is from Detroit," Frank pointed out.

Rushworth blinked at him. "I thought your family was British. You know, Winston Churchill. Your grandpa?"

Frank sighed ruefully, reaching behind Darcy to pat Rushworth's shoulder. "I think someone's been messing with you, Rush. And anyway, that's my mother's family—Churchill. My father's family are Westons."

Not a dog to let go of a bone, apparently, Rushworth persisted. "But your last name is Churchill."

Now the usually unflappable Frank looked a little discomfited. "Well, I was adopted by my mother's family—her aunt, actually. It's a long story."

He looked like he didn't especially want to get into it, but Caty, for one, was intrigued. She hadn't realized that Frank was adopted, too.

Across the table, Jane spoke up suddenly, uncharacteristically drawing the attention of the room to herself. "Why would being on Isabella's list make them murder suspects?"

"Maybe a romantic encounter went wrong that night on Box Hill. Isabella could be a little…aggressive, and not everyone appreciated it." It was a flimsy theory, at best, but Caty didn't want to have any loose ends, and anyway, Emma had insisted on an even number of place settings.

Outside the wind howled by, once again rattling the windows. Caty took the opportunity to lock Knightley in her gaze. "And last but not least, Knightley. The Theta graduate RA, meant to make sure all the undergrads are following the rules. But who ensures that *you're* following the rules, Knightley?"

Knightley looked outwardly exasperated, though Caty thought she detected something else—something *panicked*—in his gaze. "Look, this has been a creative exercise in dinner theatre, but as the legally responsible adult in the room, I'm going to have to put my foot down. We're not supposed to be in this building, we're not supposed to be drinking—" He motioned to Tilney's rum on the table, "—and we certainly shouldn't be accusing each other of murder." He started to rise to his feet, the legs of his chair scraping against the floor. "I think it's time we—"

All at once an eerie howl tore through the night air. The group collectively froze, taking a moment to recognize the sound: tornado sirens.

For a moment, they all stared at each other in stunned silence. Then Caty met Knightley's gaze. "I don't think any of us is leaving anytime soon," she said, not bothering to hide her triumphant smile.

. . .

FROM THE FILES OF CATY MORLAND:

[TEXT RETRIEVED FROM CATY MORLAND'S CELL PHONE]

EMERGENCY ALERT: TORNADO WARNING IN THIS AREA UNTIL 9:45 PM CST. TAKE SHELTER NOW. CHECK LOCAL MEDIA. - NWS

P hones around the table began lighting up and buzzing as the emergency alert went out, signifying the impending threat. Knightley sprang into action, herding everyone toward the hallway. "Come on. We need to get away from the windows."

"I'll just cover everyone's soup…" Emma tried, letting out a squeal of protest as she was dragged from the room.

As the group huddled in the hallway, everyone scrolled for as much information as they could find on the storm. "A tornado watch is in place for the parish for the next hour," Darcy informed the group, and Lizzy added, "There was one spotted just outside St. Francisville."

Caty looked to Knightley, raising one eyebrow, a challenge. "I guess, as the responsible adult in the room, it would be pretty irresponsible to let us risk driving home in that weather. Wouldn't it, Knightley?"

"I drove my motorcycle," John said, rather un-helpfully, then checked to see if anyone looked impressed.

A long moment passed, in which the signs of an internal war raged its way across Knightley's face. Nobody much liked not getting their own way, Caty mused, but Knightley was one step worse—he was *unaccustomed* to it.

"Fine," he said at last. "But as soon as the weather clears, we leave. And we won't be discussing murder."

"Are you trying to police my right to speak?" Caty asked, watching from the corner of her eye as Marianne perked up, the gauntlet effectively thrown.

Knightley rolled his eyes. "I'm not policing anything. This is absurd, and deeply irresponsible—surely I'm not the only one who sees that."

As the other Thetas exchanged glances, Caty quickly realized her error. If Knightley refused to comply, the others would likely fall in line. The rich backing the rich. Trying to bully Knightley into anything clearly wasn't the right approach.

"It's just, we're all here anyway. We have nothing better to do. And we still have Emma's amazing food to look forward to."

Caty cast a beseeching gaze to Emma, who seemed still not entirely ready to forgive not being told she was a suspect, though the praise of the food she'd so carefully instructed Rita to prepare seemed to mollify her a little.

"It seems pointless to let the dinner go to waste," Emma said at last. She met Knightley's gaze. "It's just a conversation. If it's really so far-fetched, what can it hurt?"

Tilney took the opportunity to insert himself into the discussion. "I, for one, was really looking forward to some murder talk."

In the distance, the whir of the tornado sirens faded, leaving only the ominous howl of the wind outside. Knightley scoffed a little to himself, as if he couldn't believe what he was agreeing to. "One hour. We eat, we talk, we keep things civil."

Okay, Dad, Caty thought to herself, but decided she didn't want to push her look. "Great! Back to the dining room, everyone. Who else can't wait to finish their bisque…?"

$$\pi \kappa \Sigma$$

39

Once they were all safely installed back in their seats, Caty once again called the group to attention. "As many of you know, I've spent the week since Isabella's death interviewing most everyone in this room, as well as others connected to Isabella, to put together the most likely scenario of why she was killed. For the sake of full disclosure, I also have one further piece of compelling evidence that I would like to show everyone in the room."

From her messenger bag, she drew another sheet of paper, crisp and terribly official-looking. Across the top, the words POLICE DEPARTMENT were inscribed in dark, serious letters, and underneath was listed the following:

1 LAPTOP
   1 BACKPACK
   1 DAY PLANNER
   1 iPAD
   MAIL – INCLUDING 1 PHONE BILL
   PRESCRIPTION STRENGTH MEDICATIONS – BIRTH CONTROL, ACNE CREAM, AND ALZAPRONE

Tilney helpfully read the list aloud to the table, before looking to Caty with open admiration. "Is this the list of items taken for search by the police department from Isabella's room? How did you get this?"

Caty tried not to preen too much at the praise. "It's public record." This, as though she were in the habit of applying for official police documents, and hadn't just read the tip online in one of her true-crime forums. "Feel free to pass it around. Does anything of interest stand out to anyone?"

"I thought you were supposed to be the detective," Karoline grumbled as she obligingly handed the paper on. Seeing she'd garnered some attention with this statement, and a raised eyebrow from Caty, Karoline shrugged. "What? I didn't come to a party to *think*."

"Where do you go to think, Karoline?" asked Lizzy, and without waiting for the other girl to reply—or to register the offense—she changed the subject, looking to Caty. "The thing that sticks out the most is the Alzaprone. What is that?"

"Poison? A rare, exotic opiod?" Tilney sounded entirely too excited by the prospect.

From the Files of Caty Morland:
[*Retrieved from WebDr.*]
ALZAPRONE - A sedative that treats anxiety and panic disorder.

Side effects: Can cause headaches, low blood pressure, constipation, lethargy, and nausea.

WARNING: May be habit forming. Take only under observation from a licensed medical professional. Combining with alcohol or other mood-altering substances can lead to lowered heart rate, slowed breathing, and possible death. Please consult a doctor if pregnant.

"Nothing that exciting. Just anxiety medication." Caty, too, had had some brief excitement at the unfamiliar medication name, until she realized what it was for. It was surprising to learn that Isabella had been taking anxiety medication, she supposed, but she didn't know how that could lead to her murder. More likely, knowing her friend's personality, was that Isabella might kill somebody to keep them from revealing she used prescription-strength acne cream. "Nothing worth killing for."

"Nothing on this list is worth killing for," Frank agreed, then seemed to second-guess himself, looking to Caty for confirmation. "Right?"

"So it seems," Caty agreed. "But it did make me think of another item that Isabella was rumored to have had in her possession—an item that, I believe, could have been incendiary enough to lead to her untimely death."

Caty held her breath, waiting. She'd practiced the words a dozen times in the mirror, but she hadn't been able to rehearse the response she would get. It did not disappoint. Most of the occupants of the table looked confused—the exceptions being Tilney, who looked intrigued, and Knightley, who looked annoyed.

Tilney raised an eyebrow. "You don't mean…?"

"You can't be serious," was Knightley's related, if less enthusiastic, response.

"Marla Bertram's diary," Caty pronounced, watching the ripple effect across the room at the mention of the erstwhile Kappa sister's name. "I thought it was unrelated. I thought it was a red herring. But now I know, with certainty, that it was the key to everything all along."

❧ 6 ❧

(JANUARY - ABOUT TWO MONTHS
EARLIER)

The first time Caty heard any mention of Marla Bertram or her diary was at a breakfast with Mrs. Allen, a close family friend. It was a Saturday morning, and Caty was in the thick of Rush Week. The week leading up to the spring semester was Rush at Austen University, which meant all the sorority hopefuls had to visit every sorority house affiliated with the campus to be eligible to receive a bid. Since there were eleven houses in total, this was no task for the faint of heart. All week long, Caty had been schmoozing, socializing, and networking—a trial by fire for a natural introvert.

Tonight would be yet another party hosted by the Kappas and the Thetas, but Caty half-wished she could spend the evening in pajamas instead of heels and a cocktail dress, listening to her favorite true crime podcast: *The Mysteries of Udolpho*, hosted by A.W. Radcliffe, which investigated the historical records of a Victorian madhouse in the suburbs of London.

But instead of hibernating the day away, Caty was here, exchanging small talk with Mrs. Allen. She owed a lot to the Allen family—and, as her brother James drilled into her before she left for school, undergrads never, *ever* turned down the opportunity for free food.

They met up at the Crescent, a thriving coffee shop just off campus. Mrs. Allen had offered to take Caty to an actual restaurant, but Caty liked the shabby-casual vibe of the café, which made her feel like she was a real-life college student. Which, technically, she was, but it made her *feel* that way. Plus the place had the best scones in town, and Caty had been into the British aesthetic ever since she'd gotten into the *Udolpho* podcast.

Mrs. Allen was already waiting for her at one of the back tables, blinking through owlish reading glasses at her iPad and every so often giving it intermittent shakes and pokes. She was one of those people who might cause some surprise upon learning she was a Very Important Person. She was not particularly beautiful, intelligent, or accomplished, and had an air of speaking which always made her sound much younger and vaguely confused, with every sentence ending as though in a question. Though always well-dressed, accessorized, and with the latest technological innovation on-hand, she usually reverted to talking about one of three subjects: her clothes, her dog Princess, and tennis, and upon each subject she had nothing new or interesting to say.

Nonetheless, she was kind, generous when it struck her to be so, and in the small college town of Highbury, a very important person indeed.

Upon seeing Caty, she did not utter a greeting, just held out her iPad. "What happened to my email . . .?"

Caty was able to resolve the problem quickly, then sat in patient silence while Mrs. Allen scrolled through her new messages, looking up every so often to inform her of the latest news from people she had never heard of before.

This regalement, fortunately, lasted for only a few minutes before Mrs. Allen finally put the tablet away. "Good morning, dear. I've already ordered us some sweet tea, but feel free to get anything you like?"

Caty grimaced. She didn't like sweet tea, and had told Mrs. Allen this many times, though the older woman always forgot.

Normally she didn't say anything, just let the drink sit untouched on the table, but today she'd already resolved on something else. "Actually, I was hoping to try some Earl Grey."

Earl Grey and scones for breakfast sounded like the height of elegance. It was the tea that A.W. Radcliffe often mentioned drinking in *Udolpho*, and Caty had gone back and forth about spending her small grocery allotment on buying a box, but she thought it might be better to test it out first.

"Of course, honey. I'll just call over a waitress?"

In all the times Caty had spent at the Crescent, she had never once seen wait staff; people were meant to order their food and drinks at the counter. Just as she was about to explain this to Mrs. Allen, however, a girl appeared at their table, breathless at the thrill of being summoned.

"Did you need something, Mrs. Allen?"

"We were hoping to change one of those iced teas to—?" She looked to Caty.

"Earl Grey."

The waitress, whose nametag read 'Lucy,' nodded eagerly. "Of course. I'll get those out to you right away."

Mrs. Allen again looked to Caty, uncertain. "And maybe we should order some breakfast, too? Oh dear." She squinted as she struggled to read the items on the board. "Hmm . . . oh my . . . there are just so many options? And everything looks so good?"

This hemming and hawing went back and forth for another few minutes, even after Lucy fetched a small handheld menu that Mrs. Allen could peruse. "There are just so many options . . .?" she said for roughly the fifth time in a matter of minutes. Rather than losing her temper, though, Lucy the waitress seemed elated by the prospect of being of service to Mrs. Allen. She returned to the kitchen after promising to personally put together a sampler plate of all the best breakfast offerings so the older woman wouldn't have to make any taxing decisions.

It was all a bit ridiculous, Caty thought. But then, she supposed, there had to be a few perks to being wife of the vice-president of the university.

"What a morning." Mrs. Allen sounded as flummoxed as if she'd spent the day studying for exams instead of checking her email and ordering breakfast. "How was your break, honey? And all your lovely family? We were so sorry we didn't get a chance to come down to see them."

The Allens often traveled to visit Mrs. Allen's sister in Baton Rouge, where for decades now they had been regular patrons at Caty's parents' restaurant whenever they were in town. It was partly from the Allens' encouragement that Caty had even thought to apply to AU, and knowing they'd be there to help keep an eye on her helped persuade her parents to let her go.

"Everyone's good, Mrs. Allen. Mom and Dad said to tell you hello."

"Hello to them, too!" Mrs. Allen waited, as if she thought Caty might extend the courtesy that very moment.

Luckily, Lucy returned with their drinks and food within moments, interrupting what elsewise promised to be an awkward lull. "Please let me know if there's *anything* else you need, Mrs. Allen. And may I say on behalf of the student body, how lucky we are to have you and your husband."

Caty choked on her Earl Grey, and not just because it was stronger than any tea she'd ever tried before.

But Mrs. Allen just smiled benignly, as though used to hearing this sort of thing—and doubtless she was. "What a sweet thing to say?" she returned, and after a moment Lucy understood no further comment was forthcoming and retreated behind the counter.

"This all looks so nice?" A sudden thought seemed to strike Mrs. Allen. "Can you help me take one of those food pictures to post on the web?"

She began shuffling through her bag for her iPad, as Caty once again clenched her jaw. Already she envisioned another fifteen minutes of trying to get just the *right* shot, and at least another five trying to explain to Mrs. Allen how to upload it.

By some happy miracle, they were interrupted by a cheerful, booming voice. "Sheila!"

Mrs. Allen looked up, her mouth an O of surprise. "Dolly Jennings, how nice to see you?"

A big, broad-shouldered woman made her way to the table, oblivious to the stares she drew from both her loud voice and equally loud outfit. She wore a sort of Mumu-dress that was watermelon green, a pair of bright pink crocs, and a matching bright pink purse that looked stuffed to bursting. On her way over to the table, she knocked over not one but three sugar dispensers. Still, her smile was genuine as she took in both Mrs. Allen and Caty—and as she drew closer, Caty saw with some surprise that her bag was a Birkin.

"It's been how many months now—four or five? You and Phil must have been positively reclusive this holiday season, my word." Before Mrs. Allen could think to answer, the woman rounded on Caty, appraising her. "And what a pretty little thing you are! That darling long hair and those dark eyes. I bet you have to beat the boys off with a stick."

There had been no beating of any boys with sticks (that would require actual boys, who had to show actual interest), but Caty didn't have to do much more than force a smile because Mrs. Jennings was already moving on.

"I've been running wild this last week. It's Rush, you know—so many things to do! Activities every day and whatnot. I don't know if you've heard, but I'm a House Mother now." Mrs. Allen started to respond, but Mrs. Jennings barreled on, "I know! At my age. I thought I'd retired from all that nonsense a long time ago. But these poor distant cousins of mine came to me and said they were making a new house, they heard about my Panhellenic connections and could I help them, and one thing led to another and what do you know but I'm *sponsoring* them so they can have their own little house. An 'alternative sorority' they call it—isn't that funny? We all think we're so alternative in college, don't we?"

She laughed to tears at her own observance, wiping at her eyes, before launching back into conversation. To Caty: "And I suppose you're pledging somewhere, young lady? But of course you are! It would be a waste otherwise, such a pretty little dear. Anyway, you've probably made up your mind already, but don't count out my girls quite yet—the Deltas? Oh, well, you know they're terribly poor, but such smart girls. I don't know half of what they're saying most of the time, such big words! And pretty, too, lucky for them, but bless their hearts, so *poor*. I stopped in last night for Rush and saw they only had some chips out, and I said to myself, Dolly, you must buy them some cheesecake. So I went down to the Costco and found the nice kind—you know, with all the different flavors to sample, the chocolate and raspberry and whatnot—and I bought ten. I just knew that would make all the difference. Did you have any of the cheesecake?"

Before Caty had the chance to respond, Mrs. Jennings was off again. "Well, they won't be winning any popularity contests, poor dears, but at least I don't have to deal with Barbara Norris's group. Can you even *imagine*? Those Kappas, supposed to be so prim and perfect, but you know what happened to that poor girl—"

"Dolly?!" Mrs. Allen jerked her head toward Caty, who held her tea at her lips, waiting with bated breath.

Mrs. Jennings's eyes widened. She mouthed an "oh" and winked at Mrs. Allen before mimicking turning a key and locking it over her lips. "Right. Yes. Well. Nothing very interesting there, I'm afraid. Old news, old news."

She cast perhaps the most unsubtle side-eye at Caty of all time to ascertain if this transparent subterfuge had worked. (It had not.) "Well, I should get going. So much to do today. We must brunch together soon, Sheila!" And with that, she was off, her crocs squelching across the floor as she departed.

Caty stayed still, hoping through sheer mental willpower she could convince Mrs. Allen to reveal more information. What Kappa, and why was she such a "poor girl"?

But after a long moment of silence, all Mrs. Allen said was, "I wonder if Princess needs a vest. It can get brisk at night, you know, and she's just had her hair cut?"

So Caty sighed, biting into a cream-slathered bite of scone. But the mystery of the Kappa girl chafed her mind through the rest of breakfast, and later as she walked back to her dorm. This seemed like the kind of thing A.W. Radcliffe might research, if she were here. It felt like a pity to just ignore it, as Mrs. Allen clearly wished she would.

And just like that, suddenly the Kappa party that night seemed infinitely more promising.

FROM THE FILES OF CATY MORLAND:

INTERVIEWEE: SHEILA ALLEN (WIFE OF AUSTEN UNIVERSITY VICE-PRESIDENT)

[EXCERPT FROM TRANSCRIPT OF INTERVIEW]

MRS. ALLEN: PHIL SAYS I'M NOT TO SPEAK TO ANYONE? EXCEPT FOR THE POLICE? I'M SORRY, HONEY, BUT I HAVE TO PUT MY FOOT DOWN THIS TIME . . . ?

INTERVIEWEE: DOLLY JENNINGS (HOUSE MOTHER TO DELTA LAMBDA EPSILON)

MRS. JENNINGS: OH, WELL, IT'S ALL VERY SCANDALOUS. VERY SCANDALOUS. I DON'T KNOW QUITE WHAT HAPPENED, MIND YOU —IT WAS ALL HEARD FROM A FRIEND OF A FRIEND SORT OF THING, YOU KNOW WHAT I MEAN, BUT I DO KNOW THERE WERE DRUGS INVOLVED, AND I'M PRETTY SURE PROSTITUTION WAS A PART OF IT. OR MAYBE IT WAS HUMAN TRAFFICKING? OR ARE THOSE THE SAME THING? ANYWAY, FROM WHAT I UNDERSTAND IT STARTED WITH DRUGS AND BY THE END THERE WAS SOME KIND OF SEX RING AND WOMEN WERE PULLING THEIR DAUGHTERS OUT OF PI KAPPA SIGMA LIKE IT WAS THE SALES BIN AT NORDSTROM'S ON BLACK FRIDAY. IF IT HADN'T BEEN FOR EMMA WOODHOUSE, THAT WOULD HAVE BEEN THE END OF IT THEN AND THERE, BUT SHE HELD THAT HOUSE TOGETHER THROUGH SHEER DETERMINATION. THAT IS, UNTIL ALL THIS BUSINESS WITH ISABELLA THORPE. NO ONE COULD SAVE THEM FROM THAT, NOT EVEN A WOODHOUSE . . .

7

Before Isabella Thorpe had become known as the dead Kappa and the centerpiece of Caty's murder-mystery dinner party, she had been Caty's best friend, roommate . . . and a terribly slow dresser. The night of the Kappa/Theta party, she tried on every single outfit in her closet at least twice, seeming anxious about looking just right—which was odd, as she'd spent the entire day telling Caty she didn't know why she was bothering to go, since she'd already "crushed it" during her interviews with all the houses, and none of the boys could even hold a candle to James.

"What do you think of this one?" Isabella asked Caty as she examined herself in the full-length mirror.

"You already showed me that one."

"Yeah, but not with these shoes."

Caty's irritation must have shown on her face, because Isabella turned, all contrition. "I know, I'm being so extra right now. But it's not the same for me as it is for you. You know you'll get at least a few bids because ..." She motioned in Caty's direction. "You know."

Caty did not know. "What?"

Isabella huffed a little, as if put out to have to spell out what was obvious. "Most of the sororities need more diversity, so I'm sure you'll get lots of bids."

It sounded like a compliment, like Isabella genuinely thought her Vietnamese heritage was a lucky break, though Caty didn't get how being chosen for her ethnicity was a good thing.

"Plus you're super cute and nice, and they'd be lucky to have you." Isabella pouted at her. "Please don't be annoyed with me, Caty. I just don't want to be the frumpy bestie who holds you back."

So that was what was at the root of all of this. That was just like Isabella, to worry about everyone before herself. Caty ventured a smile. "It's all right. That dress is really pretty."

"It is, right?" Isabella examined herself, nodding. "I'll go with this one."

That decided, Caty rose to leave, when Isabella halted, glancing back at her closet. "I have a pair of white shoes. Don't you think the white would be better . . . ?"

Deciding a trip to the bathroom would be a better option than homicide, Caty escaped from the room, chatting with a few girls in the hall about their excitement for this house or that. By the time she returned, Isabella had put on a new outfit, as well as a repentant smile. "Don't be mad, Caty-cutie. You're still my best bestie, right?"

Caty hurried to reassure her that of course she was—as if a little annoyance over being late to a party could ever change that!—but before she could quite finish the sentiment, Isabella interrupted her. "By way of penance, I have something that I think will make the party even more fun. A little pregaming." She produced a silver flask. "You want?"

"I thought we weren't allowed to drink at these events."

"That's why we're drinking before. Hence the *pre*?"

Caty had never been much of a partier before coming to college. She and her high school friends usually just watched TV together, and getting dressed up for an event meant they were going to a convention. Her kneejerk reaction was to decline; but then, weren't her parents always encouraging her to get out there and enjoy the college experience . . . ?

πκΣ

Caty understood now why sororities and fraternities were traditionally known for drinking. Socializing was *so* much nicer after a few sips of whatever foul-tasting thing Isabella had in her flask. She couldn't imagine how much more fun it would be if everyone was drinking. Caty knew she was killing it, too, because the group of Phi Omega girls she was talking to thought she was hilarious.

"Listen to how she says 'orange,' Harriet!" one of the girls called to another passing by, and Caty was obliged to repeat it yet again, to a chorus of enthusiastic giggles.

What did the administration at AU have against drinking, anyway? Drinking was *so* nice, yet all week when Caty had been visiting the different houses, each one had loudly affirmed it was following the alcohol ban to the letter. At one house, one girl had made such a big deal about "root beer" being the only "beer" they allowed that Caty half-wondered if she thought she was an undercover cop.

Harriet, the Phi Omega dragged over to hear Caty say 'orange,' seemed appropriately impressed. She reached out to touch Caty's long dark hair. "Wow, you speak such good English."

Before Caty could stammer a reply, one of the other Omegas corrected, "She's from Baton Rouge, Harriet."

Caty felt the other girls watching to see how she would react. Not wanting to make anyone uncomfortable, she just laughed, and the others joined her, seeming relieved.

The Omega girl who'd spoken up in her defense continued on, emboldened. "You said your parents own a restaurant?"

She made it sound like her parents were running some kind of five-star establishment. Caty doubted they'd all be listening so eagerly if they saw the plastic-laminated menus and found out about Family Tuesdays, When Kids Eat Free!

"I bet the food is really authentic." The Omega girl's tone was conspiratorial, like she and Caty were in on a shared secret. "We summer in Vietnam every few years or so. You can always tell the difference between real Pho and the fake stuff."

A part of Caty was tempted to go along with it. It was an honest mistake to make, kind of. She wasn't planning on pledging Omega anyway, so these girls would probably never know any better. But then, she already felt herself flushing at the prospect of having to pretend she knew anything about *real Pho*. "My parents don't have a Vietnamese restaurant. It's Tex-Mex."

She could see the wheels turning in the girls' minds and felt her skin begin to itch at the long, in-depth explanation this confession would necessitate. Caty's parents were both from New Mexico, and they were both white as the driven snow. The same went for her older brother, James, and most of her younger siblings, except for her youngest sister, Sarah, who was born in El Salvador. Some of them were her parents' biological children and others had been adopted, Caty included. For most of her life she'd had to deal with the confused looks whenever her family was in public together, the not-so-veiled questions from strangers about who belonged to whom and who was "really" family. In her mind, her parents were just her parents, her siblings were just her siblings. Sometimes they irritated her and sometimes she missed them and sometimes she was glad to be away. No, she had never tried to track down her birth parents. No, she felt no special kinship to Vietnam, Vietnamese food, Vietnamese films, and she had no particular resentment about the Vietnam War. Her parents did their best to give her a connection to Vietnam, taking her to cultural events and restaurants, but in truth she preferred her mother's homemade tamales to canh chua, and she was more into *Harry Potter* than V-pop. Oh, and she'd never been back to Asia, but thanks for asking.

These types of questions were why Caty wanted to come to Austen University instead of following James to LSU. As much as she loved her family, she craved four years of not having to answer questions about her odd mishmash family.

The Omega spokesperson wrinkled her nose, trying to figure out how two people that she obviously still assumed were Asian had come to own a Mexican restaurant. "So, did your parents, like, spend a summer abroad in Mexico or something?"

"Try refugees from the war," came a voice from Caty's left: Isabella, playing up the drama. "They owned the only Vietnamese restaurant in Mexico City, until the drug cartels drove them out and they ended up here in Louisiana."

Caty bit back a smile as she watched the shock playing out across the Omega girls' faces. Isabella linked her arm with Caty's. "Unfortunately she can't talk about it. Orders from El Chapo." And with that, she dragged Caty toward the center of the yard, where people were dancing along to loud music pumping over the loud-speakers.

They dissolved into giggles. "The looks on their faces!" Isabella shouted over the music. "It's true what they say—Omegas really are the dumb blonde house."

"Won't they be mad once they figure it out?"

But Isabella clearly didn't care, closing her eyes as she began to aggressively dance to the music, and so Caty did the same. The liquid courage did its trick; Caty felt more daring than usual as she allowed herself to really let loose. She even caught a few boys checking her out, and instead of just blushing and looking away, she winked—before blushing and looking away, and then retreating when one of them tried approaching, because as much as she liked the attention, she had zero idea what to do with it.

The "liquid" part of the liquid courage took a while to catch up with her, but once it did the carefree exuberance of the night started to fade, leaving behind a swirling head and a sloshing stomach. Caty shouted over the music that she needed to sit down, then pushed her way to an empty table.

After her stomach began to settle and her head to clear, Caty's eyes fell upon the chair next to hers, where she saw a pretty, expensive-looking purse, with no one nearby who could claim it. Pulling it into her lap, she opened it to see if she could find some I.D.

"Is that my purse?"

Caty froze, looking up to see a beautiful, blurry blonde angel standing over her: Emma Woodhouse, the president of Pi Kappa Sigma.

Face burning, Caty stood up and thrust the bag toward her. "I was just looking for I.D. I wouldn't take anything—from anyone's purse, but especially not *yours* . . . "

When she blinked back up at Emma's face, the older girl didn't look angry. In fact, she was smiling. "I met you earlier this week. It's Caty, right?"

Caty just gaped back at her. She couldn't believe Emma remembered her, much less her name. "Yeah, that's me." For some reason, she found herself doing a curtsey, and blurting out, "You look like a Disney princess."

"You're sweet. Do you need me to help you get a ride home?"

Caty shook her head. "No, my friends are here." All of this was going wrong somehow. She was supposed to make a good impression. "I'm sorry about your purse."

"That's what I get for entrusting it to a boy. I asked my friend Knightley to watch it while I went to the bathroom, but he seems to have disappeared." Emma sighed. "Lesson learned. Knightley can't be trusted."

"Knightley can't be trusted," Caty agreed, even though she had no idea who Knightley was.

"Are you sure you don't need a ride home?"

"No, thank you. Good night." And with another mangled curtsey, Caty turned and plunged back into the crowd, determined to find Isabella.

She hadn't counted on just how difficult this task would be with so many people in the crowd, along with the ground refusing to stand still.

After fifteen minutes or so passed, Caty was feeling both soberer and more overwhelmed by the entire situation. She wished she hadn't opted to leave her phone at home, but Isabella had assured her she would take care of calling the ride.

—which meant Isabella still had her phone. Caty didn't usually memorize numbers, but she happened to know Isabella's because she'd used it as her emergency contact on several forms. All she had to do now was find somebody with a phone who wouldn't mind lending it to her.

Caty's eyes landed on a guy who was standing on the sidelines of the party, leaning up against the side of the house and using his cell. Perfect. She made a beeline for him, fueled by a resurgence of courage.

It wasn't until she was nearing him that Caty remembered how much she hated approaching strangers, especially when those strangers were boys (and therefore a different species altogether). She slowed as she neared, trying to think of the best way to broach the subject.

"You aren't going to mug me, are you?" the boy asked, not glancing up from his phone.

Caty stopped in her tracks. "Huh?"

"You don't look the type, but then maybe that's your strategy. Look all cute and innocent, but secretly be deadly."

Caty didn't know quite what was more surprising—being asked if she was a mugger in disguise, or being told she was "cute." And by a boy who wasn't hard on the eyes, either. Though he wasn't exactly handsome, he was pretty darn close to it. He wasn't the heartthrob pretty-boy type that Isabella liked to gush over on Instagram, but he was tall and wiry and had kind of a cool, Harry Potter-vibe about him with his dark floppy hair and glasses.

"Well," Caty weighed her words carefully, "I guess I'll let you off easy since you saw through my clever disguise. But only if you let me use your phone?"

The boy looked up at her at last, offering a little side smile. "I don't let strangers use my phone."

Caty flushed with embarrassment. "Oh, sorry—"

"—but seeing as we share a dark, terrible secret, I'll make an exception."

Her head was still swimmy, so it took a moment to realize he was teasing her. She grinned so hard it hurt, catching herself from swaying forward too far. "Wow. Thanks. You're the beans."

Where had that come from? She'd meant to say "you're the best." Stupid liquor. She was never going to touch it again.

But the boy only laughed, handing her his phone. "Uh, thanks. You, too."

Caty didn't mean to snoop, but as he handed her the phone, she couldn't help but see the browser that was open. "You're a Udolphite?" She had conversed with several other members of the *Mysteries of Udolpho* fandom, but only online. He was the first person she'd met in real life who not only listened to the show, but also visited the forums.

The boy blinked, then grinned—a full one this time, both sides of his mouth. "'Obsessive nerd' is the term my father always uses, but yeah, I prefer Udolphite." He extended his hand. "Tilney."

"Caty." She remembered she was supposed to be contacting Isabella. "I'll just call my friend now . . ."

"Good idea. But after that we're going to have to talk about the barber episode, because I did *not* see that whole sheep thing coming."

"I know!" Caty gasped, and it was a full ten minutes before either one of them remembered she was meant to be using his phone.

"Go ahead and program your number in," Tilney told her. "We're going to have to continue this conversation later."

Face burning rather more pleasantly this time, Caty complied before calling Isabella. Unfortunately, the call went straight to voicemail, as did the subsequent two after that. And as much fun as Caty was having talking to the very cute, very cool Tilney, she was now sober enough to realize she should be about a thousand times soberer if she wanted to keep making a good impression.

Sensing her distress, Tilney steered her toward the crowd. "Come on. I'll help you find her."

They braved the dancing throngs together, but despite the advantage of Tilney's height, no progress was made until the booming music quieted and Caty heard a familiar, loud laugh coming from nearby.

"Isabella?"

She and Tilney found a very drunk Isabella talking to a group of frat boys, including Darcy, whom she recognized from various events as the president of the Thetas. Standing next to him was Rushworth, well-known around campus for his infamous streaking across the quad during finals week fall semester; and next to him was another boy Caty didn't yet recognize, but would later learn was a recent transfer to AU, Frank Churchill.

"Oh yeah," Isabella was saying about three decibels louder than she needed to, even with the loud music playing nearby, "my sister's a pharma rep, and she lets me go through her samples all the time. I could *totally* get that for you—"

Caty didn't know what the 'that' in question was, but guessing by the looks on the three boys' faces—disdain on Darcy's, second-hand embarrassment on Frank's, and interest on Rushworth's—she knew it was time to get her tipsy friend home. "Isabella! I've been looking for you."

Isabella turned with unfeigned joy, practically jumping into her arms. "Caty! Oh my god. My pretty friend!" She looked back to the boys. "Isn't she so pretty? I could just make out with her right now . . ."

She seemed to somehow be even more inebriated than when they'd first shown up at the party. Someone else must have snuck some alcohol in past the watchful eyes of the house mothers and GRAs. "I think we should get you home," Caty said, praying Isabella didn't try to kiss her. She looked to Tilney. "We'll just call a ride."

"One of the designated drivers will help you back. Come on, I'll help you find them . . ."

Between the two of them, they somehow managed to convince Isabella it was time to leave and half-guide, half-carry her out to the row of waiting cars. After helping her sloshed friend buckle up inside, Caty turned back to Tilney, smiling. "Thanks for your help. And sorry if we ruined the party for you."

"Parties are lame. You were by far the most interesting thing that happened all night."

A slow smile crept across Caty's face. She was pretty sure that was the nicest thing any boy had ever said to her. Feeling bold, she reminded him, "Well, you do have my phone number now."

"Good. We still have a lot to discuss . . ."

Caty grinned the whole way home after that, even though Isabella decided she had to scream-sing along with the radio the whole way back. Tilney. Cute Tilney, who liked *The Mysteries of Udolpho*. And, apparently, her.

She was so swept up in the good feelings from the cute boy and the alcohol still swirling in her system that it wasn't until the bright harsh hangover of the next morning that she realized she'd forgotten to ask anyone about the secret at the Pi Kappa Sigma house, and the "poor girl" Mrs. Allen hadn't wanted her to know about.

FROM THE FILES OF CATY MORLAND:

[EMAIL FROM WINSTON COLLINS, ASSISTANT TO THE PRESIDENT OF AUSTEN UNIVERSITY—EXCERPT]

[. . .] PRESIDENT DE BOURGH REMINDS CATHERINE MORLAND THAT INFORMATION REGARDING OUR STUDENTS IS CONFIDENTIAL, AND AS THIS REMAINS A SACRED TRUST BETWEEN YOUNG PUPILS AND THEIR ESTABLISHMENT OF LEARNING, WE ARE NOT AT LIBERTY TO DISCUSS ANY RUMORS PERTAINING TO WHAT MAY OR MAY NOT HAVE HAPPENED TO ANY STUDENTS SUCH AS MISS BERTRAM IN PI KAPPA SIGMA OR ELSEWHERE ON UNIVERSITY CAMPUS [. . .]

❈ 8 ❈

Caty was awoken by a loud, incessant buzzing next to her ear—far too loud, considering how much she'd had to drink the night before, and far too early, considering how late she and Isabella had been up stalking Tilney on social media.

"Kill me now," Isabella moaned from the top bunk.

"Sorry." Caty fumbled to find her phone, cracking one eye open to look at the screen. "I don't recognize the number."

"Then decline it."

"It might be Tilney." She had given him her number, after all, but he hadn't given her his.

"Decline it anyway. Any self-respecting undergraduate should know not to call before noon."

But Caty was already out of bed, stumbling for the hallway. "Hello?"

It was not Tilney, but rather a bright, preternaturally cheerful voice, considering the time of day. "Caty? This is Emma. Sorry if I woke you."

Emma. Emma Woodhouse. It took Caty a moment to process it, not only because she was hungover, but also because it seemed way too bizarre that Emma Woodhouse should be calling her first thing on a Sunday morning. "Oh, hi, Emma. No problem. I was up anyway." A flagrant lie, but if Emma woke up early on Sunday mornings, then so did Caty.

"Oh, good. I thought I detected a fellow morning person, but you can never tell for sure."

By now, Caty was in the hallway. She slid down, her back to the wall. "So true."

"I was wondering if maybe you wanted to meet up and go for a jog? Say 9:00? I can pick you up."

Jogging? Caty felt her stomach plummet at the prospect of this fresh new hell. She'd always enjoyed soccer and kick-the-can and other outdoor games with her siblings, but senseless running? With no goals to score or cans to kick? What was the point?

Still, it was nice that Emma was reaching out to her, and she didn't want to blow her chance of starting a friendship. And who knew—maybe she liked jogging now? The last time she'd tried it had been in middle school, and there were lots of things she liked now that she didn't then. Like... asparagus. Maybe jogging was the "asparagus" of the exercise world.

"Sure," she said, with as much enthusiasm as she could muster. "See you then."

$$\pi\kappa\Sigma$$

It turned out, jogging was *not* the asparagus of the exercise world. Only ten minutes into their route through Box Hill, Caty already hated her life. Granted, that might have been due to the hangover headache that had not entirely dissipated (despite the copious amounts of coffee she'd drunk since hanging up the phone) and not to the exercise itself.

Emma, on the other hand, seemed to be in her element. Not only was she un-winded, but she also looked flawless, even without a spot of makeup on. Plus she seemed fine carrying on a conversation that luckily didn't require much more than a grunt in response.

"So, you're from Baton Rouge, right?"

Grunt.

"And you're rooming with Isabella Thorpe?"

Grunt. And so forth.

Caty tried to distract herself with the scenery, even as her head and innards declared a mutiny on the rest of her body. Box Hill was just far enough outside of town that they felt secluded amongst the thick trees and rocky paths. Louisiana didn't have much by way of hilly terrain, but Box Hill provided a rare exception that made it feel like they'd slipped out of the marshes and swamps and into a different world altogether. This illusion was aided by the thick fog that hadn't quite cleared away by mid-morning and loomed along the ravine and forest floors.

Noticing her interest, Emma informed her, "If you get here early in the morning or late at night, the fog's even thicker. You can barely see a few feet ahead of you. It feels like something out of a Gothic novel."

Caty felt a delicious chill run through her at the thought. That sounded just like the atmosphere she always imagined for *The Mysteries of Udolpho*. "Cool," she huffed.

"We can do an earlier jog next time, if you want to see it."

So they would be jogging again. Earlier. Caty felt torn. On the one hand, the fog sounded intriguing, but. . . running. *Before* nine. Then again, if it was Emma's thing and Emma was the kind of person she'd like to be someday, maybe jogging was the way to get there. "Sure!"

She must not have been doing as good a job of pretending to enjoy herself as she thought, because Emma gave her a sympathetic smile. "It's not too much farther. And the view will make it worth it, I promise."

"Not much farther" proved to be much farther than Caty would have liked, although she did feel pretty good now that the running part was over, and the view *was* amazing. Perched atop the highest point of the hill, they were able to overlook the entirety of the town below, as well as the water and swamplands stretching out beyond that. A few places were pretty steep, with sheer drops down to the ground, but Emma and Caty settled on a part of the crest that flattened out, offering a bit more stability.

"Beautiful, isn't it?" Emma settled next to her. She removed her pack and reached inside, handing Caty a thermos. "I made us some green smoothies, with blueberries, kale, banana, chia seeds, and almond milk. My dad's kind of a health-food nut, and I guess it rubbed off on me. But I swear by these things. They're the best energy boost after a run."

Caty opened the thermos and looked at the dubious contents inside. She could see the blue from the blueberries, but it also had a murky greenish-grayish hue that was less than appealing. Bracing herself, she took a sip.

"Oh wow," she said, and found she only had to dial up her enthusiasm a little bit. "That's much better than it looks."

"I know, right? They're my favorite snack."

'Snack' seemed an odd choice of words since in Caty's world, this terminology referred to chips and cookies and French fries and *chocolate*. The smoothie, on the other hand, tasted like the kind of thing she ate so she could feel like she deserved a snack later. Then again, Emma was in awesome shape and had the clearest, most perfect skin Caty had ever seen. (But at what *cost*??)

"And... they're much better for you than whatever you had before you came to the party." Emma gave her a knowing look.

A flush worked its way up the back of Caty's neck. "Oh, yeah. That was—"

Emma held up her hands. "Look, what you do on your own time is your business. But they take that stuff seriously at AU. If Mrs. Norris caught you, that would have been the end of your chances with the Kappas."

The thought was a rude awakening. Caty had her heart set on Pi Kappa Sigma. It had been her favorite house to visit during Rush Week. The whole atmosphere just oozed class, and the girls were by far the coolest and prettiest. Which, as Isabella pointed out as they tottered away from the house in their heels, meant they'd get to socialize with the hottest guys. ("For you," Isabella had insisted coyly, "I'm already taken.")

Plus the Kappas were supposed to get lots of scholarships, which would make Caty's parents happy. Even though she had a full-tuition scholarship for being in the top ten percent of her high school class, they were always hinting she should use the money she'd saved from her summer jobs carefully, as well as look for new ways to earn a little extra, so long as it didn't interfere with her studies. She had to maintain a 3.75 GPA to keep her scholarship for the next year, after all.

She swallowed, realizing just how close she'd come to ruining everything. "I won't drink again. Ever," she promised.

Emma was still smiling, though the expression looked like it had shifted into something almost . . . businesslike. "Well, you're probably wondering why I asked you here."

Actually, Caty *had* been wondering that. Emma didn't strike her as the kind of girl who had any shortage of friends, nor as the kind of girl who shied away from going jogging by herself. Plus her previous encounters with Emma—including the Theta party the previous night—had been fairly embarrassing, so she wasn't sure why she'd been singled out.

It struck her that maybe she hadn't made the cut, and Emma had brought her here to try to be nice and break the news to her in person. Like a breakup, but worse somehow, because it wasn't just some boy saying he didn't feel like kissing you anymore, it was a cool, confident girl telling you she didn't want to be your friend.

"We technically aren't handing out bids until this afternoon," Emma continued, "but I wanted to let you know that Pi Kappa Sigma wants you. And we're hoping you'll choose us."

Caty had been so certain it was bad news that for a moment she could only blink at her. "Are you serious?"

"I'm serious."

"Oh my god!" Caty forgot herself and half-lunged forward, embracing Emma. By the time she realized that was a super weird thing to do, Emma was, fortunately, laughing. "The Kappas are my first choice. Of course I'll accept!"

"That's so great!" Emma beamed back at her. "And I also wanted to let you know, before we give out the bids, that there's going to be a room open in the Kappa house. I was thinking maybe you and Isabella would want to fill it."

Caty hadn't thought moving into the house would even be a possibility until the next year, when a few of the older Kappa girls graduated. Even then, she'd been warned it would be competitive to get those spaces, and might require some major networking and schmoozing. Yet here was Emma, offering a room to her on a silver platter. And with Isabella, too. Everything was falling into place.

"It's just, you seem like you would be a good fit in the house." Emma was talking faster now, sounding almost . . .nervous? "You have the kind of energy that I think the Kappas need moving forward."

Caty wasn't sure what that meant, but it sounded like a compliment. "Thanks? I mean, I would love to. I just don't know if we'll be able to get out of our contracts."

"Oh, Mrs. Norris will be able to help y'all. The university can't say it officially, but school housing has an understanding with the Greeks, and they won't kick up a fuss."

Caty was, of course, excited to be a Kappa because they were the coolest sorority on campus, but she was almost as intrigued by the old historic house in which she would get to live. Visions of attics, secret compartments, and forbidden west wings danced through her head. It was all too good to be true. She grinned back at Emma, not quite sure how she'd earned this honor, but thrilled it had been bestowed upon her. "Then, yeah! Totally. I can't wait to tell Isabella . . ."

It didn't strike Caty until later, when she and Isabella were getting ready for the bid ceremony, to wonder why there was suddenly space open in the Kappa house. If any girls graduated in December, then surely it would be common knowledge that beds had opened up, and others would be vying for the spots. Something else must have happened to make it possible for Caty and Isabella to move in.

Mrs. Jennings's words came back to her, about *"that poor girl"* from Pi Kappa Sigma. And Caty had to wonder if the conveniently available space in the Kappa house wasn't quite so convenient after all.

FROM THE FILES OF CATY MORLAND:

INTERVIEWEE: KAROLINE BINGLEY (JUNIOR AT AUSTEN UNIVERSITY, VICE-PRESIDENT OF PI KAPPA SIGMA)

KAROLINE: A KAPPA GIRL SHOULD BE SMART, SOPHISTICATED, SEXY BUT NOT SLUTTY, WELL-TRAVELED, COSMOPOLITAN, AND JUST HAVE THAT "IT" FACTOR. YOU SHOULD ALWAYS BE WONDERING WHO SHE IS WHEN SHE WALKS IN THE ROOM, AND SHE SHOULD BE ON YOUR MIND LONG AFTER SHE LEAVES IT.

CATY: THAT'S A PRETTY IMPRESSIVE LIST. BUT WHAT IF THERE WAS A KAPPA WHO WAS MISSING, SAY, ONE OR TWO OF THOSE QUALITIES? OR HAD OTHER TRAITS THAT DIDN'T QUITE FIT THE MOLD?

KAROLINE: WELL, THEN MAYBE THAT PERSON WASN'T CUT OUT TO BE A KAPPA.

CATY: SO THEY SHOULD—WHAT, LEAVE THE SORORITY?

KAROLINE: IDEALLY.

CATY: WILLINGLY? OR DOES THAT MATTER?

KAROLINE: YOU MAKE IT ALL SOUND SO SORDID. THIS IS A SORORITY, NOT THE CIA. PEOPLE CAN COME AND GO AS THEY PLEASE.

CATY: AND IF THEY REFUSE TO GO? LIKE ISABELLA?

KAROLINE: ISABELLA WAS INITIATED INTO THE KAPPAS FAIR AND SQUARE. ONCE THAT HAPPENED, SHE BECAME MY SISTER. AND I WOULD NEVER TURN ON A SISTER.

CATY: LIZZY BENNET SEEMS TO THINK OTHERWISE.

KAROLINE: LIZZY BENNET CAN SHOVE IT UP HER ASS, OKAY? SISTERHOOD IS FOR LIFE.

❦ 9 ❦

It was the second time within a short period that Caty's brother had been called upon to help her move, so she anticipated some kind of bribery would be necessary. At the very least, his own large pizza and wings, and probably dessert, too—and there was no telling if even that would be enough of an incentive. James was a good brother, as far as brothers went, but he did not like to give up his precious LSU weekends for the family.

(After his mother reminded him once that they were only a short drive away and he could visit them for more than just holidays, James responded with, "I have friends, Mom," and that had pretty much been that.)

What Caty hadn't considered was that James wouldn't just be helping her move—he'd be helping her and *Isabella* move, and this proved to make all the difference.

It hadn't taken a great detective to pick up on the chemistry between the two during Isabella's brief visit at New Year's. James, who normally spent his winter holidays hanging out with friends, sure found an awful lot of reasons to hang around the house when Isabella was there. When he and Isabella figured out he was in the same fraternity as her brother, John, at LSU, she gushed to Caty late into the evening about destiny and true love. Now James was the source of all the texting Isabella was constantly doing, sometimes even late into the night, and first thing in the morning, too.

YEAH, OF COURSE, James replied before Caty even had the chance to offer him compensation. *I'D BE HAPPY TO HELP. AND MAYBE I CAN TAKE YOU BOTH OUT FOR DINNER AFTERWARD.*

That was when Caty knew her brother had it pretty bad. Not only was he not expecting any free food out of the deal, he was also offering to treat *them*. In the world of James, that was pretty much a declaration of love.

What she hadn't taken into account was that James would bring along Isabella's brother, John. At first it seemed like a great idea—the more helping hands, the merrier!—but that notion quickly dissolved upon meeting John. In addition to doing very little of the actual helping (seeming to prefer pointing out what others were doing wrong to doing anything himself), his running commentary on the other girls in the sorority was setting Caty's teeth on edge.

"I can tell if a girl's a slut just by looking at her," John informed Caty as he followed her up the stairs. She was carrying a box of textbooks; he had a pillow under each arm. "It doesn't matter what she's wearing. That's where most people get it wrong. You can tell more by the way she carries herself…

"I'm worried about you and Isabella in this place," he continued, unbidden, as they returned to James's truck for another round. "I've seen a lot of things about wild sorority girls. Stuff on the Internet—sets my teeth on edge. Wet t-shirt contests and kissing each other and all that nonsense. If I found out a sister of mine was acting like that, I'd lock her in my basement and only feed her bread and water until she learned how to act like a good, God-fearing girl again."

Caty glared at him sidelong as she hoisted out another box. "Maybe if you hate those kinds of videos so much you should stop watching them."

"It's not my fault if people put them out there. I'm just saying, thank God that's not *my* sister. For her sake."

Predictably, Isabella and James seemed too wrapped up in each other to notice how terrible John was being. "I just think you better prepare yourself for what you'd do if another girl tries to kiss you," he told Caty their eighteenth or so trip up. "It's all fun and games if it's at a party or something, and there are boys around to watch, but you'd better remember she might actually be a lesbian. Then what are you gonna do?"

"Caty!"

Teeming with gratitude, Caty turned as Emma approached. At the sight of the Kappa president, John's eyes bulged to almost cartoonish proportions.

"Do you and Isabella need any help moving in? I can round up some of the other girls and call over the Thetas."

"No need for that, sweetheart." John's voice had mysteriously dropped about half an octave lower. "I've got all the muscle you need right here."

For a long, unblinking moment, Emma just stared at him. Then, she looked back to Caty. "Let me know if you need anything. *Anything.*" She gave the younger girl a meaningful look before retreating.

Caty looked after her wistfully, wishing she'd never called her stupid brother and he'd never brought his stupid friend. They could have a bunch of cute fraternity boys helping them now if it weren't for this idiot. Maybe Tilney would have shown up, and they could have picked up where they'd left off at the party.

John let out a slow whistle as he watched Emma leave. "It just goes to show, the only reason a girl can't look like *that* is if she doesn't diet and exercise. It makes you wonder why every girl doesn't just take care of herself."

Caty glared at the back of his head. "I don't diet or exercise."

"Yeah, well, you're not fat. Thank God."

Just when Caty thought she might murder John, she turned to see James and Isabella, each with an armload, both grinning with a slightly dazed look at the bliss of getting to be near each other. It would have been cute, if Caty hadn't been so irritated about being left alone with John for so long.

"I think there's just one more round after this," James informed them, after they'd all deposited their respective hauls. "John and I can manage."

"Of course we can," John sniffed. "I've barely even broken a sweat."

And with that, at last, he was gone, if only for a moment. Isabella turned to Caty, all heart-eyed and besotted. "Your brother is *so* nice," she gushed, half-collapsing back on the unmade bunkbed. "Like, *so*, nice . . ."

As Caty could not offer the same compliment in return, she opted to throw a distracting pillow at her friend's head instead. "He's nicer when you're around," she teased.

Isabella just giggled. "Hey, what do you think about John? I don't care if you want to make out with him, or whatever."

Luckily, the boys returned before Caty was forced to answer that particularly unappealing offer. "I'm starving," John announced, dropping a box onto the ground with a loud THUMP. "What do you say, Caty? Want to hop on my hog and drive around this dump to find something edible?"

"Um," said Caty. "I thought we were all going to eat together?"

"Ooh, come on, Caty," laughed Isabella. "We'll look so hot and mysterious getting driven around town by some biker dude."

"What 'we'?" John retorted. "I didn't buy a Thundercat to drive around my chubby sister."

"Shut *up!*"

"I thought we were all going to eat together?" Caty said again, louder this time.

At long last, James intervened. "We can all take my truck. Caty, do you know any good Tex-Mex food around here? It won't be as good as Mom and Dad's, but Isabella's never had fajitas before—"

John interrupted with a haughty shake of his head. "No, no, no. I know what Caty will want." He winked at her. "Vietnamese food, right? I took the liberty of looking up the best Asian restaurants in Highbury. There's supposed to be a good Thai place nearby—good by Highbury standards, anyway."

Caty spoke as if she hadn't heard him. "I could go for some Italian. How does Schedoni's sound?"

"Maybe we can do some shopping afterward," Isabella suggested, "pick up a few things for the room."

Caty blinked at her in confusion. "But we just moved in all our stuff."

"Yeah, but we're in the Kappa house now." Isabella motioned around the room. "We need to be Pinterest approved. The other girls will expect it. I'm sure it won't cost more than two hundred or so apiece."

"Two hundred?" Caty gaped at her. That would be all her fun money for the semester, blown in one go, just to get some matching comforters and wall decals. "Bella, I don't have that kind of money to spend."

Isabella sighed. "Fine. But . . . maybe you could talk to Mrs. Allen sometime this week?"

Caty frowned. Why would she talk to Mrs. Allen about stuff for the room? Just because the Allens had offered to sponsor her sorority fees didn't mean she could turn to them every time she wanted some spending money.

"Maybe," she hedged, because she was tired and hungry and wanted to end the conversation as soon as possible. There was no way she'd be asking Mrs. Allen for that money.

"I'm starving." This from John. "Can we save the girly chit-chat for later?"

The other three moved toward the door, but Caty remained in place. She needed just a minute to herself, to regain her sanity.

"You coming, Cootie?" James asked from the doorway.

"I just need to find my phone. Two minutes, promise."

Caty waited until James left to sink down on the bed and look around the room. It was hard to tell since it was so messy, but it was much smaller than the one they'd given up in the dorms. Still, there was a nice view out to the garden below—much better than the parking lot they used to overlook.

She moved over to the window, leaning across the desk to look out at the detached guest house where Mrs. Norris lived. As she did so, Caty noticed something bright red in the dark gap between the back of the desk and the wall.

Reaching down, she fished for a moment before her fingers closed on something. It was a red, leather-bound diary, with an old-fashioned lock. Flipping it over, Caty saw a few words carved in black ink into the back. *Property of Marla Bertram. Luke 8:17.*

Marla Bertram. She must have been the girl who'd had the room before them. Caty imagined she'd be pretty upset when she realized she'd left behind her diary. She should probably give it to Emma or Mrs. Norris so they could get it back to its owner.

Caty's phone buzzed, interrupting her train of thought. *GET UR HOT ASS DOWN HERE, SLUT!!*

Sighing, Caty tucked her phone into her pocket. She debated a moment before slipping the diary into her pillowcase so it wouldn't get lost amongst the move-in clutter, then headed outside to meet the others.

FROM THE FILES OF CATY MORLAND:

INTERVIEWEE: JOHN THORPE (SENIOR AT LOUISIANA STATE UNIVERSITY, BROTHER OF ISABELLA THORPE)

JOHN: I KNEW THAT PLACE WAS BAD FOR HER AS SOON AS WE SAW IT. ALL THOSE HALF-DRESSED GIRLS PARADING AROUND IN SKINTIGHT CLOTHES. THE GIGGLING AND THE TICKLING AND THE PILLOW FIGHTS. TOO MUCH ESTROGEN. IT'S ALL NONSENSE WHEN YOU COMPARE SORORITIES TO FRATERNITIES. FRATERNITIES ARE ABOUT HISTORY, BROTHERHOOD, FORMING BONDS THAT YOU CAN TAKE INTO THE REAL WORLD. SORORITIES ARE JUST PLACES FOR GIRLS TO TRY OUT BEING LESBIANS—WHEN THEY'RE NOT HOOKING UP WITH RANDOM GUYS AT PARTIES. WELL, ISABELLA WASN'T LIKE THAT. I DON'T CARE WHAT ANYONE SAYS. THEY'RE JUST TRYING TO SELL NEWSPAPERS OR WHATEVER.

CATY: SO ISABELLA CONFIDED TO YOU ABOUT HER LOVE LIFE?

JOHN: SHE DIDN'T HAVE TO. BECAUSE SHE KNEW IF I GOT WIND OF HER ACTING LIKE A LITTLE SLUT, I'D HAVE TO DO SOMETHING ABOUT IT.

❧ 10 ❧

"*N*urse Desmond had the unsettling sensation of being watched, all through her late-night shift that began on the night of December 18th and continued into early the next morning. Later, she would write in her journal that as she walked up and down the poorly lit halls, she had to convince herself that it was all in her imagination, and for a while, it worked. Of course, that was before they found the severed hand . . . "

Earbuds in, Caty listened with bated breath as she made her way up the darkened stairway of the Kappa house. It was her third time listening to this episode of *Udolpho*, but still she shuddered as she imagined being Nurse Desmond, walking up and down the corridors of the madhouse, feeling a pair of murderous eyes tracing her every move . . .

The thought elicited a delicious chill. Despite the creaking staircase and old bones of the Kappa house, Caty had been disappointed to learn just how un-Gothic the building felt with the constant hustle of girls coming and going at all hours. With so many other people around and the constant refrain of Selena Gomez drifting through the walls, Caty had yet to feel frightened in the old place.

But tonight . . . tonight she was coming home late from a biology lab, and most of the girls, including Isabella, had opted to go out for ladies' night at the local piano bar. That meant the Kappa house was all but empty. Caty planned on getting dressed and joining her new sisters, but she would allow herself a good twenty minutes to wallow in the dark corridors, the shadows cast by the old linen curtains, and the sound of the wind-struck tree branches scratching against the windows.

"Nurse Oliver had been missing for almost thirty minutes, though nobody knew it yet. Some thought her shift must have ended already, others thought she was busy helping a patient. What none of them could have anticipated was the door that had been left ajar, and the ripple of events that would forever change the way the nursing staff practiced their protocol . . ."

Caty turned down the hallway leading to her room, reveling in the shadows and the silence on her floor. That was, until she noticed something *moving* in the dark. She stopped in her tracks, staring in dumb silence at the doorknob to her bedroom, which was unmistakably being turned from inside. A dark figure emerged, stepping into the hall.

For a moment, Caty was too petrified with fear to move, to even blink. But then, as the figure turned to face her, instinct took over, and she screamed bloody murder.

As lights turned on and footsteps approached, Caty watched the dark figure with wide-eyed terror, her back pressed to the wall, afraid to look away for even a moment.

"What's going on?" Emma appeared, brandishing a lacrosse stick. She followed Caty's petrified gaze, poised to strike—

And let her arms fall back down to her side again. "Mrs. Norris?"

The house mother seemed just as rattled as Caty, one hand clutched to her chest, the other holding a white-knuckled grip on her cane. "Good God. Is this the thanks I get for taking out the trash?"

A mortified Caty did her best to explain. That the hallway was dark, that she hadn't expected anyone to be home, that she'd been listening to *The Mysteries of Udolpho*. She apologized again and again, until Emma put her hands on her shoulders and guided her to her room.

As they passed Mrs. Norris, the older woman sniffed, turning up her nose. "This is what comes of corrupting your mind with that useless technology," she said, motioning distastefully to the phone in Caty's hands.

"She's going to hate me now," Caty moaned, dropping her bag on the floor and half-collapsing onto her bed.

"She hates most people. I wouldn't take it too personally." Emma patted her shoulder sympathetically. "I'm going to rinse off. Then I think we should join the other girls at the piano bar, get your mind off it."

"Okay." Caty listened as Emma shut the door behind her, continuing to wallow in mortification. She wondered how she would be able to look Mrs. Norris in the eye again.

Only . . . the more Caty thought about it, the stranger the whole thing seemed. Why had Mrs. Norris been collecting trash from her bedroom at almost 9:00 at night? She strained her memory to recall if Mrs. Norris had been carrying any trash when she left the room. She glanced over to see that the basket was empty, but she didn't know that anything had been put into it; it was one of the new purchases Isabella made to spruce up their shared space. But what other reason would Mrs. Norris have for sneaking into their room?

With a sudden flash of foreboding, Caty sat up, feeling inside her pillowcase. She found Marla Bertram's diary, just where she'd left it. Was it possible that this was what Mrs. Norris had been looking for. . . ?

No, Caty told herself. It was simply her imagination running away with itself again, and that was what had gotten her into this embarrassing predicament in the first place.

$$\pi\kappa\Sigma$$

At the dinner party, Caty's story was briefly interrupted as Rushworth snorted. "Well, that's obvious, isn't it? If the diary led to Isabella's death, and Mrs. Norris was in your room looking for the diary, then Mrs. Norris killed Isabella." He sat back, looking infinitely pleased with himself for having made the deduction—and rather spectacularly stupid, with a healthy rim of bisque coating the skin around his mouth.

Caty was actually kind of impressed that Rushworth had been able to follow along so well. He'd always struck her as not being the sharpest tool in the shed. But it also didn't escape her attention, just how eager he'd been to foist the blame on Mrs. Norris.

Across the table, Jane spoke up. "It makes sense, if Isabella was killed to get her out of the sorority. There's no one who's more devoted to the Kappa's honor than Mrs. Norris."

Karoline, too, seemed strangely eager to follow this line of investigation. "And she was dead set against voting Isabella into the house, y'all."

"So were you, Karoline, as I recall." Emma's gaze was a challenge. Apparently she hadn't completely forgotten those rumors about Karoline trying to oust her as Kappa president.

Karoline blinked back at her, annoyed at having been called out. "Yes, but I had my reasons, didn't I?"

This little drama could quickly derail the evening again, so Caty spoke up once more, putting things back on course. "It's an interesting theory, but of all the people I interviewed, no one saw Mrs. Norris at Box Hill that night."

"And she has that cane," Frank pointed out. "So she couldn't climb the hill, could she?"

Tilney took a sip of his rum, looking amused. "I'd just like to point out that no one is saying Mrs. Norris *wouldn't* have killed Isabella, just that she *couldn't* have. Cheers to Austen University's stellar hiring practices—putting a woman that we all agree is capable of murder in charge of a group of college-aged girls . . ."

πκΣ

A loud buzzing noise sent Caty's pulse racing again. Her phone, that was all. Fishing it out of her bag, she saw a text from an unfamiliar number.

Hey Caty, this is Tilney, your rescuer from the party and fellow Udolphite. Coffee? Next Saturday?

She was excited enough she could have written him back right away, but even Caty was not *that* naïve. Instead, she opened her message thread with Isabella and sent her the following:

OMG!!!! BELLA!! It happened! A text from my future husband!!

She was obviously joking about the husband thing (because she was only eighteen and not, like, religious or planning to turn into a vampire bride or anything), but Isabella would know that. Caty forwarded Tilney's message to her, then added a follow-up message to her friend. *What should I write?? What should I wear???*

Caty sat perched at the edge of her bed, watching her phone with eager anticipation. A few seconds passed, and nothing. She pulled up an Internet browser just to pass some time while Isabella wrote her back. When a few minutes passed and still nothing from her best friend, she told herself Isabella must have her phone in her purse or something and hadn't seen the message. She would just have to tell her all about it when they met up at the piano bar.

Fortunately, Emma was a tolerably receptive audience in Isabella's place. "I approve of a fun, freshman-year fling. You don't want anything serious before you're 25, anyway."

She . . . didn't? Caty hadn't known this about herself, but Emma said it with such authority that she was probably right. Anyway, a fun fling with a boy as cute as Tilney was more than she'd been hoping for out of her freshman year, so she'd take it!

Emma helped her compose the perfect response text ("Not too forward, but not too coy either. He put himself out there by reaching out to you. We always want to reward good behavior with boys, so they know how we expect to be treated"), then instructed her to send it in about half an hour.

"Yay, date!" Emma crowed with her. "Now, let's go find the girls . . ."

By the time they arrived at the piano bar, the place was in full swing. Apparently they weren't the only sorority taking advantage of ladies' night. Only fifteen more minutes of free drinks remained, so Emma hurried off to the bar to get in under the wire. She didn't drink often, she told Caty on the drive over, and never on university property as per the Panhellenic rules, but free booze was free booze.

Because Caty was underage, the bouncer had drawn two huge black X's on the backs of her hands so the bartender would know not to serve her, which was a bummer. Fortunately, she already felt pretty buzzed thanks to her upcoming date with Tilney. She just hoped the X's washed off by then.

Caty searched the crowd for Isabella, eager to tell her the news. She still hadn't heard anything back from her, so she assumed she must be too busy having fun. Sure enough, Isabella was smack dab in the middle of the party, dancing closely with another girl from their house. Like, *closely*. It looked like their pelvises were sewn together. As Caty watched on, Isabella and the girl leaned in and kissed each other. With tongue.

Caty looked away, embarrassed and confused. If she'd seen Isabella kissing another boy, she would have to tell James, but—did it count if it was a girl? Was that still cheating? She was pretty sure Isabella would have told her if she was bisexual, since her friend had zero problems telling her all kinds of other intimate, even uncomfortable details about her life. So if it didn't turn her on or anything, maybe it was just for fun, or something? In which case, would James even be mad if he were here to see it . . . ?

Spotting her in the crowd, Isabella let out a screech that rivaled Caty's terrified scream earlier that night, in volume if not in pitch. She barreled through the crowd and wrapped Caty in a tipsy embrace. "Bestie!"

She smelled of booze. Caty puzzled, wondering how Isabella had gotten alcohol. She should have the same dark X's on her hands as Caty did, yet there was no trace of the underage mark of shame. Did she have a fake I.D. she hadn't told her about?

"You took forever to get here!" Caty had to help Isabella get onto the stool so she wouldn't topple over. "Oh my god, it's been SO fun. We should come here every week."

"I've been texting you." Caty raised her voice to be heard over the loud, off-key karaoke at the front of the room. Someone was singing Adele like it was personal. "Do you have your phone?"

"Oh, whoops! I put it away for safekeeping." Isabella reached into her ample cleavage and began fishing around, oblivious to the free show she was putting on in the process. Caty looked away, spotting two boys at a nearby table watching appreciatively.

At last, Caty reached over and stilled Isabella's arm to get her to stop. "You can find it later. I'll just tell you." She leaned across the table so she could lower her voice. "Tilney texted and asked me out for coffee!!"

She expected squeals, cheers, exclamation points. Instead, Isabella looked distracted, her eyes focused on something over Caty's shoulder. Glancing over, she saw the two same boys, grinning at Isabella. She grinned back.

"Um." Caty tucked a strand of hair behind one ear. "So, I'm pretty excited."

"Oh my god, me too," Isabella returned, in a tone that told Caty she had no idea what she was talking about. She leaned in closer. "So, don't look now, but those boys are totally staring over here."

They might not be staring so much, if Isabella weren't so blatantly staring back. Caty refrained from pointing this out, folding her arms. "We could move to a different table."

"No way. It's not *my* fault they're practically drooling. They should be the ones that have to move." Isabella looked to her, squeezing her arm. "Don't worry, Caty. James is the only boy I could even dream of being my boyfriend. He's worth a thousand of those losers."

Her eyes darted back to the two boys at that, checking to see if they were still looking, but still, Caty felt reassured. Isabella liked to flirt and have a good time, that was all. James was the one she cared about.

"Aren't you so excited for Saturday?"

Caty smiled, pleased. So Isabella *had* been paying attention. "Yeah. I mean, I know it's just coffee, but hopefully we can get to know each other better."

"Coffee? I'm talking about New Orleans." Seeing the look on Caty's face, Isabella groaned. "Ugh, I must've forgotten to tell you. James and John are taking us to New Orleans. There's, like, this ghost/murder tour in the French Quarter. It sounds *so* spooky and fun."

Caty hesitated, torn. On the one hand, the murder tour *did* sound interesting. She got goosebumps just thinking about all the weird, creepy stuff they could learn about New Orleans history. Maybe she could even get enough ideas to start her own podcast, like A.W. Radcliffe. But, even worse than the requirement of spending the day with John Thorpe, the trip would mean she'd have to bail on Tilney.

"I can't. I already told Tilney I'd meet him for coffee."

For a moment, Isabella looked outright annoyed. Then suddenly, she smiled at Caty. "We'll see."

FROM THE FILES OF CATY MORLAND:

[EXCERPT FROM AN ARTICLE PUBLISHED BY LIVEWIRE NEWS ABOUT ISABELLA'S DEATH]

. . . ONE UNDERGRADUATE, ROBBY FERRARS, DESCRIBES HIS BRIEF ENCOUNTER WITH THORPE AT THE CROWN INN: "I REMEMBER SEEING HER THERE AT LADIES' NIGHT. SHE WAS A LITTLE, YOU KNOW, OUT OF CONTROL. SHE FLASHED ME AND MY FRIEND, TOM. LIKE, HER BREASTS. AND SHE WAS STARING SUPER AGGRESSIVELY. LATER THAT

NIGHT I SAW SHE'D SOMEHOW FOUND OUT MY NAME AND FOLLOWED ME ON INSTAGRAM." THOUGH FERRARS SEEMS TO HAVE FOLLOWED ISABELLA BACK, HE SAYS NOW, "SHE WAS HOT BUT IT WAS A MAJOR TURNOFF. TOO DESPERATE-STALKER FOR MY TASTE."

❧ 11 ❧

It happens every so often that even the best of friendships are tested. At least, this was what Caty told herself on hour four of not speaking to Isabella. She'd assumed she could reason with Isabella about changing her plans with Tilney once her friend was sober. But the next morning—even hungover and bleary-eyed —Bella continued to pester Caty about whether she'd canceled with Tilney yet.

Of course not, was Caty's reply, because having coffee with a fellow Udolphite (who just happened to be oh so cute and a very good kisser—or so she imagined) was more important than tagging along on Bella's date with James to New Orleans, especially if it meant spending the day with John.

They bickered about it, but not in a way that Caty took seriously. Isabella had pulled her whiny, pleading act before, about dumb things like getting the top bunk or borrowing Caty's computer. And usually, it must be said, Caty eventually caved, so it must have been a surprise when she continued to hold her ground. Isabella's badgering became so irritating that Caty decided to give them both some space and went to find Emma, who had offered to go over her academic course plan for the next three years.

Perhaps because she was so tired from all the firm "nos" to Isabella, Caty found herself agreeing to more business classes than she'd been planning on taking (which was not a difficult number to achieve, as she'd been planning on taking none).

"Even private detectives have to know how to market themselves," Emma informed her. "And, you never know. You might get bored of this whole crime thing and decide to go a different route down the road. Maybe even international business?"

"Not likely. I'm really into murder."

"Hmm," said Emma, then after a beat, suggested Caty switch to green teas, which were supposed to have more health benefits than the Earl Grey she'd finally caved in and purchased.

Carrying the three boxes of green tea Emma insisted she take ("Just to try"), Caty braced herself for round two of her argument with Isabella. Instead, she found her roommate sitting on the edge of her bed, painting her toenails a sparkly purple. She smiled before averting her gaze back to her feet. "Hey, babe. Sorry about before. I bought you a latte. And a muffin."

At the edge of the desk, there was, indeed, a grande to-go cup and a poppy seed muffin—

"Oh," said Isabella, applying another layer to her big toe, "that's already been fixed."

"So, we're going next week?"

"No, this weekend. I texted Tilney and he said it's fine."

"You—what?"

Isabella still didn't look up at her, which at last struck Caty as strange. No pedicure was *that* all-absorbing. "I texted Tilney. He said you could do it next week, maybe."

"How could you text Tilney? You don't have his number."

At this, Isabella at last had the good grace to blush. "I used your phone."

The whole truth of it came out then, as Caty scrolled through the message chain. Isabella hadn't clarified that she wasn't Caty, nor offered any explanation as to why she was breaking their plans. She had also greatly exaggerated about the benevolence of Tilney's response. He had not suggested "next week" as Isabella claimed; his exact words were *Ok Some other time*, which everyone knew was boy code for "never."

As Caty gathered her things together, trembling with rage, Isabella became irritatingly rational. "Babe, you can't leave. John and James are gonna be here in half an hour. The plans are already made—you can fix things with Tilney later."

"I'd rather study," Caty returned, sweeping the untouched coffee and muffin into the wastebasket.

$$\pi\kappa\Sigma$$

It was an act of moral superiority she would soon come to regret, as she got to the library and remembered her financial aid hadn't yet come through. If she wanted to be able to buy groceries for the next week, she'd have to forego a snack from the library café. Caty told herself it was better to go hungry than to take an emotional bribe, though her stomach did not agree.

The physical science homework she'd been planning on doing would never be able to distract her from her growling belly. Instead, Caty decided she should be far more productive and look up Marla Bertram.

So far her search on the mysterious previous occupant of her room had proven to be less than fruitful. Once she'd managed to pry open the diary's lock, she discovered the entire thing was written in what appeared to be gibberish. This was a daunting obstacle, but nonetheless thrilling. People didn't write in code unless they had something to hide, after all.

Still, Caty had as yet to break said code, which meant she'd learned very little about Marla from the diary itself. No one in Pi Kappa Sigma had any information to offer beyond what Caty already knew: that she'd lived in her old room, and that she'd left campus suddenly at the end of fall term. Even Emma, who enjoyed telling Caty little tidbits of gossip about this girl and that, clamped up at the mention of her name. "I think she got pneumonia?" was all she'd say on the matter.

The almighty Google was the next obvious solution, but between Isabella breaking into her phone and Mrs. Norris sneaking through her room, Caty felt a little paranoid about using her laptop to search for anything. She could always just clear her search history, she knew, but what if she forgot one time, or left her laptop open while she ran to the bathroom? If Norris knew she was interested in Marla, she might redouble her efforts to find the diary; and if Isabella found out, the entire house would know, too. A school computer, however, would offer some blessed privacy, free from prying eyes.

There was not much news on Marla alone, but as a family unit, the Bertrams were fairly prolific online. The family's patriarch, Reverend Thomas, was an evangelical preacher of some renown. He and his wife had four natural children and one foster daughter. Marla was the oldest girl, the third oldest child. Looking through pictures of them, Caty couldn't shake a sense of unease. They were all blonde and beautiful in a pale, homespun kind of way, except for the foster daughter, Fania, who appeared to have Arabic ancestry and wore a Hijab. She looked decidedly out of place in the otherwise fundamentalist household, making Caty wonder if Reverend Thomas was more open-minded than his reputation suggested. (And she could only imagine the kind of questions *Fania* got about "belonging" to her family.)

Aesthetically, Fania should have been the one to stick out like a sore thumb in the family photos, but Marla was the one who claimed that advantage. Though she had the same almost-white hair, the same bright blue eyes and seemingly Amish-inspired clothing as her parents and biological siblings, she looked at the camera with a knowing smile that differed from the others' wan expressions.

Caty zoomed in on that smile now, feeling an eerie connection with Marla Bertram. This was exactly the sort of girl who would write a diary in code, exactly the sort of girl who would keep secrets.

I could tell you a thing or two, her smile seemed to say.

"Gotcha!"

Caty jumped about a mile out of her chair, heart pounding in her chest as she turned to see Tilney standing over her. "Busted," he said, folding his arms.

$$\pi\kappa\Sigma$$

Over coffee, which Tilney insisted on paying for (very date-like, no?), Caty explained what happened with Isabella and the case of the forged text message. "She sounds kind of unstable," Tilney returned, sipping at his Americano.

Caty bristled. It was one thing for her to think Isabella was behaving irrationally; it was another to have someone else say as much. Isabella could definitely rub people the wrong way, and she could be selfish, and sometimes she could even be downright mean. But, she was also the first real friend that Caty had made at Austen University. It would have been impossible to explain to anyone who had never felt so out of place and *alone* what it meant to find someone like that. Not just someone to watch TV with and gossip about boys, but who would always have her back, even if she went about it the wrong way sometimes.

"She has some boundary issues," Caty hedged loyally, "but I don't think she meant any harm. She just . . . likes getting her way."

"Well, she's lucky she has such a good friend." Tilney offered a diplomatic smile, and Caty softened. Cute, a true-crime fan, *and* understanding. The boy was proving to be more and more of a catch every time she spoke to him.

"So," said Tilney with an impish glint in his eyes, "what have you written about me in your blog?"

"My . . . blog?"

"Let me guess: the entrance of a dapper, handsome stranger livened up an otherwise pedestrian party at the Theta Gamma Nu house. Well-dressed, well-read, well-spoken . . . is he the elusive perfect man, or simply too good to be true?" Tilney grinned, pleased with himself. "Warm, or cold?"

"Cold. Definitely cold."

"Hmm." Tilney stroked his chin. "That's what I would have written in *my* blog, if I had one, and if I got the chance to meet me . . ."

"What even makes you think I have a blog?"

He scoffed. "You're a child of the digital age. Going by gender alone, I'll veer on the side of stereotype and guess . . . Tumblr?"

Caty's cheeks pinkened. "I can neither confirm nor deny that hypothesis, sir."

"Let me guess. An occasional ramble about life, but usually you just repost other peoples' artwork of your various fandoms, and an obscure literary quote here and there to give it a more esoteric vibe."

Caty continued to smile, though she was beginning to wonder if she was being insulted. "Is it all blogs you think are ridiculous, or just my hypothetical one?"

"It's everything that's ridiculous, Miss Morland. But nothing more so than me."

There he went, softening her again, just when she'd begun to fear he was insufferable. Caty was starting to see that conversing with Tilney was going to be a bit of a tightrope act. Instinct told her that he was the sort of person who could take advantage, if left unchecked.

Tilney took a long sip of his coffee. "Well, I'm hurt that you chose not to write about our auspicious introduction. It isn't every day that two Udolphites meet in the flesh, you know." He raised an eyebrow at her. "Or is your blog dedicated to writing about your own mysteries? You're bound to find at least one, especially in Pi Kappa Sigma."

Caty went very still, trying her best not to give anything away. Was he only teasing, or did he know something? "What do you mean?" she asked in what she hoped was her most neutral tone.

"What do you know?"

In a rush, Caty confided everything she'd gleaned about Marla

Bertram—the secondhand information from Mrs. Jennings, the strange behavior from Mrs. Norris and the other Kappas, and most importantly, the coded diary. (So much for playing it cool.)

Tilney looked intrigued, no hint of sarcasm in his eyes now. "Do you have the journal with you?"

"I keep it with me all the time now, ever since I saw Norris snooping around the room."

Caty handed it to him, and together they looked at the scrawling handwriting, the indecipherable gibberish. "Weird," Tilney pronounced at last. "But pretty in keeping with what I knew of Marla."

"You knew her?"

"Distantly. I'm positive she wouldn't have any idea who I was— not a lowly sophomore to her godly senior."

Caty considered that. "She was a senior when she left, with only one semester to go before she graduated. Doesn't that seem—off?"

"Marla was pretty off, as a rule. But yeah, it does seem strange, even for her." Tilney pondered a moment. "There are rumors around the Sigma house, of course—that she overdosed, that there was a hidden sex ring. Overall I wouldn't put much stock in any of them. The Sigmas en masse are—how should I put this delicately . . . ?—idiots. But where there's smoke, there's fire, and the Kappas are working just a little too hard to keep it all quiet if she just got sick like everyone claims."

It was Caty's turn to brood, wondering how she was supposed to piece this all together if the Kappas weren't talking and the Sigmas knew nothing, and Marla herself was absent and toyingly obscure.

"You know who would know? Your RA."

"Anne?" Caty wanted to pretend it was a good idea, because he was cute and she would really like to kiss him at some point, but alas, acting had never been her strong suit. "Why would she talk to me about it when none of the other Kappas will?"

The naughty gleam found its way back to Tilney's eyes. "Who said anything about 'talk'? If Anne's anything like my Graduate RA, Brandon, she'll have to keep files on any problems that happen with the girls under her care. And she can't be in her room all the time."

Caty felt a delicious chill run through her. She couldn't break into Anne's room and break into her files—could she?

Tilney put his hands behind his head, leaning back in his chair. "Now that would be something to write about on your blog."

Caty bit back a smile, not wanting to encourage him too much.

The bell over the door rang as it opened, and Caty looked up to see one of the other Kappa pledges, Jane Fairfax, walking into the shop. She almost called out to say hello, until she noticed she was with someone who looked distinctly older than her—maybe in his late 20s. If she was here for a job interview or to meet with her professor, Caty didn't want to distract her.

But no, Caty realized as she took in the man's face. She recognized him from the Kappa party. He was the Theta Graduate RA, Knightley. She'd seen him in passing; he was a family friend of Emma's, and they were always acting vaguely exasperated but still fond of each other, as only people who have known each other for a very long time can do.

What was he doing here with Jane? There had been rumors going around the Kappa house—that Jane had been having some sort of affair with her professor back in Vienna, which was why she'd had to transfer to AU at the semester break. Caty didn't usually put much stock in talk like that, but maybe Jane had a thing for older men.

She was distracted from this thought by Tilney, reaching for the diary she'd left out on the table. "An honest to God secret diary in code." He flipped through the pages, shaking his head. "Some girls have all the luck." A beat passed as Tilney considered the book. "I could bring it home with me, try to take a crack at the code, if you like."

A small frisson of unease coursed through Caty. He was only curious, she knew, as any true-crime aficionado would be. But even so, it was *her* first real case, and she knew she couldn't afford to trust the diary out of her hands. "Thanks for the offer, but I think I'll try again myself this weekend."

Tilney closed the book, handing it back to her. "Ambitious," he said with an easy smile, his eyes flickering back to the red-leather cover as Caty slipped it into her bag.

FROM THE FILES OF CATY MORLAND:

INTERVIEWEE: HENRY TILNEY (SOPHOMORE AT AUSTEN UNIVERSITY, MEMBER OF SIGMA RHO)

CATY: YOU'RE FROM LOUISIANA, CORRECT?

TILNEY: BORN HERE. RAISED HERE. WILL DOUBTLESS DIE HERE, AND HAUNT ANY HIPSTERS WHO DARE TO RENOVATE THE FAMILY HOME.

CATY: SO IN SOME WAYS, YOU'RE SORT OF AN INSIDER WHEN IT COMES TO SOUTHERN LIVING. BUT, FORGIVE ME FOR SAYING SO—

TILNEY: HOW DARE YOU.

CATY: —YOU DON'T REALLY SEEM THE FRATERNITY TYPE.

TILNEY: OH, WELL. THANK YOU. I RETRACT MY MOCK OUTRAGE.

CATY: I'M GUESSING THERE MUST BE SOME FAMILY INCENTIVE FOR JOINING?

TILNEY: YOU SAY INCENTIVE, I SAY MANIPULATIVE EMOTIONAL BLACKMAIL. POT-AY-TO, POT-AH-TO.

CATY: CARE TO ELABORATE?

TILNEY: MY FATHER IS GENERAL TILNEY. HE USED TO BE SIGMA RHO PRESIDENT, BACK IN THE DAYS BEFORE THE INTERNET AND JOY, AND NOW HE RUNS THE UNIVERSITY'S ROTC PROGRAM, AND MY LIFE.

CATY: SO YOU'RE A LEGACY. WHICH MEANS, YOU KIND OF HAVE THE INSIDE TRACK. IN YOUR EXPERIENCE, DO YOU THINK IT'S POSSIBLE FOR SOMEONE TO BE SO OBSESSED WITH THE REPUTATION OF A SORORITY THAT THEY'D KILL ONE OF ITS MEMBERS TO KEEP HER FROM DAMAGING IT?

TILNEY: FRANKLY, I'M SURPRISED IT DOESN'T HAPPEN MORE OFTEN.

❀ 12 ❀

(FEBRUARY - A FEW WEEKS BEFORE
ISABELLA'S DEATH)

"Thank y'all for coming out to the third official planning meeting of the Pi Kappa Sigma Talent Show Committee, now in session."

Caty did her best to keep smiling. Emma made it sound like they had a choice in the matter, but in reality, it had been stressed in the last two planning meetings (and the bi-weekly emails) that the annual Pi Kappa Sigma Talent Show was as mandatory as mandatory got. Though the Kappas had banned hazing a few years before (a fact of which Caty reassured her parents in every phone call since bid day), the talent show acted as a sort of mild pledging ritual. There would be no forced drinking, parading around in bikinis to have her body parts rated by fraternity brothers, or any of the other dangerous or degrading rituals outlined in the frantic emails sent to Caty by her mother; but all pledges were required to participate in the talent show, whether as onstage talent or backstage crew.

As far as hazing went, Caty knew they were getting off pretty light. If only they didn't have to have so many meetings. Frankly, she didn't understand how there was so much to plan. It was a *talent show*, not high tea with the queen.

"So far fifteen of you have signed up for acts. Thank you for doing so." Emma appraised the room. "As for the rest of you . . . While all pledges are required to participate, the older sisters should also strongly consider contributing. Dig deep, think about what talents you can summon." She cast her gaze about the table. "Like . . . Jane. Maybe you could play the piano for anyone who wants to do a musical number?"

Jane looked a little out of it, like she hadn't been paying attention. "Um. Sure."

"Fantastic."

Emma went back to business, explaining why every Kappa should feel it was her duty to bolster her sisterhood, but Caty continued to watch Jane. It was hard to explain, but she sensed something was off. Jane always seemed kind of aloof—nice, but not one of the girls who was going to spend her free time gossiping in the Kappa house. Over the past few days, though, she'd withdrawn even further into herself, like she was burdened by something. Like maybe she was carrying a dark secret...

Once again, Caty reminded herself to focus on one mystery at a time. Too much was at stake to get distracted, she reminded herself, turning her gaze once again to the front door.

Emma's instructions on the best way to distribute fliers were interrupted by a chime from her phone. Her face lit up as she read the screen. "Good news, y'all. Frank Churchill is on his way over. He's a genius at this sort of thing—Knightley says he pretty much single-handedly planned that amazing Theta mixer at the beginning of the semester."

Karoline arched an eyebrow. "Yeah, I'm so sure that's why he's coming over, Emma. Because he's super into planning events."

Emma smiled, not correcting her.

Movement at the front door. Caty straightened, watching as Anne slipped out, her backpack straining with books. She wore track pants and an oversized AU sweatshirt, her hair in a messy bun atop her head. All the details added up to one thing: she was heading to the library. Which meant her room, and all those files, would be left unattended for a few solid hours.

Caty forced herself to wait ten minutes before rising to her feet.

"Oh, shoot. I just remembered I have to upload my paper. Be back in fifteen."

She hurried out of the room before anyone could stop her, were they so inclined, and raced up the stairs. The halls were dark since everyone was at the meeting downstairs, and Caty felt a thrill at her own cleverness. All those murder podcasts hadn't been for nothing. She had basically figured out how to commit the perfect crime.

Once inside Anne's room—which, thankfully, wasn't locked— Caty felt less sure of her own deductive skills. Where to start? She began opening and shutting drawers, hoping she would know what she was looking for when she found it.

"What would A.W. Radcliffe do?" she murmured to herself. After brief deliberation, Caty started on the wastebasket. In movies, people were always throwing away important information that could be used for clues.

There. Amid a few granola bar wrappers and used-up sticky tabs was a piece of paper crumpled into a small, tight ball. Whatever was written on it had been crossed out so intently that dark ink bled through the other side.

Heart hammering in anticipation, Caty grabbed the balled-up paper and hastened to smooth it out. She squinted at the scratched-out lines, trying to make out the words underneath. That first one looked like coffee, and the next one was . . . milk?

Oh. It was a grocery list. Deflated, Caty threw the paper back in the bin.

Okay, so this was starting to feel less thrilling and dangerous than inept and ridiculous. Caty worried her bottom lip as she hoped for the burst of detective-ly insight that would lead her to some heretofore unknown information about Marla Bertram. It wasn't like Anne would go to the library and conveniently leave her laptop behind, but maybe—

Oh, wait. There it was: Anne's laptop, stored up on a shelf above her desk. God, everything was so tidy. Anne made Caty feel like a pig in comparison. And if she was a pig, Isabella had to be a wild boar or something, because despite her professed interest in having a room that was "Pinterest approved," she had thus far used her laundry basket as a purely decorative item.

Reaching into her back pocket, Caty pulled out the rubber kitchen gloves she'd brought along, just in case, so she wouldn't leave behind fingerprints. True, the giant yellow monstrosities weren't the most aesthetically pleasing way to commit a minor crime, but in a pinch, they would work.

Gloves in place, Caty opened the laptop, crossing her fingers that it didn't have a password. (Metaphorically crossing her fingers, that was, as the thick rubber didn't allow for much flexibility.)

Tonight must be her lucky night, because not only had Anne left her room unlocked and her laptop behind, but her computer was also a model so old that it required no password. Someone should talk to her about safeguarding her things. Not Caty, of course, because that would be both incriminating and stupid, but *someone*.

After that, it was all pretty simple. Anne was as organized with her personal files as she was tidy with her bedroom. A quick click into a folder marked 'RA' revealed several files, including (Caty saw with a rush of euphoria) a folder entitled 'Marla Bertram.'

Practically salivating at the discovery, Caty clicked on the folder —only to find that on this, at least, Anne had possessed enough foresight to create a password.

"Shoot," Caty grumbled, though in actuality, she was pleased. The truth about Marla Bertram couldn't be all that juicy if it weren't stored inside a secured folder, could it? Maybe Tilney could help her brainstorm what the password might be. (Cuddled up on a couch next to a fire . . . And so on, and so forth.)

For now, she made a copy of the locked file to email to herself. One of Anne's tabs already had her email pulled up. Using Anne's email address felt risky, but it would save Caty the trouble of opening another window, her own email, then deleting all the history to make sure Anne never noticed it.

Alas, this part of her subterfuge proved to be more difficult than anticipated. Not because anyone appeared at the door, or Anne happened to log into her email address from another computer, as Caty feared, but because Anne's laptop was *so* slow. There were plants that grew faster than this thing loaded. She was starting to understand why Anne had so conveniently left it behind.

Vowing to herself that she would buy Anne a new computer if she ever came into some unexpected money, as a sort of Karmic retribution for sneaking through her things, Caty waited. And waited. After a while she resorted to doing some lunges around the room, because she hadn't had time to work out that day, and cardio health was important—or so Emma was always telling her.

Finally, the folder loaded, and the email was sent. Caty set about cleaning up her virtual mess so Anne would never realize she'd been there.

Unfortunately, she accidentally clicked on the drafts folder instead of the sent items folder, and so had to wait while the computer loaded the wrong page. Ten years later, the drafts folder finally came up. As Caty moved to click back, one of the subject lines caught her eye: I don't know if I should send this.

Intriguing. Judging by the date stamp, it had been written a few days before, so clearly Anne was still deliberating on whether it should be sent. Maybe, by some strange coincidence, it had something to do with Marla Bertram . . . ?

Caty clicked on the message, doing some squats as she waited for it to load. Since the email was only a few lines, it took less time than the other page, and she was able to quickly peruse its contents.

To: WENTWORTH_FREDDY@IBERVILLEPD.COM
SUBJECT: I DON'T KNOW IF I SHOULD SEND THIS
MESSAGE:
HI, IT'S ANNE. I HOPE ALL IS WELL. IT'S BEEN

That was where it ended. Though Caty hadn't gotten very far, something about the message still felt too intimate. Almost more intimate than if the email had been finished and sent, because at least then it would have been intended for one more person to see; as it stood now, Anne had chosen for whatever reason to keep it to herself, and Caty had violated that. Relaying a silent apology, she exited the message.

Once the sent items folder loaded, Caty moved to delete her email so she could put the laptop back where it belonged and get out of the room. Had she been gone for more than fifteen minutes? She'd have to come up with a backup story, just in case someone asked her what had taken so long.

But before Caty could delete the email, another sent message caught her eye. It had been sent to Knightley a day before, and the subject line read, *THOUGHT THIS MIGHT HELP.*

Not two minutes before, Caty had vowed to uphold Anne's privacy. Still, there was something about that email that just begged for her attention. Ever since seeing Knightley with Jane at the coffee shop, Caty had wondered about him. It was possible, of course, that they were just meeting up to discuss something school-related— coffee was the platonic drink of choice, after all. But then, there was Jane's history of dating authority figures…

Just for sake of thoroughness, Caty decided she should make sure the email had nothing to do with Marla Bertram. A.W. Radcliffe always said intuition was an investigator's best friend, after all, and what was this irksome sense of distrust if not gut instinct?

To: SIR_KNIGHTLEY@AU.EDU
SUBJECT: THOUGHT THIS MIGHT HELP
MESSAGE:
HEY, THIS IS THE PASSAGE I WAS TELLING YOU ABOUT. LOOKS LIKE IT'S PRETTY OFFICIAL. ☹
HANDBOOK, PG. 164, SECTION 3
A FEW MONTHS CAN GO BY QUICKLY, THOUGH.
-A

An innocuous enough message on the surface, but Caty's Sherlock senses were tingling. She scoured Anne's bookshelf and desk, searching for the handbook she'd referenced.

Stacked into a neat pile of books on the desk was a binder marked 'Resident Advisor Handbook.' Caty flipped open to page 164, searching for section three, and felt her blood run cold.

SECTION 3: RELATIONSHIPS WITH UNDERGRADUATE STUDENTS

IT IS THE UNIVERSITY'S OFFICIAL POLICY THAT GRADUATE RESI-DENT ADVISORS ARE STRICTLY FORBIDDEN FROM ENTERING INTO ROMANTIC OR OTHERWISE SEXUAL RELATIONSHIPS WITH UNDERGRAD-UATE STUDENTS DURING THE TERM OF THEIR EMPLOYMENT, EVEN IF SAID UNDERGRADUATE STUDENT IS NOT UNDER THEIR SUPERVISION. ANY VIOLATION OF THIS RULE WILL RESULT IN IMMEDIATE TERMINA-TION, AND THE RESIDENT ADVISOR MAY ALSO BE SUBJECT TO FURTHER ACADEMIC CENSURE DEPENDENT UPON THE CIRCUMSTANCES.

"Oh my god," Caty blurted aloud. Okay, so she didn't know quite what it meant, but she knew she had the same feeling she got when she was listening to *The Mysteries of Udolpho* and A.W. Radcliffe came across the clue that was going to break everything wide open.

Hands shaking with adrenaline, Caty forwarded the Knightley email to herself before deleting both messages she'd sent. She replaced the laptop, then deliberated a moment before removing page 164 from the RA binder. There was a chance Anne might notice it was missing, but it was a chance Caty would have to take. This clue, she knew, was too important to leave behind.

Afterward, Caty returned to the meeting, doing her best to act like she was invested in making this the best Kappa Talent Show in the history of Kappa Talent Shows.

But all the while, her mind was churning. Was Jane the girl Knightley was interested in dating—or was it somebody else? And why did Caty's gut tell her this had something important to do with Marla Bertram's disappearance?

$$\pi\kappa\Sigma$$

A tense quiet fell over the dinner table as everyone processed this new piece of information.

John Thorpe was the one to break the silence, gesturing back and forth between Jane and Knightley with his fork. "So the two of you have been...?" He made an extremely inappropriate gesture with his hands.

"Um," said Jane, staring down at her plate.

"Hey," Frank protested, his voice coming out sharper than Caty had ever heard it. Sensing the surprise from around the table, Frank shifted back into his usual easy, affable charm. "That's a little aggressive, John. No way to talk to a lady."

"The two of you were meeting up for coffee?" This from Emma, who was looking at Knightley with a slightly stung expression. Clearly she had not been in on the loop.

Knightley met her gaze before looking to Caty with a tight, clenched jaw. "You broke into Anne's room, went through her private files and emails without her permission." He looked beseechingly to others at the table. "How are we still encouraging this behavior? Clearly this has gone too far."

Marianne gave him her most disdainful look—an impressive accomplishment from the younger Dashwood sister, as many of her expressions were the definition of scornful. "Sounds like something a sexual predator might say to gaslight his accuser."

With a sigh, Knightley took his napkin from his lap and tossed it onto his plate.

πκΣ

After the talent show meeting (finally!) adjourned for the night, Caty was surprised to find Isabella in their room. She felt a little disappointed at the sight of her friend—not just because things had been weird between them ever since the Tilney-texting incident, but because she'd wanted some time to think over what she'd found that night in Anne's room, piece it all together.

"Hey," she said.

"Hey," said Isabella back.

"You weren't at the meeting."

"I had a group project to work on. Emma said I could make up points by helping set up chairs at the talent show."

"Oh."

An awkward lull stretched. This was how it had been ever since last Saturday. Two girls who had once been inseparable, attached at the hip, now acted like two overly polite strangers. Caty hated it. She almost wished she'd just gone to New Orleans with the others, if only to have spared them both the discomfort. Not that it was right, what Isabella had done, but . . . enough time had passed that she didn't feel angry anymore. She just missed her.

For a moment, she deliberated letting Isabella in on her scoop—the diary, the email, everything. Then they could solve this thing together, like old times.

Before she could decide one way or another, Isabella's phone buzzed. She looked down, her face registering surprise, then a flushed pleasure as she read through the text.

Caty temporarily forgot that they weren't speaking anymore. "You okay, Bella?"

Isabella blinked at her, as if she'd forgotten she was there. Her cheeks were rosy, her eyes unnaturally bright. "Fine. I just have to… study. I'm going downstairs."

She left without saying anything else, taking only her phone with her, no books or laptop. Caty frowned after her, but told herself it must be something romantic and gushy from James. In which case, good riddance. One of the few perks of not speaking with Isabella was not having to hear all the details about her friend and her brother.

Besides, that left Caty time to ponder over what she'd discovered that night and figure out what it all meant.

· · ·

FROM THE FILES OF CATY MORLAND:

INTERVIEWEE: JAMES MORLAND (JUNIOR AT LOUISIANA STATE UNIVERSITY, BROTHER OF CATY MORLAND AND "BOYFRIEND" OF ISABELLA THORPE)

[INTERVIEW CONDUCTED VIA PHONE CALL]

JAMES: WE WERE STILL TEXTING, BUT NOT NONSTOP. IT WAS LIKE THAT IN THE BEGINNING, I GUESS, BUT IT HAD BEEN A FEW MONTHS AND . . . YOU KNOW.

CATY: WERE YOU STILL INTERESTED?

JAMES: OF COURSE. WE WERE BOTH JUST BUSY WITH SCHOOL, AND ... THAT'S JUST HOW THINGS GO. I ALWAYS TEXTED HER BACK AS SOON AS I COULD. AND . . . I WOULD TEXT HER FIRST THING IN THE MORNING AND LAST THING AT NIGHT. KIND OF LIKE A GOOD MORNING, GOODNIGHT.

CATY: I'M SURE SHE APPRECIATED THAT. DID YOU TEXT HER EVERY MORNING, EVERY NIGHT? WITHOUT FAIL?

JAMES: I THINK SO. UH—NO. WAIT. I BROKE MY SCREEN AND HAD TO GET IT FIXED, SO FOR A FEW DAYS THERE WASN'T MUCH COMMUNICATION.

CATY: CAN YOU REMEMBER WHEN THAT WAS?

JAMES: I THINK IT MUST HAVE BEEN A WEEK OR TWO BEFORE THE TALENT SHOW? UM—A WEEK, I GUESS. IT HAPPENED DURING A PICKUP GAME WITH SOME OF MY FRIENDS.

CATY: SO THE WEEK LEADING UP TO THE TALENT SHOW, YOU WOULDN'T HAVE BEEN TEXTING WITH ISABELLA?

JAMES: NOT UNTIL THURSDAY OR FRIDAY, WHENEVER THE PHONE WAS FIXED.

❧ 13 ❧

Caty was settling in to do her cleaning duty after community dinner when her phone chimed, and she saw with a giddy thrill that she had a string of messages from Tilney. Truth be told, it was difficult to know if the excitement came from the fact that it was Tilney texting, or that he might have made progress with the password-protected file on Marla Bertram. The exhilaration of playing detective was pretty much on par with the exhilaration of flirting with a cute boy, Caty was learning

No luck, Nancy Drew. Yet.

There's a Sigma who's majoring in computer science who said he could take a crack at it.

I've sworn him to an oath of silence—and am also helping him with his English paper. He'll keep quiet, or EVERYONE's hearing about his comma splices, so help me god.

Caty's face hurt from how hard she was smiling. Progress in the case, AND a cutesy nickname from Tilney. She thought Emma would agree that he was falling madly in love with her—if she could tell Emma about their Marla Bertram investigation, which she absolutely could not. She and Tilney had pinky sworn and then gotten wasted together, or maybe that happened in reverse. Either way, the vow was sacred.

NICE WORK, WATSON, she typed back. *WE'RE MAKING PROGRESS.*

A few seconds later, another chime: *I LET YOU BE N.D., BUT YOU MAKE ME BE WATSON?? DUDE.*

She giggled. *SORRY. I'M THE SHERLOCK IN THIS RELATIONSHIP.*

Caty hesitated before sending, afraid she might be coming on too strong with the word 'relationship'. But then again, as Emma was always saying, "The only way to get the best treatment is to never put up with anything else." Maybe that was the secret to boy-kind—assuming their flirty banter meant something, in order to make it so?

A response chimed from Tilney. *GREEDY. ;)*

Caty grinned, thoroughly besotted. A winky face was subtle, but —she felt—significant. You didn't send a winky face to just anybody.

The good feeling evaporated as she put aside her phone and began washing the dinner dishes, and not just because somebody left the lasagna dish out without letting it soak. She hadn't told Tilney this yet, but she'd already begun forming some ideas about what had happened to Marla Bertram. No doubt, Tilney would remind her that A.W. Radcliffe was always saying they should keep an open mind and not jump to conclusions before all the evidence was present, but Caty felt confident that she'd made some important connections already.

The first piece of evidence? That Marla Bertram kept a diary in code, which meant she was hiding something—a secret important enough that Mrs. Norris broke into Caty's room to try to keep it quiet.

The second piece of evidence? The email between Anne and Knightley which suggested he was investigating the possibility of having a relationship with an undergraduate student.

The third piece of evidence? That Marla Bertram abruptly left the school, one semester before she was due to graduate.

The conclusion? Knightley and Marla Bertram must have been involved in a secret relationship. When Knightley found out how much trouble he could get in with the administration, he'd tried to break things off. Maybe she'd blackmailed him, threatened to go to the president of the university, and Knightley had to take some drastic measures to keep her silent . . .

Caty backtracked. Okay, that might be too extreme. She thought there was something weird going on with Knightley, but she didn't know that she quite believed he was capable of physical violence. In the subtle digging she'd done with Emma, she'd learned that Knightley was overall a quiet, studious guy, who didn't go out much, and definitely didn't have a string of girlfriends. Which didn't sound much like a lothario abuser.

Unless . . . Knightley had a thing for younger co-eds. And it only *seemed* like he never had a girlfriend because he was conducting secret affairs with girls from the neighboring sororities. He'd keep it up until they graduated, then move on to his next target. Except, Marla hadn't gone quietly. Maybe she'd had a nervous breakdown. Maybe she'd gotten pregnant. So Knightley had to get her out of the way without anyone realizing he was involved. Maybe that was why there was so much secrecy about Marla's disappearance— because Knightley was leading everyone astray.

Granted, it didn't explain why Mrs. Norris would be helping him cover things up. Or why Anne had been emailing him just a few days ago about that part of the handbook. That threw a wrench in Caty's theory, unless...

Unless Knightley had already set his eye on another undergraduate girl. Caty remembered seeing Jane Fairfax with him at the Crescent. If she was his next victim, it would explain why Jane seemed so weird and distant at the talent show meeting, why the two of them were meeting up for coffees together.

Caty's phone buzzed again, startling her from her thoughts. She dried off her soapy hands, hoping it was Tilney.

At the sight of John Thorpe's name on her screen, any excitement dissolved. He'd been texting her ever since "helping" with the move into the Kappa house. She'd hoped her lack of enthusiasm would be enough to give the hint that he should discontinue, but apparently not.

Hey you

How could such a simple, unpunctuated statement make Caty's skin crawl so very much? It was somehow worse than him saying something vulgar or rude, because it assumed a familiarity that there was no way to get out of. If she ignored him, he just persisted until he got an answer; if she responded, it looked like encouragement; if she told him to stop, he'd tell her she was overreacting, being a snob, he was just trying to say hello. There was no winning with the John Thorpes of the world.

She agonized over it for a few minutes, long enough to receive another impatient chime from him.

HEY

She typed a simple *STUDYING,* then put her phone on silent.

$$πκΣ$$

By the time Caty finished with the dishes, the light was on in her bedroom, which meant Isabella was back from her night class. Things had thawed between them over the past few days, but mostly because Isabella spent all of her time texting. James must have been on the receiving end of those messages, because she seemed particularly happy lately—happy enough that she'd even asked Caty to watch the latest episode of *The Cases of Otranto* together. And even though she'd spent most of the time texting through the show, Caty could still recognize an olive branch for what it was. She was glad Isabella and James were so happy together.

Sure enough, Isabella was on her bed, texting, as Caty entered the room. She looked up with a smile so big it must have hurt. "Hey, girl! How were dishes?"

"Filthy, but I whipped them into shape."

Isabella laughed as though this was especially witty. Caty shifted, uncomfortable. She was happy they were getting along again, but it felt kind of weird that they'd been so angry at each other, then just swept everything under the rug and gone straight back to being best friends again.

Then again, it wasn't like Caty had tried to bring it up. As strange as it felt to ignore all the unsettled business, she didn't want to go back to fighting.

"What've you been up to?" She motioned toward Isabella's phone. "Texting with James?"

"Mm-hmm." Isabella averted her gaze. It was kind of sweet, that she could still get embarrassed about messaging with her boyfriend. "He says hello."

Caty rolled her eyes. "No, he doesn't."

"No, he doesn't," Isabella agreed with a guilty smile.

An awkward pause stretched out between them. Caty took in a deep breath, deciding it was time to move past the weirdness. "So things have been progressing, with Tilney." The name hadn't been spoken between them, since he'd been the issue that instigated their fight before. But if they were going to be friends again, Isabella would have to get used to it.

"That's great," Isabella returned, and it sounded like she meant it. In fact, if Caty didn't know any better, she would never have suspected that Tilney had ever been a source of tension between them.

"I mean, it's nothing serious yet. Mostly just texting."

Isabella looked at her, wide-eyed and solemn. "Texting means a lot more than people think it does. That's how you get to know someone, you know? Face to face you can be distracted by hormones or whatever, but when you're texting . . . that's when you get to know what someone is *really* like."

The words hung in the air, strangely earnest. "Yeah," Caty returned, for lack of anything better to say.

Then Isabella's phone buzzed, and all her focus returned to the screen, her face lighting up at whatever she read, fingers flying to send back a hasty response.

Though her friend was preoccupied, Caty nonetheless went through her nightly ritual of exaggerated yawning, setting her alarm, and rubbing her eyes, before she crawled into the lower bunk.

The first thing she'd done when she moved in with Isabella was to rig up a series of curtains that obscured the lower bunk from the rest of the room and gave her a little cube of privacy. Caty loved her new friend, but she'd quickly learned that unless she set up some boundaries, being Isabella's bestie would be a full-time position. This conclusion only took a few days of Isabella's head popping into view, ready to engage Caty in immediate and lengthy conversation, regardless of whether she was reading, watching TV, or even working on homework.

The one boundary Isabella did respect, however, was sleep, so Caty made up an excuse about having trouble sleeping with any light in the room, built her little fortress, and pretended to go to sleep early, sometimes hours before she drifted off. As much as she liked Isabella, and people in general, Caty needed time to be herself, all by herself. Isabella seemed to think she was just goofing around when she was on her phone, but to Caty, that was invaluable me-time, when she got to be alone with her thoughts.

Tonight, once the curtains were carefully drawn, Caty fished under her pillow, where she'd been hiding Marla Bertram's diary.

To her dismay, there was nothing there. Frantically, Caty picked up the pillow, then felt around behind the mattress, peering down to see if it had fallen down between the bed and the wall. But there was nothing there.

Marla Bertram's diary had vanished.

From the Files of Caty Morland:

[Tumblr post from Marla Bertram, username: Caged Starling]

Did you know that most birds are fucking miserable in captivity? Like, you're at the pet store looking at these

LOVEBIRDS THINKING, AWW, HOW CUTE, BUT THEY'RE THESE ELEGANT BEAUTIFUL CREATURES THAT ARE JUST LONELY AND WEIGHED DOWN AND DOING CRAZY SHIT LIKE PULLING OUT THEIR OWN FEATHERS AND REFUSING TO EAT SO THEY CAN JUST FUCKING DIE ALREADY. GOD, I HATE HUMANS.

❧ 14 ❧

(MARCH, AGAIN)

A t least some of the guests of the dinner party seemed appropriately impressed by the missing diary—though not, as Caty had anticipated, all. "So what?" John Thorpe, the self-appointed voice of the dissidents, spoke up. "It wasn't Isabella's diary, was it? Who cares if it went missing?"

Darcy looked a little put out about belonging to the same group as John Thorpe, though he, too, voiced his qualms. "The diary and Isabella's death don't seem to have anything to do with each other."

"Well," said Lizzy from across the table, "Isabella did die just a week or so later. It could be connected."

Darcy scoffed at this; his grandfather, Caty remembered hearing, had been a judge. "Circumstantial."

"Yeah," Karoline spoke up, seeming eager to agree with anything Darcy had to say. "And it's just a coincidence, too."

Lizzy ducked her head, trying to hide a laugh, and Darcy's naturally embedded frown deepened.

Caty took the awkward pause as an opportunity to regain control of the conversation. "In the chaos that followed—the talent show, Initiation, and of course, Isabella's murder—I actually forgot about the missing diary for a while. I know, hard to believe. I told myself that I must have just misplaced it. It wasn't until after Isabella's death, when I saw it in the possession of one of the people at this very table tonight, that I realized it might all be connected."

Glances were exchanged across the table, everyone trying to suss out the guilty party—save be the guilty party, who looked rather conspicuously pale.

"But how could the two things possibly be related to each other?" Caty continued. "Isabella didn't even know Marla Bertram. And what could be in a diary that would possibly be worth killing over?"

She let the question linger in the air for a moment before pressing on. "That thought was at the forefront of my mind as I conducted interviews this last week, with those nearest and dearest to Isabella, and even those only peripherally connected to her. Almost everyone was happy to help—with a few notable exceptions." Another moment as Caty allowed everyone in the room to draw their own conclusions over who the difficult parties might be. "Some of the resistance I had expected—like John, who'd voiced his doubts about Isabella being murdered from the beginning."

"Fake news," confirmed John.

"But one person in particular surprised me with his consistent avoidance and refusal to see me." Caty waited a beat before letting her gaze land on Knightley. "George Knightley, the Theta GRA, pledged to help the students under his care through their tumultuous undergraduate years. Too busy to answer a few paltry questions about the death of a girl that, arguably, as the 'responsible adult' of the group, he should have prevented?"

Knightley sighed, his shoulders tensed, as though he had been bracing himself for this all evening. "I already apologized for that. It was a busy week—"

"Murder waits for no one, Knightley," said Caty, as outside, a peal of thunder clapped through the sky.

πκΣ

(A FEW DAYS EARLIER)

Out of everyone at Austen University, Knightley was proving to be the most elusive when it came to pinning him down for an interview about Isabella's death. Caty's previous observations about him during their brief interactions—such as the rendezvous with Jane Fairfax at the Crescent, and the email to Anne about dating undergraduates—weren't exactly proof of murder, but they were odd. And Caty was beginning to learn that it was in the oddities, those things that didn't quite add up, that the truth was often buried.

(...Okay, so that was something A.W. Radcliffe said in one of her podcasts, but Caty really was beginning to learn that for herself. Regardless, the Knightley thing deserved a little more time and attention, even if it led nowhere.)

In fact, *nowhere* was where the thread of investigation seemed to be going, since Knightley had become evasive ever since word got around that Caty was investigating Isabella's death as a murder.

"Busy," Emma protested her terminology, "not *evasive*. His master's thesis is due at the end of the month. Cut him some slack."

Caty tried, she did. Not wanting her bias to cloud her judgment, she was determined not to jump to any conclusions about Knightley. She just wanted to ask him a few questions, and she told him as much over the phone. When he sounded distracted and cagey, Caty generously ascribed that to his impending deadline. When he informed her that he was sorry but he didn't have time for her, Caty tried to make it easy for him. Could she send him an email, which he could answer when he got a moment? After obtaining a reluctant yes, Caty read and re-read her message to make sure it was as simple, straightforward, and non-accusatory as possible, before sending. When days stretched on and still no response was forthcoming, Caty tried a polite reminder, and when that was ignored, she tried sending a text, and when that was left on read, she knew that Knightley was a murderer.

. . . That was a joke. Mostly. Caty wasn't jumping to conclusions, but it did seem a little suspicious that he couldn't bother to reply to a text. He was busy, but he wasn't dead. In fact, he still had time to meet with Emma for their weekly brunch.

"He has to eat," Emma chided her when Caty brought this to her attention. "It's not superfluous time. It's time he would be spending eating anyway, he just chooses to do it with me."

At that, a sudden idea struck Caty. "Could he choose to do it at your house this week…?"

Caty was perhaps not as clever as she thought, since when she sprang upon Knightley at the Woodhouse residence, he didn't seem surprised, just resigned. ("Sprang" was Emma's word, for the record. Caty maintained that she merely greeted him with an ever-so-slightly higher amount of enthusiasm than one might normally use to greet an acquaintance.)

To be fair, Emma did her fair share of springing on Knightley, too, pestering him about *was he eating* and *it was still important to get exercise* and *self-care was a necessity, not a want.* "You look haggard," Emma said to him, reaching for his forehead. "Are you feeling sick?"

Knightley avoided the touch. "I haven't been sleeping well."

Was it only Caty's imagination, or did he dart a quick, guilty glance in her direction as he said it?

Emma brightened. "I have something that could help. Some L-Theanine, and some lavender…"

"What do you want to know?" Knightley asked Caty over the egg-white frittatas that Emma had ordered for them. This was the only time period he would allot to answer questions about Isabella from this time forward, he informed her in no uncertain terms.

"I just wondered what you remember about Isabella? Anything that stands out?"

Knightley shook his head. "I don't know that I ever met Isabella. I mean, maybe in passing, but I can't remember ever having a conversation with her."

Caty perked up at that, her Sherlock senses tingling. "Are you sure?"

"Pretty sure, yeah."

"That's strange. I thought I remembered seeing the two of you talking at the talent show."

Knightley chewed for a few moments, and Caty could practically see the wheels turning in his mind. He took a long sip of his fresh-squeezed orange juice. "Was she the—um, nun? That's right. I think we did talk. Briefly." He furrowed his brow a little at Caty. "You must have been paying close attention."

Caty just gave her best bland *Bless your heart* smile that revealed absolutely nothing. "Emma, didn't you tell me that Knightley had something to do with your decision to vote Isabella into the Kappas?"

Emma was looking at Knightley quizzically. "You remember. We had a whole discussion about it. You said she deserved another chance."

"Most of us could." Knightley continued eating, wolfing down his food as he glanced at his watch. "You didn't tell me names, remember? I just knew there was a Kappa bid who'd gotten into a bit of trouble. And I know what Karoline and Norris can be like when they smell blood in the water." He thought it over. "I guess if I'd put my mind to it, I could have figured out it was the girl from, um, the talent show. But I was a little preoccupied at the time. And still am." He looked, pointedly, at his watch again.

"Well." Caty forced a smile. "I guess Isabella was lucky to have you to speak up for her."

"You see?" Emma crowed to Caty afterward. "There was a perfectly logical reason behind it." She shook her head with an affectionate eye-roll. "Knightley is way too boring to be a murder suspect."

Caty wished that were true, for Emma's sake. Boring was something she certainly wouldn't have minded a little of after the whirlwind of Isabella's death. What she couldn't understand, and what was becoming increasingly frustrating, was Knightley's insistence on being so cagey. What was the point of dodging phone calls, giving half-answers, and even outright lying, if he didn't have something to hide?

πκΣ
(*MARCH, AGAIN*)

"Then I saw the stolen diary, while I was conducting interviews," Caty informed the table. "And suddenly, everything fell into place."

Half a dozen pairs of eyes looked to Knightley inquisitively. He cleared his throat. ". . . I don't have the diary, if that's what you're trying to insinuate."

"No," Caty agreed, then looked to the guilty party. "But Jane Fairfax does."

VOLUME TWO

"Seldom, very seldom, does complete truth belong to any human disclosure; seldom can it happen that something is not a little disguised, or a little mistaken."

Jane Austen, *Emma*

All eyes in the room shifted now to Jane—who under the best of circumstances shied away from attention, and who now looked like she wanted to crawl underneath her chair.

"Is it true, Jane?" Lizzy asked her in the gentle tone one might use to coax a wild animal, or a toddler. "Do you have the diary?"

Bright pink splotches bloomed on Jane's cheeks, her chest. "Y-yes. I mean, I did, but——"

"It's all right, Jane." Caty gave her an encouraging smile. "I know you didn't realize what you were doing. You were tricked into it. By *him*."

She hardly needed to have raised the index finger she now pointed in Knightley's direction; anyone who had been following even remotely along with the evening could have predicted where this was all heading. Still, a pointed finger helped add to the drama of it all. Caty only wished a clap of thunder might have pealed right then, but there was no controlling the weather.

And before Knightley could offer another one of his feeble protests, Caty barreled on, laying out the entirety of her case.

Knightley had been dating Marla Bertram in secret, but something went wrong between them in their relationship, causing

Marla to leave school a semester before graduating. (Caty's bet was on an unplanned pregnancy, but she had no proof to verify this.)

The coverup after Marla left was very hush-hush, and somehow Knightley lucked out by avoiding having his name dragged through the mud. He should have been on his best behavior, laid low for a bit, but instead he almost immediately began pursuing a relationship with another undergraduate—this time Jane Fairfax, a recent transfer with a known history of carrying on illicit affairs with authority figures.

Unbeknownst to Knightley, Marla had left behind her diary in her old bedroom—a diary that told the truth about his manipulation and abuse of power. Isabella must have found the diary in Caty's things and been blackmailing Knightley. Knightley convinced his new girlfriend, Jane, to steal the diary—and that was why Caty had seen it in her room the previous week when she went over to interview her.

Unfortunately that hadn't been enough for Knightley. Isabella already knew too many of his secrets, with or without the diary in her possession.

"So he waited for her in the fog that night on Box Hill," Caty concluded. "Maybe lured her away from the crowd to get her on her own. And he pushed her over the edge, ensuring that she would never tell a soul."

The room was silent, crackling with anticipation, and Caty felt a little rush of pleasure run through her that was better than a crush, better than chocolate, even. She had just solved her very first murder.

Emma was the first to break the silence. "It's not true. Even if all the pieces added up—which they don't—Knightley wouldn't have killed someone to save his reputation. He's one of the most decent people I know."

"Agreed," said Darcy, folding his arms, and Frank and Rushworth did the same in solidarity.

Caty held her ground, refusing to budge. "Everyone is capable of murder, under the right circumstances."

"Um, why would Knightley date Jane Fairfax? She's a nobody."
Karoline looked across the table, pulling a face. "No offense, Jane."

At Jane's side, Lizzy scoffed. "Typical. Challenge one of the rich
and privileged, and the rest close ranks as soon as possible."

Marianne nodded in emphatic agreement. "I, for one, have no
trouble believing that a white privileged male wouldn't think twice
about murdering a woman to silence her."

"No one had to silence anyone," John retorted resentfully. "The
Thorpes have plenty of money, thank you very much—my sister
wasn't so hard up that she'd have to resort to blackmail."

"Who said it had to do with money?" Caty countered. "Maybe
it was influence she needed. Like Knightley persuading Emma out
of nowhere to vote Isabella into the Kappas."

She thought she'd scored a point there, but when her eyes
landed on Tilney, she was dismayed to see he looked unconvinced.
He gave her an apologetic grimace. "I'm sorry, V.M., but I feel like
we may have taken a few leaps of logic. What is there that connects
Marla to Knightley?" He held up a hand to ward off Caty's reply. "I
know there's that weird email to Anne, but that was sent *after* Marla
left university. Everything else is conjecture. And without that
motive, what reason would Knightley have to kill Isabella?"

Silence fell over the table. Caty felt, for a moment, as if she
couldn't breathe—like a fish dragged out of water, gutted, and
filleted. There had been no doubt in her mind whatsoever that
Knightley was the guilty party. She searched her mind desperately
now for the thing that proved it, that connected all the pieces
together, but she realized with a cold dread that Tilney was right.

Her mouth worked, but no sound came out. She looked, desperately, to Jane—her last hope that the kaleidoscope might twist one
more time and bring the picture back into focus. "But… the
diary…"

"I did have it," Jane agreed. "But I didn't steal it. Isabella gave it
to me, right before she died."

$$\pi\kappa\Sigma$$

Jane's relationship with her murdered Kappa sister had been a strange one, she explained to her rapt audience. She and Isabella were in the same Louisiana History class, taught by Professor Weston—Frank's father. Jane hadn't realized this until the day she and Isabella both received bids from the Kappas, but after that Isabella made a point to save Jane a seat in every class.

"I thought she seemed over-friendly, but nice," said Jane. "Maybe a little lonely."

In the few minutes before class, they sometimes passed the time exchanging idle pleasantries, but nothing that had stuck out to Jane as being significant, even after Isabella's death. "She liked to gossip, and she told me some things about a few of the Kappa girls. Nothing huge. Nose jobs and things like that." Jane hesitated. "She did mention Marla Bertram to me, but only vaguely. Said there was a Kappa girl who'd been kicked out of school, but she didn't seem to know much more than that."

To Jane, it was an entirely superficial relationship, one that existed only because she and Isabella happened to be in the same sorority and happened to be taking the same class: "We didn't even follow each other on Instagram."

That night on Box Hill, Isabella approached Jane when she was getting a drink. They'd compared their new Kappa pearls, and then out of nowhere, Isabella handed Jane the diary. "Remember that Kappa girl I told you about? The one who left AU? I found her diary in my room. I think it's written in code. Weird, right?"

It was weird, but Jane wasn't particularly interested, and she had no intention of keeping the diary. But Isabella disappeared into the crowd of dancing bodies before Jane could hand it back to her. Not knowing what else to do, Jane put it in her bag, deciding she'd give it back to Isabella the next time she saw her.

"Believe it or not, I forgot about it, with everything that happened. It wasn't until the police told me I might have been the last person to speak to her that I remembered it and realized it could be significant."

"So the police have it now?" asked Caty. At least there was that. Even if she hadn't managed to solve the murder, the key evidence was in safe hands.

Jane cleared her throat, seeming to shrink in on herself a little, as if she dreaded what she was about to say. "Actually, no. It was ... stolen."

As she'd anticipated, this response produced no little amount of interest around the table. Jane rushed to explain, seeming to want to get it all over with as quickly as possible. "It wasn't just the diary— my entire book bag was taken. I went to the Crescent to do some studying, and afterward I was going to stop by Charlotte's house to drop it off—she's my aunt's girlfriend, and one of the lead detectives on the case. I got up to go to the bathroom and left my bag at the table, and when I came back . . . gone."

Stunned as she was by learning her theory about the murder had been incorrect, Caty still could not be entirely insensible to the intrigue of these new developments. It could be a coincidence, of course, that the diary had been in Jane's bag when it was taken . . . but what if it wasn't?

Karoline clicked her tongue at Jane. "That was very careless of you, Janey. You should never leave your things unattended in public. You really must learn to take better care of yourself."

Jane flushed, looking irritated. "I didn't—" But she stopped herself, suddenly, looking down at her plate.

"Well, you just told us you did, Janey, so there's no use getting worked up about it . . ."

But Caty ignored Karoline, focusing on Jane's expression, the set of her jaw. "You weren't alone," she guessed. "Someone else was with you at the Crescent." As a force of habit, her eyes darted over to Knightley, who gave her an exasperated look.

"*Really?*" he asked.

Jane's blush, seemingly impossibly, had deepened. "That's my business. It doesn't have anything to do with the diary or Isabella or—"

Quite unexpectedly, Frank cleared his throat, interrupting her.

"Jane," he said, his voice softening as he met her gaze across the table, "it's all right."

FROM THE FILES OF CATY MORLAND:

[EXCERPT FROM JANE FAIRFAX'S FACEBOOK PROFILE]
RELATIONSHIP STATUS: IT'S COMPLICATED

❧ 2 ❧

I t should have come as no surprise to anybody that Jane Fairfax
had some secret motivation in pledging Kappa. Jane was not
the kind of girl one would expect to find in a sorority. She was
neither tan nor blonde, she did not know how to perform a keg
stand, and she had never uttered a single "whoo" in the throes of
excitement. Jewish by birth and agnostic by practice, she had yet to
be saved by Jesus, and she had no intention of getting a Chinese
symbol tattooed on her body. Her degree would be in music performance and composition, not interior design, nutrition/fitness, or
elementary education. She was not a frequent gym-goer or
smoothie drinker, and though she did own an Instagram account, its
main use had been posting pictures of scenic Vienna, not taking
selfies in bathroom mirrors.

To anyone who pointed out these discrepancies, Jane would say
she was interested in the sorority because of the scholarships offered
to the Kappas, the networking systems available after she graduated,
and the opportunities that having such a connected sisterhood could
afford her.

However, despite these very logical reasons for joining a sorority,
in truth this was not why Jane begrudgingly agreed to go Greek. In

reality, Jane was doing it for a reason that meant she had no room whatsoever to turn her nose down at any sorority girl, stereotypical or elsewise.

She was doing it for a boy.

A particularly cute boy, it was true, and one who made her believe in things like fate and romance and Hallmark movies, but a boy nonetheless. The feminist in her recoiled at the idea, the jaded New Yorker in her warned her she was being ridiculous, but Jane was in love. And lovers—much like angry people and sports fans— are not always wise.

Besides, Jane had spent the first twenty years of her life being prudent, and it turned out it was much more fun being twitterpated.

It has been said that love comes when one least expects it, and that was precisely when Frank Churchill arrived. Or, to be even more precise, it was back in October, when Jane was still living in Vienna. Jane was sitting in Café Hawelka, immersed in transcribing some sheet music, when she heard a booming voice at her left ear.

"Shall I compare thee to a summer's day?"

Startled, Jane looked up to see a handsome, dark-haired boy kneeling next to her, a single daisy in his hand. His voice was loud and confident, thundering throughout the small café. As he finished the sonnet, he didn't stumble once over the words, even though—as Jane soon gleaned from the glassiness of his eyes and the slight sway of his torso—he was quite drunk. People around them whispered and pointed, some even recording on their phones, but his eyes remained trained on hers.

Unfortunately for the would-be Romeo, Jane had almost as little experience dealing with spontaneous poetry from strangers as she did playing team sports, which was to say none. Her focus on becoming a classically trained musician afforded little time for distractions such as boys and dating, a lifestyle choice that felt vali-dated by the dearth of interest. On the rare occasion a boy came sniffing around her, he was generally put off by her one-track-minded pursuit of her goal, which necessitated long hours of prac-tice and study and little time for partying, drinking, and romantic shenanigans.

There was no reason now to suspect this boy would be any different, familiarity with Shakespearean sonnets aside. Still, the impromptu poetry had been a sweet gesture, so Jane offered a smile and a "thank you" before returning to her work.

The loud guffaws from the other side of the cafe, coming from a group of college-aged, American boys, confirmed to Jane that the whole thing had been part of some dare. She didn't take it personally, but she didn't particularly want to become the butt of a joke, and anyway, she had work to do.

So it surprised her when she glanced up to see the boy still on his knees before her, crestfallen. "You didn't like it?"

His tone was so earnest, his eyes so *honed* on her, that Jane couldn't help it: she blushed. Of all the banes of pale-skinned persons, this particular one was the worst. It created such an involuntary intimacy, allowing others a glimpse into emotional turmoil they had no business seeing.

(Of course, later Frank confided the blush gave him the courage to keep trying, so it wasn't all bad, in the end.)

The boy reached for a napkin. Taking the pencil out of her hand without asking, he wrote something down.

It was his phone number. Jane's blush deepened, and she took a moment to compose herself before meeting his gaze.

He was waiting for her with a wink. "Don't break my heart, Fraulein."

She didn't call him, of course. Not only did Jane have no time for drunk American boys who accosted people in coffee shops, but the boy had also been too wasted to even pick her out of a lineup. Furthermore, anyone who could be that charming at the drop of a hat was doubtless too practiced in the art to ever be taken at face value.

So when she saw him sitting at what had been her table the next time she came to that same cafe, she told herself it was just a coincidence. When he spotted her, and his face broke into a broad grin, she reminded herself that she was very busy and goal-oriented and that this boy did not fit into her five-year plan.

But when he rose to his feet and told her, "Thank God. I've

been coming here every day since the last time I saw you"—Jane knew she was in trouble.

As the afternoon wore on, she learned the boy was Frank, a fellow American in Austria on a study abroad from Tulane.

And that was how it was for them, after that, falling in love to music. Frank loved bluegrass, whereas Jane preferred instrumentals, though they found common ground in the beauty, the passion, the secret language of melody.

As it often happens once love has gotten involved, discussion of future plans began to intersect and include each other, like the label Frank could open in New Orleans, where Jane would have access to his studios to work on her compositions. Plus, as he told her with a sparkle in his eye, they could get season tickets to the Louisiana Philharmonic Orchestra, and go to the Hi-Ho Lounge any time they wanted. The best of both worlds.

Only the more they talked about this hypothetical future, the more it began to seem impossibly distant. Frank couldn't transfer to Vienna; his great-aunt was adamant about him finishing the business degree before he pursued music, and she was the one footing the bill. Neither could Jane transfer to Tulane, since she'd been informed there was a waitlist for the composition program.

By way of total chance that seemed very much like fate, they discovered a coincidence almost too perfect to be true. Jane's only tie to Louisiana was an aunt who was an instructor at a school about two hours from New Orleans—a small college called Austen University, where it just so happened that Frank's father had recently earned tenure in the history department. The two had drifted apart over the years, with Frank mostly being raised by his great-aunt and uncle, but now felt like a time when they could finally reconnect, as adults.

Not only was it possible for both to finish their respective educations at the school, but their separate connections to the university made it *plausible*. Jane could cite a desire to spend more time with her favorite aunt, who doted on her like a daughter, and Frank could reconnect with an estranged father. It was perfect. It was destiny.

πκΣ

It was also, thought Caty, the most she had ever heard Jane Fairfax speak, and it completely changed her perception of the quiet, reserved girl who had seemed so out of place at all the Kappa functions. Jane wasn't boring and distant. She was passionate and secretive—and a little bit insane to leave behind Vienna for Highbury, Louisiana, for any boy, no offense to Frank.

Her eyes had become so accustomed to returning to Knightley throughout the evening that Caty found them going there again now—surprised to find that his gaze, in turn, was focused on Emma.

Emma, who Caty now recalled, had been flirting up a storm with Frank ever since he arrived in Highbury. Caty thought of that talent show performance with the two of them and cringed internally on Emma's behalf, realizing now that he'd had a girlfriend the entire time. Poor Emma.

The girl in question looked stunned, her face markedly pale in comparison to Jane's crimson flush and bright eyes. "But…" the blonde stammered, "Jane and her professor…the affair…"

Frank looked chagrined. "I made that up. I was afraid you and Karoline would put together that Jane and I had both been in Austria at the same time, so I thought I should throw you off the scent." He looked to Jane across the table, expression sheepish. "Jane wasn't very happy about that particular solution."

"No, I wasn't." Jane sounded wry, but there was an edge to her voice that suggested she wasn't entirely over it, at least not yet.

"Why all the secrecy?" Tilney asked the couple. "No offense, but you don't exactly have paparazzi following you around. Who were you hiding from?"

A grimace from Frank. "My aunt. Great aunt, actually. I know it sounds strange, but after my mother died and my father left, she raised me. I owed her a lot, and she had some very particular ideas about what my future should look like. That's the reason I'm a business major, not a music major." He looked again to Jane. "Aunt Bernadette would have preferred for me to date someone from an old Louisiana family."

Rich, Caty thought was the subtext of that, though Frank was far too Southern to say it so bald-facedly.

"But the heart wants what it wants," Frank concluded, smiling at Jane. "Since Aunt Bernadette passed so recently, Jane and I decided to wait a while before we made it public, but...I guess the cat's out of the bag now."

"Your aunt passed away?" Knightley seemed to be hearing this information for the first time, which was a bit strange, as he was the GRA overseeing the wellbeing of Frank and his fellow Thetas. Thinking back on it, Caty thought she had always detected a little coolness between the two young men, though now Knightley looked —she hated to admit it—genuinely concerned for Frank. "I'm so sorry. That must have been so difficult for you."

"It happened the morning of Initiation. That was why I wasn't there that night, at Box Hill." Frank gave a strained smile, a self-deprecating little shrug. "She was old, and life goes on." Another smile at Jane, who was watching him anxiously from across the table; despite his bravado, Caty could see from Jane's reaction that it had been enormously difficult for him. "But at least now Jane and I can be together."

Emma blinked rapidly. "Well, that's..." Her face broke into a broad, relieved smile. "Fantastic. I'm happy for you both." She met Jane's gaze, holding it. "Really."

"So cute," Karoline chimed in, smiling, though the rest of her face looked as though she'd sucked on a lemon. "How clever of you, Janey, snatching up one of the richest, cutest boys before anyone else even had a chance with him."

Frank turned his most charming smile to Caty. "So, sorry to throw a wrench in your theory. But Jane couldn't have been secretly dating Knightley, because she was secretly dating me."

That was true, Caty realized with a sinking sense of dread, as she once again met Knightley's gaze across the table. Her entire theory revolved around the premise that Knightley had manipulated Jane into taking the diary. Without it, she had nothing.

Still, that email to Anne nagged at her; Knightley wasn't all he was pretending to be, no matter if she'd connected the dots the wrong way before. It could still be him.

Only, the more Caty thought, the less logical it seemed. Why was she so certain that Knightley had an underhanded plot to corrupt undergraduate girls, again? In all her sneaking and digging, she realized, nothing connected him to Marla Bertram. Nor was it damning proof to have seen Knightley and Jane getting coffee together, in a public place where they were likely to run into people they knew. For the first time it struck Caty that if Knightley was a nefarious seducer of the young and impressionable, he was being very obvious about it.

"Marla Bertram," Caty blurted, grasping desperately at this last and final hope. "Knightley still could have had something to do with her disappearance, and maybe Isabella found out…"

Even as she said the words out loud, Caty knew how flimsy it sounded. Knightley did not so much as flinch at the name of either girl, his expression more resigned than anything. *Here we go again*, he seemed to be thinking, and Caty found she could not blame him.

Still, she pressed on. "You know what happened to Marla." It was meant to be a definitive statement, but it came out sounding like more of a question. A plea, even.

Knightley sighed, but before he could say anything, Emma spoke up. "If he does, it's only because I told him. And if he hasn't mentioned anything, it's only because I asked him not to." Drawing in a beleaguered, ever-so-slightly melodramatic breath, Emma braced herself. "But if telling the story will clear Knightley's name, I'll do it. There's no way I'm protecting Marla's sneaky ass over him…"

From the Files of Caty Morland:

> **From:** EWOODHOUSE@AU.EDU
> **To:** SIRKNIGHTLEY@AU.EDU

Subject: Bless her soul...

Message: Hypothetically speaking, how much trouble would one get in for killing Marla Bertram? Asking for a friend.

XOXO

P.S. Send dark chocolate

3

Marla Bertram was to Emma's presidential term over the Kappas as the iceberg was to the Titanic: a catastrophe which threatened to sink what had elsewise seemed unsinkable.

Despite her choir-girl facade and her reputation as the renowned Reverend Thomas's daughter, Marla seemed to be something of a troubled soul. She drank—not just socially, at parties and sorority events, like any other fun-loving Kappa, but her morning coffee was always a little Irish and her orange juice was always a touch Russian.

She stole, too; valuable items around the Kappa house could usually be traced to her bedroom, and had to be quietly returned to avoid a scandal.

Also, she smoked, which was not technically against Kappa rules, except she would sometimes do it while falling asleep, which caused more than one incident with the local fire department.

"She was not," Emma put it as diplomatically as she could, "Kappa material. Bless her soul."

The final straw came just before winter break, when Marla passed out in the tub after polishing off a bottle of wine on her own.

Marla had nearly drowned; an ambulance had come, as well as the police, and the firemen who now knew the Kappas as regulars.

Mrs. Norris, a friend of the Bertram family who had signed up as Kappa House Mother to keep an eye on their wild-child daughter, swore up and down that it had been an accident, that there was no way Marla could have been trying to kill herself. Reverend Thomas came personally to try to smooth things over with the administration, but by then it had already been one incident too many and the university didn't want to be liable for what Marla might do next.

A compromise was reached. Marla would leave, a semester before graduating; the university wouldn't formally expel her; and the administration would double down on drinking restrictions at Greek functions to put up a show of taking care of the problem.

No one would speak about it. The hope was that the rumors would leave Austen University just as quietly as Marla did.

Of course, as the events leading to this confession indicated, this proved to not be the case. If anything, all the secrecy caused the rumors to take on a life of their own. Marla had now apparently been connected to drugs, sex rings, human trafficking . . . and affairs with older men.

The truth of it wasn't really that interesting, in the end. Marla was just a troubled girl from a well-connected family, and her time at Austen University was now over.

It was a rather anticlimactic ending to the Marla Bertram saga, and to Caty, it felt like another defeat. "But…the diary. She must have been hiding something. Why else would she write it in code?"

"Because she was a basic bitch who loved attention and drama." Karoline blinked at the reactions across the table to this, digging in. "Well, am I wrong?"

"She was hot, though," said Rushworth. Aside from this, no one seemed too inclined to disagree with Karoline's assessment.

So the diary had been meaningless. The reddest of all the red herrings. There was no mystery surrounding it whatsoever. Jane hadn't taken the diary; Isabella had given it to her. There was nothing to connect Knightley to the missing diary, nothing to connect him to Marla Bertram. Nothing to connect him to Isabella.

It was all, Caty realized, a complete and total dead end.

Darcy cleared his throat. "I think someone owes Knightley an apology."

He was right. Caty knew he was right. She had accused Knightley of something truly heinous, put his character and reputation through the ringer, and all on wild speculation. She wasn't a detective. She had no idea what the hell she was doing. She should never have presumed to interfere in something like this. She was just a nosy freshman who'd been jumping to conclusions and harassing poor Knightley.

But somehow, saying it out loud, felt like admitting she'd been wrong about everything—even Isabella being murdered in the first place. And Caty found, as all eyes at the table turned to her expectantly, that she couldn't do that. Couldn't let down Isabella any more than she already had.

"I," she started, mouth dry.

She was saved by the sudden whine of tornado sirens. The whole party dispersed, heading once again to the hallway. Caty rose to her feet to follow, then impulsively stopped, crawling under the table instead.

Think, think, Caty told herself. The eerie cry of the sirens made it difficult, but she tried her best to focus. She was missing something. There had to be *something.*

Movement appeared at the corner of her eye. Caty looked up, surprised to see Tilney crawling under the table to join her, his smile sympathetic. "Hey, V.M. You doing okay?"

Caty buried her face in her hands. Scorn, she could handle; disdain, she could deal with. But sympathy made her want to crawl into a hole and die. "I'm a ridiculous person. I was so sure that something terrible happened to Marla, and that I was the only one who could solve it. Save her. And Jane, too. I'm so delusional."

"Yes, but you're very pretty, so…"

Caty laughed at that, and Tilney joined in, wrapping an encouraging arm around her shoulders. "You went down the wrong investigative path. It happens to all the great detectives."

"Not Poirot," Caty sniffed.

"Yeah, but, he's an insufferable bastard. Even his creator hated him."

Caty laughed again, wiping away some snot and tears with her sleeve. Touched that Tilney would go to so much effort to comfort her, she leaned into him. "Well," she summoned a deep breath for courage, "at least I wasn't wrong about one thing."

"What's that?"

She kissed him.

It wasn't quite the fireworks she'd been anticipating, but he smelled nice, and his lips were soft, and it was *Tilney*. When they broke apart a few moments later, Tilney smiled, squeezing her hand. "So, there's something I should tell you . . ."

$\pi\kappa\Sigma$

Caty sat for a moment, processing. "So, boys and girls, huh?" For lack of anything better to say, she heard herself blurting, "It must be nice to have so many options."

"It's more about the person, for me. The connection." Tilney cleared his throat. "I've only had girlfriends in the past. When I was younger, I thought that was all I was interested in, but when things started to change in high school, I think I was in denial, or maybe I just didn't want it to get back to my father."

He tightened his grip on her hand. "I promise, it's not you. I think you're smart and funny and cool, and I love how wonderfully morbid your mind is. But to be honest, right now I just don't feel open to that. Now that I've admitted the truth to myself, I sort of want to explore that other part of me, you know? Not take the easy route, for once."

He said this all in one linked chain of verbal vomit, hardly stopping to breathe; he was shaking, Caty saw. She had never seen him anything but charming, witty, unflappable. He was so afraid, she realized. Afraid of how she might respond, what she might say to him.

She smiled at him, nudging him with her shoulder. "So you're calling me easy, huh?"

Tilney gave a choking, relieved laugh. "Well, if John Thorpe's bathroom-stall graffiti is anything to go by—yes."

They smiled at one another. Caty hesitated, then extended her arms. "Can I?"

Tilney reciprocated instantly, clinging onto her, still shaking.

This was *so* not how Caty expected this to go. And, if she was being honest, it was a little disappointing. She'd harbored such a crush on him, lived out so many secret little fantasies in her mind of what it would be like to be his girlfriend, to wear his sweatshirt when it got cold, and keep a spare toothbrush at his room, and have someone so cool and smart be her somebody.

But...she had a choice in front of her now. She could either nurse her hurt feelings, and lose Tilney's friendship altogether. Or she could get over it, and keep around somebody who made her laugh, liked the same shows, and suspected his acquaintances of murder, just like she did.

Maybe that was part of growing up—realizing that not everybody who would play an important role in her life had to be a romantic partner. That maybe it was just as special and miraculous to find somebody who could be that rarest of rare things: a true friend.

They pulled apart, and she smiled at him. "Still each other's best weirdos?"

"Always," said Tilney.

He sat up, sniffing and running a quick hand over his eyes. "Okay, enough of the saccharine. You have a case to solve, and—" he checked his watch, "ninety-two minutes left of the tornado warning forcing everyone to stay in the house while you piece it all together."

"Oh. That." Caty burrowed down into her shoulders, trying to disappear as much as possible. "I think I'll just stay down here for the rest of the night. Let me know how the trifle is . . ."

Tilney ducked out from under the table, pulling her along with him and up to her feet. "Enough wallowing. Your best friend is dead and somebody in that room did it. Probably. So how are you going to prove it?"

Caty thought about it, her mind racing. She was very glad, suddenly, that she no longer had to worry about Tilney thinking if she was cute or not, because her thinking face—as Isabella had pointed out to her on more than one occasion—was particularly unattractive. "I think I have an idea. Can you stall for a few minutes?"

"Caty, darling, I was *born* to stall for a few minutes. Take all the time you need."

FROM THE FILES OF CATY MORLAND:

[EXCERPT FROM AN INTERVIEW WITH A.W. RADCLIFFE, GIVEN TO PERFECTLY PERFECT MURDERS]

PPM: DO YOU EVER MAKE A WRONG TURN SOMEWHERE IN YOUR RESEARCH AND COME UP WITH A DEAD END?

RADCLIFFE: OH, GOD. OF COURSE. OF COURSE! IT'S INEVITABLE THAT NOT EVERY LEAD ULTIMATELY PANS OUT. BUT ACTUALLY, I TRY TO THINK OF THESE NOT AS WRONG TURNS BUT CROSSED WIRES. 'I FEEL LIKE I SHOULD HEAD IN THIS DIRECTION, BUT IT DOESN'T GO ANYWHERE, BUT I TRUST MY INSTINCT, SO...' (LAUGHING) YOU KNOW, WHAT IS MY GUT *REALLY* TRYING TO TELL ME? I THINK THE ONLY REAL FAILURE IS IF YOU STOP TRUSTING YOURSELF.

❧ 4 ❧

The sirens had long-since faded during Tilney's and Caty's tête-à-tête, and the pair found the others gathered in the kitchen, broken into smaller groups. Off to one side were Marianne and Lizzy, and on the other side of the kitchen were the Kappas and the Thetas—Emma, Karoline, Tilney, Darcy, and Rushworth. In between them, rather poetically equidistant between these two poles, were Frank and Jane. And, perhaps just as symbolically, was John Thorpe, standing off to the side by himself and pretending to text on his phone.

At the re-entrance of Caty and Tilney, all conversation stopped. Caty wavered uncertainly in the door, feeling her confidence rush out of her in a great leaping whoosh at those ten pairs of wary eyes.

Tilney reached down to give her hand a brief, reassuring squeeze. "Was anyone there the night Robert Martin crashed his motorcycle into the Sigma Rho pool?" he asked, going over to divert the attention of the Theta-Kappa group, while Caty took the opportunity to duck over to the Deltas. Luckily, Frank and Jane were much too absorbed with each other, and John Thorpe was much too absorbed with himself, to need much distracting.

"You were so brave in there," Marianne said to Caty, reaching out to grasp her hand as she approached. "I stan a strong queen not afraid to challenge authority. What can we do to help you?"

Oh. Well. That had been easy. Caty had thought she might have to do a little more sweet-talking to get Marianne and Lizzy to cooperate, after her earlier behavior. "I just have a few more questions, if you don't mind. Not about the murder, necessarily. But I can't help but notice there seems to be some bad blood between y'all and the Kappas." She met Lizzy's gaze. "You and Karoline, in particular."

Lizzy gave a dry, bitter laugh. "There's certainly no love lost between Karoline and me, but I really don't see what that has to do with Isabella. And, no offense, but I don't especially want to get dragged through the ringer like Knightley just was."

Caty had expected as much. "I understand. Would it help to know that I'm also considering Karoline? And that what you say could very well prove she's a murderer?"

Lizzy took a moment, considering this new information. "Well, when you put it like that…"

πκΣ

A glass of rum later, and the story had been revealed in its entirety. Karoline Bingley, the vice-president of Pi Kappa Sigma, was assigned to Lizzy as her "big sister" during Initiation—a choice which Lizzy retrospectively described as a twist of fate "even crueler than Sisyphus's". The two butted heads right from the beginning, with Lizzy taking umbrage to Karoline's superiority complex, foul attitude, and rude behavior, and Karoline taking umbrage to Lizzy's face.

"She didn't like me from the first moment she saw me," Lizzy groused. "I could have revealed a secret lineage to Princess Diana and it wouldn't have changed her mind."

Of course, as no direct relation to the former Duchess of Windsor could be established, this was impossible to say for certain. However, since everything else about Lizzy filled Karoline with so much sheer loathing, it seemed safe to assume that there could have been no salvaging the relationship. Karoline reacted with outrage when she found out Lizzy had four sisters, and that they grew up sharing bedrooms. ("Dear God, Bennet! Haven't your parents ever heard of birth control?!") When she learned Lizzy was at AU on scholarship, she nearly—as Lizzy so eloquently put it—"shit a brick."

That wasn't to say the beautiful, rich, well-connected Karoline couldn't be charming when it suited her purposes. "She was nice to my sister, Nora, the first few weeks," Marianne spoke up. "Nora thought they were friends."

"Until Karoline's brother, Charlie, started sniffing around her."

Marianne gave an indignant toss of her head. "Imagine turning on another woman because she isn't rich enough to date your brother. How despicable. How petty. How . . . un-sisterly."

Luckily, as Lizzie summarized with a smile, the whole process drove her and Nora together in solidarity, and the two became fast friends. They decided that Pi Kappa Sigma was more trouble than it was worth, especially since they could start their own sorority without the social hierarchy, strict rules, and astronomical fees.

Naturally, this secession was not taken well by the Kappas, Karoline in particular. If she didn't like Nora and Lizzy before, there were at least the laws of sisterhood that gave them some protection. Now? She seemed to have taken it upon herself as a personal mission to make their lives at AU miserable.

"I don't usually condone woman against woman bashing," Marianne concluded, "but Karoline Bingley is practically patriarchal."

Caty wasn't entirely sure what this was supposed to mean, but she smiled along, nodding. "Thanks. Y'all have been so helpful." She made eye contact with Tilney, signaling that she was almost finished, before looking back to Lizzy and Marianne. "Do you think you could do me one last favor and help Tilney convince everyone to go back into the dining room? There's one quick thing I need to do..."

$$\pi\kappa\Sigma$$

Caty raced up the stairs to the bedroom she'd once shared with Isabella, knowing she had to be quick. After all, once the tornado warning dissipated, she would be deprived of her unwittingly captive audience.

In the darkened room, she sat down on the ground and over-turned the wastebasket, sorting through the accumulated clutter until she felt the familiar piece of crumpled paper. It was still there, thank goodness. Caty didn't know if the cleaning crew was leaving the room as-is due to the open police investigation or if they'd been forced to stay away by the university shutdown; either way, she was enormously grateful to find the letter she'd at one point vehemently wished to never see again. Thank goodness she hadn't followed through on her first impulse to set it on fire.

FROM THE FILES OF CATY MORLAND:
[DELIVERED TO ISABELLA'S CUBBY TWO DAYS AFTER SHE DIED]

DEAR ISABELLA,
WHAT SOUND DOES A SLUT MAKE WHEN SHE FALLS OFF A CLIFF AND HITS THE ROCKS?
SP-LUT.

Caty started to rise to her feet when she heard something—a soft but discernible creaking of the floorboards outside the door.

She froze. So, too, it seemed, did the person standing in the hall-way, as no further footsteps could be heard. What were they doing there, just waiting? Caty thought about calling out, but why hadn't the person announced themselves? She could think of only a handful of reasons why somebody would be following her through the darkened corridors of the Kappa house without making their presence known, and none of them were benign.

Another moment passed before she heard another creak of the floorboards—this time accompanied by muffled footsteps, heading away from the room. Caty wanted to feel relieved by this, but worried it might be a trap, like in *The Mysteries of Udolpho* when the surgeon got lured into the pantry by the schizophrenic chef and bludgeoned to death with a rolling pin. (*Gripping* to listen to, unpleasant to live through, she suspected.)

Inspired by the episode, she looked around the room for anything she might be able to counter-bludgeon with. Would an umbrella be heavy enough, or should she try to throw her American history textbook?

"Caty?"

The girl in question yelped at the sudden appearance of Tilney in the doorway. "You coming, Veronica Mars? The natives are getting restless downstairs."

Caty drew in a relieved breath, hoisting herself to her feet. "Okay, I'm coming." Crumpled paper gripped in hand, she followed him into the hallway, hesitating before she asked, "Did you see anyone in the hallway?"

"No. Everyone's in the dining room downstairs."

"You're sure?" The last thing Caty needed now was another reason to doubt her sanity, but she needed to know if someone had been following her.

"Emma's set out the second course, and she's *strongly* suggested that leaving the table when the entrée has been served is a major faux pas. I had to sign over the soul of my firstborn before she'd let me leave—so I'd say yeah, pretty sure."

Caty frowned. She'd been so certain. But unless someone had managed to sneak away—unlikely, under all those watchful eyes—it must have just been the old house settling, combined with the tumultuous weather and her raised adrenaline. "Okay. Let's go."

"You ready for round two, V.M.?"

She drew in a deep, bracing breath. "Oh, I'm ready."

5

The second course was herb-crusted chicken served on wild rice. As Caty and Tilney re-entered the room, Rushworth let out an audible groan. "Thank God. We can finally eat."

"We were waiting for you," said Emma with a strained smile. "It isn't polite to begin eating until all party guests are present."

If there had been any lingering fear about the food being poisoned by one of the murder suspects in attendance, once again Rushworth proved to be a ready and willing sacrificial taste-tester. He'd devoured nearly half his plate before Caty even had the chance to sit down.

Carefully smoothing her napkin over her lap, Caty let everyone take a few bites before she cleared her throat. "I'd just like to say that I'm sorry, to Jane, and especially to Knightley, for jumping to conclusions."

The words hung in the air as everyone waited to see what Knightley's response would be. He met Caty's gaze, nodding. "I appreciate that, Caty. Really." He sighed a little, cutting into his chicken. "And I know you were just trying to look out for your friend, but I'm glad we've put the murder investigation behind us for the evening."

"Oh, the investigation isn't over," Caty reassured him pleasantly. "We haven't found the murderer yet, so. How could it be?"

John Thorpe let out a dramatic groan. "God, not more of this. She *fell*. That's all. Can't we just enjoy our meal in peace?"

Despite the overt irritation in his tone, the hand holding his fork was shaking visibly. Was John battling his grief for his dead sister, Caty wondered, followed by the far less charitable thought—was someone like John Thorpe capable of real grief?

It wasn't a nice thing to think; Caty knew someone didn't have to be likable or even good to have real, human emotions. But so far all she'd seen from John was unbridled hostility. Was it possible he was trying to repress his struggle over losing his sister? Or was it some other emotion he was trying to hide?

"It's possible," Caty conceded, the words tasting like sawdust on her mouth. But she needed to regain some footing with these people, prove that she could think rationally. "Maybe Isabella did just fall. But we all know that she provoked some strong reactions during her short time here at AU."

By way of proof, Caty produced the letter she'd gone upstairs to retrieve—the anonymous piece of hate mail Isabella had received in her mail cubby a few days after she died.

"What sound does a slut make when she falls off a cliff and hits the rocks?" Tilney read aloud for everyone. "SP-LUT."

A moment of shocked silence followed. "That's disgusting," said Lizzy, as beside her Marianne quivered in silent, mouth-gaping rage.

For once, Karoline was in complete agreement with the Deltas, her nose wrinkled in distaste. "Who would send something like that?"

"Do you think it was the murderer?" asked Frank, exchanging an uneasy glance with Jane.

Caty shook her head. "I don't. But I wanted to show this as an example of the response to Isabella's death. The media, the forums —everybody was so quick to jump on the idea of Isabella being a slut. But aside from the normal dancing and partying and drinking that most college students do, what actually sets Isabella apart from anyone else in the Kappas? Anyone else at this table, for that matter?"

A moment's pause. "Her boobs were bigger," Rushworth spoke into the void, through a mouthful of rice. At everyone's blank stares, he elaborated, "Bigger than anyone else's at the table, I mean."

Caty didn't know quite what to do with that, so she just moved on. "I was thinking of one event in particular that set Isabella apart from the other Kappa pledges. One night that proved to be so incendiary it almost got her kicked out of the sorority, and made at least one person here threaten to kill her—that I overheard, anyway."

As some uneasy glances were exchanged across the table, Tilney leaned back in his chair, looking positively delighted at this turn of events. "The talent show?" he asked Caty.

"The talent show," she confirmed.

FROM THE FILES OF CATY MORLAND:

INTERVIEWEE: EMMA WOODHOUSE (SENIOR AT AUSTEN UNIVERSITY, PRESIDENT OF PI KAPPA SIGMA)

CATY: CAN YOU REMEMBER WHICH SONG ISABELLA WAS SUPPOSED TO SING ORIGINALLY? BEFORE THE LAST-MINUTE CHANGE?

EMMA: YES, I CAN. SHE WAS MEANT TO SING "STEAM HEAT" FROM *THE PAJAMA GAME.* THAT WAS THE SONG SHE GOT PRE-APPROVED DURING REHEARSALS.

CATY: HOW WOULD YOU DESCRIBE THE NUMBER?

EMMA: IT'S A CLASSIC. SEXY, BUT IN A SUBTLE, TASTEFUL WAY. VERY KAPPA APPROVED.

CATY: AND THE SONG ISABELLA ENDED UP SINGING?

EMMA : I THINK WE BOTH KNOW THAT WAS ABOUT AS FAR FROM KAPPA APPROVED AS POSSIBLE.

❦ 6 ❦

(FEBRUARY)

The yearly Kappa show was an annual tradition as old as the university itself, one which some considered to be quaint and traditional, and one which others decried as outdated and sexist. An event where a young woman showcased her talent wasn't offensive in and of itself, even to the Marianne Dashwoods of the world; what raised the ire of some were the very specific types of talents allowed to be put on display. Singing and dancing were encouraged, so long as there was nothing "vulgar" or "tasteless" in the presentation. Anything deemed "unladylike," however—like Louisa Musgrove's request to tell her repertoire of fart jokes—was rejected. It all felt a little 1950s for many peoples' tastes, but the Kappas maintained that it was part of their heritage, and thus, the show must go on.

"No, Julia's flute playing goes *after* Henrietta's ballet number," an exasperated Caty explained to the light operator. "Those cues will have to be changed..."

It was thirty minutes until curtains opened for the annual Kappa talent show, and despite all the extensive planning meetings, it was still turning out to be a total shit show. In the thick of it all was Caty, who had compensated for her own personal lack of talent by signing up to be the stage manager. This had seemed a safe choice at the time—she would still get points for participating, but no one would have to endure her off-key rendition of "Mr. Sandman." It was only now, on the night-of, that Caty realized just how much responsibility she had taken on, and just how insane it was to try to manage almost 100 adrenaline-charged girls.

"For God's sake, Louisa," Caty snapped to the girl in question, who was attempting to climb up into the catwalk to get a better look at the gathering audience, "get down from there!"

Isabella had reassured Caty that part of the magic of "the theatre" was that everything would seem like it was falling apart until the curtain parted and suddenly everything came together. Caty wanted to believe this, but it was hard to be optimistic when no one seemed to know which act was going when, the pianist was MIA, and Emma, the person who was meant to be running the entire thing, had been saying she was five minutes away for the past hour.

As she exited the lighting booth, Caty was accosted by Isabella, who was a bundle of nervous energy, two spots of color high on her cheeks. No doubt she was nervous about performing her musical number, though in truth, Caty thought the performers were the ones who had it easy. She cursed herself for her lack of talent. If only she could sing or tap dance, she could have just been one of the "artists," running around mindlessly and consumed with her own nerves. Instead, as a talentless individual, she was stuck as stage manager, with the weight of the entire production on her shoulders.

"Just the bestie I was looking for." Isabella linked her arm through Caty's as they crossed toward the stage. "I need to change my musical cue. Jane isn't going to be playing for me anymore—I have a track." She handed Caty a CD, her smile angelic.

If blood could actually boil, Caty would have steam coming out of her ears right about now. "All musical cues were supposed to be approved a week ago," she quoted Emma's email back to her room-mate. "No last-minute changes. No exceptions."

"I know. But Jane didn't show up for our last rehearsal and I need tonight to go perfectly. I already gave the track to the sound booth but they said I needed to get your approval. Please, Caty Bear?"

This was just so . . . typical of Isabella, and the buddy-buddy act wasn't cooling Caty's irritation in the slightest. For a moment, she fantasized about saying no, putting her foot down. But then she thought of the weeks, even months, of retaliation to come, with the moody silences and passive-aggressive comments, and it just wasn't worth it. Especially when Emma wasn't even here to oversee her own rules.

"Fine," Caty relented. "But you owe me. Big time."

With a squeal and a cheek kiss, Isabella was off, much more euphoric about setting up chairs than a person had any right to be. Caty shook her head after her. Some people just loved the spotlight.

The doors opened and Caty turned, hoping it was Emma, arriving at long last. Instead, with no little dismay, she watched as Knightley entered. Ever since she'd discovered Anne's email, Caty had tried to keep an open mind and not jump to any conclusions. This intention proved rather difficult, though, with Knightley always just dropping off something at the Kappa house, or passing by on his way to class, or helping out with this or that.

She wouldn't leap to any conclusions; she wouldn't. But, bless his soul, he certainly seemed to enjoy spending time around the Kappas, didn't he?

Knightley approached, smiling. "Hey, Caty. Emma just sent me an SOS text, said she's running late. I'm here to set up chairs, or hang signs, or whatever you need me to do."

Caty remained stone-faced, unfazed by his crinkly-eyed charm. That kind of thing might work on the innocent and naïve, but she had read *The Stranger Beside Me* and was immune to the charisma of handsome psychopaths.

"You can set up the concessions booth," she instructed him coolly. "You'll have to unload Mrs. Norris's SUV. And make it snappy—we're running behind."

She walked away before he could respond, relieved to see Emma approaching from the back entrance. She held her hands up in silent entreaty to Caty. "I am *so* sorry. I didn't mean to be this late, but…well, Jane Fairfax was kind of having a crisis, and sometimes there are more important things than talent shows, you know?"

Those were strange words, coming from the girl who'd told them not two days ago that there was nothing more important than the talent show—not schoolwork, not boyfriends, not jobs or family obligations, because they were Kappas, dammit, and Kappas knew how to put on a show. But, not one to quibble, Caty lowered her voice. "Is everything okay?"

"Did you hear about the performance on the Kappa front lawn?" Caty confirmed that yes, she *had* heard about the elaborate *Sound of Music* tribute that had taken place that afternoon, complete with a makeshift stage with a curtain and the whole works. "Well, that was for Jane. I'm pretty sure it was arranged by this professor she was having an affair with back in Austria, no doubt trying to win her back."

"That sounds stressful. Is she okay?"

Emma looked as though the thought hadn't once crossed her mind. "Oh, well, you know Jane. She wouldn't say anything to *me*." She waited a moment before adding, "And, I mean, she kind of brought it upon herself, you know?"

How strange that Jane wouldn't want to confide in her, Caty thought dryly, though she kept the opinion to herself.

She glanced over to Jane, who was setting up at the piano, looking tired and uncharacteristically frazzled. Caty furrowed her brow, realizing something about Emma's explanation bothered her. How could some professor who was living in Austria arrange for a stage to be built on the Kappa front lawn, and an amateur glee club to perform a medley from *The Sound of Music*? It was possible, she supposed, but it seemed like something that would be difficult to orchestrate from overseas.

Far more likely that someone close by organized it, she thought. Someone who felt like he had something to lose, and had plenty of money to throw around to get what he wanted.

She looked again to Knightley, who had found some excuse to

leave the concessions booth again and was helping Isabella set up the last of the chairs, the two of them smiling and chatting. As Caty watched on, he made his way over to the piano, where Jane was doing some last-minute warmups. She stopped as Knightley approached, looking up. He said something to her and she gave him a strained smile, shaking her head. Knightley gestured with his hands, seeming intent about whatever he was saying. As she listened on, Jane's smile faded.

$$\pi\kappa\Sigma$$

Back at the dinner party, Knightley cleared his throat. "For the record, I'd heard about what happened with the stage on the lawn and I was offering to help Jane clean up after the show. I didn't know if whoever had sent the gift—" here he carefully avoided looking at Frank, "—had thought through some of the details like that."

Caty offered her most conciliatory smile. "I'm not trying to suggest anything else. I'm just relating the events as I experienced them, at the time." She gestured to Frank. "Like, I know now it wasn't the Austrian professor who sent the gift to Jane. It must have been you, right, Frank?"

Jane and Darcy had switched seats so that Jane and Frank were now beside each other at the table. He reached over, taking her hand. "Jane and I were going through a bit of a rough patch then. Mostly because I was being such an ass."

Everyone laughed a little at that, Jane included. Caty had never seen her more vivacious than now that things were out in the open between her and Frank. Gone was the quiet, reserved girl with little to add to conversation. She had more color in her cheeks, more light in her eyes; she positively glowed now. "We still weren't telling anyone about us, and it was starting to take its toll." A laugh. "God, it feels good to have it out in the open."

Caty smiled at her happiness. Some relationships worked out, it seemed. And others… others were doomed before they even began. Thank the Lord.

$$\pi \kappa \Sigma$$

"Hey, gorgeous."

Caty was so wrapped up in watching Jane and Knightley that it took her a moment to register John Thorpe. "What are you doing here?"

"You didn't think I'd miss the big show, did you? I know how important these kinds of things are to girls."

"Oh." She shifted. "I'm sure Isabella will appreciate it."

"Not my sister, dummy. I'm here to support my woman."

A long moment passed. "Me?" Caty realized, horrified.

John laughed—a dismissive, *isn't that cute* noise. "Well, duh. We've been texting for weeks now. You're lucky you're cute enough to pull off that whole ditzy act, beautiful."

Without a word, Caty turned and walked away. She had a talent show to run, after all, and somehow in the meantime, she would also have to figure out how to get rid of John Thorpe and warn Jane away from impending doom, AKA George Knightley.

"Ten minutes until curtain!" she called, ducking backstage.

As she did so, she heard a mocking, exaggerated mimicry from somewhere in the darkened wings. "'Ten minutes until curtain,'" someone snarked, causing some of the other girls to giggle. "I guess that's what happens when you give *some* people a little taste of power."

Caty stopped in her tracks, the wind knocked out of her. She didn't recognize who'd been speaking, but whoever it was, it was obvious this was not playful, good-natured teasing. Someone thought Caty was irritating. And other people must think so, too, because they had laughed. Had the power gone to her head? She was just trying to get everything organized, make sure it all played out like it was supposed to, but maybe she had overstepped, been too pushy—

Before the thought could spiral too far, another voice spoke up in the darkness, and this time, it was one Caty recognized. "You're so funny, Julia," Isabella spoke up, making no attempt to disguise her voice or lower it, "I'm so glad that HPV diagnosis hasn't gotten you down."

More laughter, and Julia—whoever she was—made no response. Isabella continued on, louder than before, "You heard Caty. Places, bitches!"

Caty smiled her silent thanks at her friend as she heard dozens of footsteps shuffling into place. Isabella might be a mega-bitch sometimes, but it was always a true pleasure to see her harness that power for good.

That settled, Caty turned to check the AV equipment one last time, when she bumped into an older girl with brown, wavy hair. It took a moment to place her as Lizzy Bennet, the fast-talking president of Delta Gamma Nu. What on earth was she doing backstage at the Kappa talent show?

For a moment, they stared at each other in dumb silence. "Break a leg," Lizzy said at last, hurrying off into the audience.

$$\pi\kappa\Sigma$$

A moment of silence passed as everyone at the dinner table processed this piece of information. Then Karoline Bingley shot to her feet, pointing her finger at Lizzy with a triumphant gleam in her eye. "I *knew* it!"

FROM THE FILES OF CATY MORLAND:

INTERVIEWEE: LIZZY BENNET (SOPHOMORE AT AUSTEN UNIVERSITY, PRESIDENT OF DELTA LAMBDA EPSILON)

LIZZY: ...NO COMMENT.

7

I
sabella was the penultimate act of the night, to be followed by a group number performed by all of the Kappas. They would be singing "Girls Just Wanna Have Fun" en masse, and Caty was having a hell of a time rounding everyone up and making sure they were all in their right places as soon as Isabella finished. *It's almost over* was the mantra carrying Caty through the night, and she clung to it now, envisioning her quiet bed, her podcast, and the last of the Ben & Jerry's. *It's almost over.*

It was lucky, actually, that Isabella had changed last-minute to singing along to a track, since Caty wouldn't have to cue Jane in with the piano. She had more than enough responsibility on her hands at the moment, with dozens of Kappas rushing to get into babydoll dresses and jostling each other in the wings.

But as the opening chords of Isabella's song began to play, Caty realized she wasn't hearing the familiar bars to "Steam Heat." Instead of the Fosse-inspired black ensemble that Isabella had rehearsed in, she came onto the stage in full nun's regalia, wearing a long and glittering crucifix, her hands clasped as if in prayer.

As the music from the track continued playing, Caty realized she recognized the song—"A Call from the Vatican," from the musical

Nine. Caty wasn't a musical theatre buff by any stretch of the imagination, but she had a vivid memory of going to the cinema to see the film version with her father...a scantily-clad Penelope Cruz writhing around the screen in all her bombshell glory...Caty and her father both staring down at the ground in mutual, mortified silence.

"Oh God," Caty said aloud, her eyes widening not so much in horror as wonder at the sheer audacity of it.

Isabella looked up into the spotlight, winked, and began unzipping her dark robe. Someone in the audience let out a wolf whistle, which other fraternity brothers took up as Isabella tossed off her habit to reveal sexy bed-tousled hair, then kicked off her robe to show that she was wearing very tight, very skimpy black lingerie. Only the glittering crucifix remained, dangling between her voluptuous breasts.

Emma must be having a coronary, wherever she was. "What do we do?" someone asked Caty in a frantic whisper, and she realized she had no idea. She was just a freshman, trying to earn some points in her sorority's talent show for charity. This was waaaay beyond her pay grade.

And so the musical number proceeded unhindered. Unhindered, and uninhibited. As Isabella sang, she writhed around onstage, putting on quite the show. From the sounds of it, most of the fraternity brothers in the audience approved, and Isabella lapped up the attention. She shimmied out of a lacy black garter, shooting it off into the audience—where it struck Darcy square in the face.

Darcy's fraternity brothers roared in approval, elbowing him enthusiastically, though Darcy remained stone-faced—the only male in the room, it seemed, who was not enjoying the show.

Well, not the *only* male. A figure charged from the audience to the stage—a short, stocky boy with dark hair and a face flushed and mottled with rage. John Thorpe. He leapt onto the stage with one surprisingly athletic bound, grabbing Isabella by the forearm and dragging her offstage.

Isabella fought him, egged on by the shouts from the riled-up fraternity brothers in the crowd, urging an encore. Even this close, Caty could scarcely decipher what the two siblings were shouting at each other, though the words "slut" and "whore" featured prominently. She looked offstage, exchanging a moment of silent horror with Jane, both of them helpless as to how to proceed.

Then another figure darted onto the stage: Karoline Bingley, looking absolutely livid. "Get off the stage!" she shouted at the pair. "This is *so* not Kappa approved."

Either willfully ignoring her or genuinely oblivious to anything but their own domestic drama, John and Isabella continued bickering with each other, screaming, shoving, scratching. At last, seeming to realize it was a lost battle, Karoline turned her ire toward the wings. "Shut the curtains, you idiots!" And, when this wasn't accomplished fast enough, she grabbed one end of the curtain and began dragging it shut herself, until at last it swallowed them all.

Once the curtain was drawn, Karoline turned her impressive ire on the Thorpe siblings, now backstage. "Shut up. Shut up!" Something in her expression succeeded in cowing the two of them into silence, and Karoline hissed at them through gritted teeth, "Don't say another word, so help me God, or the two of you will disappear so deep in the swamps they'll never find your bones."

That was… an oddly specific threat, thought Caty, taking an instinctive step away from the Kappa vice-president.

She was distracted by some commotion happening on the other side of the curtain. Dreading what fresh hell this might be, Caty peeked out—relieved to see Emma taking the stage. Thank God. If anyone could fix this, it was Emma.

The blonde's smile was defiantly cheerful, as if everything had gone according to plan. "My, my," she said once she'd reached the mic, "some of these numbers certainly have evolved from rehearsals."

She looked to Jane, and Caty could see the wheels turning in her mind as she improvised what to do. "We're meant to go into our final number now," Emma said, "but I think we might have time for one more little song—if y'all are up for it?"

The crowd cheered its tepid approval. Undeterred, Emma glanced back at Jane, her smile tight and determined. "Sorry to put you on the spot, Jane, but do you know 'Summer Lovin' from *Grease?*"

Seeing the glint in Emma's eye, Caty pieced it together. She was determined to pull the talent show back from the erotic spectacle of Isabella's number, and back into Kappa-approved territory. *Grease* was the perfect upbeat, kitschy choice, a staple of high school theatres and diners and afternoon television that could only offend those most determined to take offense. Plus, Emma looked like she'd been born to play Sandy.

Caty couldn't hear Jane's reply, but it must have been an affirmative, since Emma barreled on, "Great. Now all I need is the perfect Danny . . ."

A few more whistles from the peanut gallery, some encouraging applause. Emma played it perfectly, putting up a hand to her face to shield the light as she pretended to survey the crowd. "What about . . ." Emma let the pause dangle just long enough, ". . . Frank Churchill?"

This suggestion was met with thunderous applause and stomping from Frank's Theta brothers. He put up a good show of reluctance, waving his hands, shaking his head, but there was no way to turn down an invitation like that, and Frank was never one to shy away from the spotlight. He warmed to a crowd the same way Emma did, the two of them becoming their best, most charming selves whenever people were watching.

God, they made a beautiful couple, Caty thought wistfully as Frank joined Emma onstage. Emma always said she wasn't interested in a serious relationship until her mid-20s, but the two of them would be virtually guaranteed Instagram fame for life if they ever decided to join forces and unleash their charm and beauty on the world.

They were both decent, though not remarkable, singers, which was almost more enjoyable to listen to, Caty thought. Soon the entire crowd was on its feet, and the unpolished, impromptu nature of the song had everyone cheering them on more whole-heartedly than they'd done all evening.

As the last notes of the song faded away, Emma and Frank turned to one another, smiling, faces glowing from the spotlight. It would have been a picture-perfect moment, had it not been interrupted by an explosive BANG coming from somewhere in the rafters. A garish yellow cloud descended from above, covering everything onstage with a thick coat of mustard-colored dust.

FROM THE FILES OF CATY MORLAND:
[EXCERPT OF A UNIVERSITY-WIDE EMAIL SENT BY THE OFFICE OF PRESIDENT DE BOURGH]

PLEASE BE ADVISED THAT THE ADMINISTRATION IS AWARE OF THE INCIDENT THAT TOOK PLACE AT THE PI KAPPA SIGMA TALENT SHOW AND WILL BE USING ALL AVAILABLE RESOURCES TO DISCOVER THE PERPETRATOR(S) RESPONSIBLE. AUSTEN UNIVERSITY HAS A STRICT POLICY AGAINST HAZING, PRANKING, AND OTHERWISE IRRESPONSIBLE SHENANIGANS. ANY HELPFUL INFORMATION SHOULD BE SENT TO WCOLLINS@AU.EDU. REMEMBER, ANYONE WHO WOULD BREAK THE RULES BY COMMITTING AN ACT OF DOMESTIC TERRORISM IS NOT YOUR FRIEND AND DOES NOT DESERVE YOUR PROTECTION.

8

Backstage, all yellow-hell broke loose as dust-coated Kappas screamed and ran around in helpless circles, waiting for someone to take charge. Emma, who would normally play this role, stood in mute, mustard silence, staring down at herself, for once not seeming to know what to do.

"Who did this?" Karoline screeched, quivering with rage. "Who fucking did this?" She began to weep, fat tears that carved streaks down her yellow-coated face as she looked down at her dress. "This is Dior!"

Clearly the Kappa leadership were in no place to take charge. Feeling a surge of something that very much resembled gumption, Caty raised her voice above the din. "Okay, girls, listen up. All freshmen report to the backstage dressing room to wash up; sophomores can use the upstairs bathroom. You have ten minutes, then you need to let the juniors and seniors rotate in. Remember, it's only dust."

Remarkably, the girls listened to her, shuffling offstage—most of them just glad, it seemed, to have someone take charge. Once the crowd thinned out, Caty searched for Isabella and John. She'd been as taken aback by Isabella's routine as anybody, but although she personally would never have done anything so provocative onstage, John's reaction was extreme. She knew the two of them squabbled like any siblings; she and James could get at each other's throats sometimes, too, but he'd never grabbed her like *that*. A part of her wondered what John might have done if nobody was watching.

Isabella had disappeared, but Caty soon found John—or rather, he found her, cornering her in the backstage corridor with his tirade about family honor: "We're not some godforsaken trailer trash. We're the Thorpes, goddammit. Our ancestor served under Robert E. Lee, and *she's* out here dancing for tips."

He continued on like this for quite some time, despite Caty's decided lack of response to his baiting. Isabella's dance was...an unusual choice, true, but the song *was* from an award-winning musical.

"I should have known this sorority would be a bad influence. Someone needs to remind Isabella that the Internet is permanent, and anyone could post a video of what she did tonight. Then the whole world will know what a slut my sister is."

Strange, Caty thought, that John seemed to have no such qualms about the videos he'd posted online of his fraternity brothers trying to light his farts on fire. Or the footage he'd taken of himself enjoying the Mardi Gras festivities in New Orleans the previous year, where some of the women were wearing far less than Isabella had onstage. Apparently the double standard was lost on him.

Mid-diatribe, John looked to Caty, eyes solemn. "I'm so glad you're not that kind of girl, Caty." He took her hand, which she was too startled to refuse. "You're the kind a guy waits his whole life to find."

Oh. No. No, no, no, no, no.

"I have to pee," Caty said, then fled.

Thankfully, John did not follow her to the backstage costume closet, where Caty sat and breathed for five minutes until she was no longer in danger of hyperventilating. When the world sufficiently stopped spinning, she pulled out her phone, sending out a desperate plea to Tilney.

HELP.

Tilney, God bless him, answered within a matter of moments. *WHAT'S UP, NANCY DREW? YOU AREN'T LOCKED IN SOMEONE'S TRUNK, ARE YOU? BECAUSE I'VE LEFT ALL MY TOOLS AT HOME ...*

Despite the direness of her situation, Caty couldn't help but laugh. *YOU DON'T OWN ANY TOOLS.*

OH, THANK GOD. Tilney replied. *I'VE BEEN LOOKING FOR THEM EVERYWHERE . . . BUT I DIGRESS. YOU'RE IN DISTRESS?*

JOHN THORPE. I THINK HE THINKS SOMETHING IS HAPPENING BETWEEN US.

Tilney: *OH, HE DEFINITELY DOES. HE'S BEEN TELLING ANYONE WHO WOULD LISTEN THAT HE'S, QUOTE, DATING THE HOT KAPPA ASIAN CHICK. (CLOSE QUOTE)*

Caty blanched, feeling sick. How on earth did John Thorpe come to such a delusional conclusion? The only time they spent together was with her brother and his sister, and she wasn't very subtle about spending most of *that* time trying to get away from him. But now . . . everyone thought she was dating the guy who boasted about his "hilarious" attempts to troll Malala Yousafzai online because she seemed "just a little too into herself" (his words).

Worst of all was the thought that Tilney might have heard John's bragging and thought, even for a moment, that it might be true. *WHAT??? No WAY. NEVER. NEVER. NEVER. NEVER. AND DID I MENTION NEVER???!*

Caty held her breath as she watched the bubbled ellipses, indicating that Tilney was responding.

YOU HAVE NO IDEA HOW HAPPY I AM TO HEAR THAT. I WAS THINKING OF STAGING AN INTERVENTION. MAYBE EVEN A LOBOTOMY.

She took a moment to enjoy the roller-coaster swooshing in her stomach. Tilney didn't want her to date John Thorpe. Because the guy was a creep, true, but maybe, maybe, it also had to do with some feelings of his own. Deciding to be bold, Caty typed a quick reply.

NO NEED. HE'S NOT THE ONE I'M INTERESTED IN.

She pressed send, then put her phone away, heart pounding. Her bravery only extended so far, after all, and she was afraid to see how Tilney might respond to that—or worse, if he didn't respond at all. She'd give it time to breathe now, while she figured out a way to deal with John.

Exiting the closet, Caty intended to search for Isabella, though she soon became sidelined by angry shouts coming from onstage. Afraid that John and Isabella were at it again, Caty hurried toward the sound.

Instead, she found Karoline Bingley shouting at a conspicuously dust-free Elizabeth Bennet, who faced down her impressive rage with a smirk.

"…jealous, that's all. And frankly, it's pathetic," Karoline finished her toddler-scale rant.

Behind her, Emma wiped off her face with a towel, uninterested in all the drama. More engaged were a boy Caty thought must be Karoline's brother, Charlie, since he looked so much like her, but somehow much nicer; and Darcy.

Lizzy looked entirely too amused by the situation. "You're right, Karoline. Jealousy *is* pathetic. My god, if I had, say, schemed to kick two girls out of my sorority because I didn't like the attention they were getting—I would feel too embarrassed to show my face in public. Just a thought."

"Oh, please. You know what you did to get kicked out."

"Oh, please," Lizzy retorted, and for the first time there seemed to be the slightest crack in her implacable veneer. "We did way less than that stripper nun did today, and I don't see anyone rushing to oust her."

"Believe you me," Karoline snapped, "Isabella Thorpe is out of the Kappas as of today."

A startled Caty looked to Emma, who avoided eye contact. Caty's mind raced. She hadn't even considered that Isabella might get thrown out, and she very much doubted Isabella had, either. Her space back in the freshman dorms was already filled, which meant if she was expelled from the Kappas, she wouldn't just be sorority-less, she would be homeless.

Lizzy shook her head. "That's not the point, Karoline. Banishing the nun doesn't accomplish anything. She wasn't the one who coated everyone in dust."

"So you're admitting it was you?"

"Nice try." For the briefest moment, Lizzy's eyes slid over to Caty, who realized with a start that she might be the only one who'd seen her backstage before the show. Then she looked back to Karoline, with that infuriatingly smug smile on her face. "But, woman to woman? I have to tell you that yellow *really* isn't your color."

With that, Karoline lost it. Screeching, she lunged at Lizzy. Her brother reacted immediately, pinning her back from behind. Darcy quickly stepped in between the two girls, blocking Lizzy from Karoline's wrath. "Everyone needs to calm down. This was just a talent show, for God's sake."

"You think you're so smart, Lizzy," Karoline snarled, "but no one crosses a Kappa and lives to tell the tale…"

FROM THE FILES OF CATY MORLAND:

INTERVIEWEE: KAROLINE BINGLEY

CATY: WOULD YOU CONSIDER ELIZABETH BENNET TO BE YOUR RIVAL?

***KAROLINE* :** RIVAL? ABSOLUTELY NOT.

CATY: THERE DOES SEEM TO BE HISTORY BETWEEN YOU—YOU WOULDN'T CALL THAT A RIVALRY?

KAROLINE: NO. I WOULDN'T. BECAUSE A 'RIVALRY' IMPLIES A RELATIONSHIP BETWEEN TWO EQUALS.

❦ 9 ❦

(MARCH, AGAIN)

"We know now, of course, that Isabella's talent-show performance caused more of a stir than even she could have anticipated," Caty concluded as everyone digested this information, along with their herb-crusted chicken. "It nearly cost her a place in the Kappa house."

The week leading up to Initiation had been awkward, tense, with Karoline and Mrs. Norris both adamant that Isabella should be voted out, Anne quietly but firmly holding her ground that Isabella deserved a second chance, and Emma on the fence. As they now knew, it was only some gentle encouragement from Knightley that had persuaded Emma to cast the deciding vote.

All the while, Isabella had never spoken once on the subject, at least not to Caty. Caty had never seen her so withdrawn, so unwilling to discuss what was bothering her. Usually any complaint of hers was voiced loudly, insistently, and often.

"And," Caty continued, "it may very well have cost her her life."

It took very little time for the peanut gallery to chime in now; they had all grown accustomed, it seemed, to thinking of each other as potential murderers.

"My money is on Lizzy Bennet," said Karoline, to the surprise of absolutely no one. "Sneaking around backstage, where she wasn't supposed to be." She leveled her gaze on Lizzy, sneering. "I knew it was you who set off that color-dust bomb, Bennet. I *knew* it. It had the stench of knock-off perfume and desperation all over it."

Lizzy opened her mouth to respond, but quite unexpectedly, Darcy beat her to the punch. "Elizabeth doesn't wear perfume."

A long, awkward moment followed, as both Karoline and Lizzy frowned at Darcy. He seemed to realize only belatedly what a strange statement this was to make, looking as flustered as anyone that rich and handsome could manage to look. "I have an unusually strong olfactory response."

Karoline's eyes welled with tears, and for a brief, foolish moment, Caty thought she might be thinking of Isabella. "You have no idea the damage you caused, Bennet. One of a kind. Do you even know what that means?"

Lizzy blinked back at her, unimpressed. "I'm sorry—are you trying to compare the destruction of your dress with the death of a human being?"

"If you can murder a dress, you can murder a person. That's all I'm saying."

Marianne rushed to speak up in Lizzy's defense. "What about you, Karoline? You threatened to kill Lizzy in front of a group of people—did you follow through with the heinous woman-on-woman crime once you got Isabella alone?"

"Do you really think I would go shoving people off muddy hill-tops in my Loubotins?" Karoline retorted.

Despite having only moments before been accused of murder, Lizzy seemed to be enjoying herself immensely. "So again, to be clear, it isn't that you wouldn't have killed Isabella for moral reasons —it's that you wouldn't have risked your shoes?"

Darcy leaned forward, placing his palms on the table. "I don't see how any of this is productive. The two of you could go back and forth all night hurling accusations at each other, but it doesn't prove anything."

"You're right, Darcy," Caty agreed. "Especially since there are other people who stand out just as much as potential suspects after that talent show. John Thorpe, for starters. And, well, you."

John Thorpe's loud protestations and red face were a stark contrast to Darcy's paling skin and silent dismay. "What?" he managed to get in finally amid John's ranting tirades about the difficulty of being a straight white male in today's world.

Caty, likewise, ignored John for the moment to focus on Darcy. "Isabella did single you out that night—by tossing you her garter. Out of everyone at the talent show, why did she choose you to throw it to?"

"The word 'throw' is a little misleading. The garter ricocheted into the audience and smacked me in the face. I doubt she could have aimed it at anyone, even if she'd tried."

"Maybe," Caty conceded. "But Isabella did express a romantic interest in you. By all accounts, she took a huge risk at the talent show that night, changing her number at the last-minute. Why do that unless she was trying to get someone's attention? And then who does she single out in the audience? You." A deliberate beat as Caty let this sink in. "Seems like a funny coincidence."

"Coincidence being the operative term there."

Jane cleared her throat. "I'm not pointing any fingers, but Isabella did seem very determined to prove something at the talent show that night. Before she switched tracks last-minute, she had us rehearse together again and again, more than any of the other acts."

"Y'all." Emma sat up in her chair, looking meaningfully around the table. To Caty's surprise, it looked like Emma had chosen to partake of some of Tilney's rum, and based on the slight slurring of her speech, she was apparently a bit of a lightweight. "There's no way Darcy and Isabella . . . No. I mean, Darcy dated *me*, so…" She left unspoken the idea that one did not go from an Emma Woodhouse to an Isabella Thorpe, though the look on her face translated her meaning all too clearly.

An amused Tilney topped up another glass with rum, sliding it down the table to her, bartender-style. "Emma, I never realized before tonight just how much I like you."

She beamed back at him, happily accepting his offer of spirits.

Rushworth had finished his plate by now and looked around the room, seeming a bit restless without something to shove into his mouth. "So which one of y'all did it?" He glanced side-eyed at Caty's half-eaten chicken. "You gonna finish that...?"

Knightley raised his hands in a calming motion—as ever, the voice of reason. "Nobody did anything. There's nothing to prove—"

"It was me," said Marianne Dashwood unexpectedly, her chair legs scraping against the ground as she rose dramatically to her feet.

FROM THE FILES OF CATY MORLAND:

INTERVIEWEE: MARIANNE DASHWOOD (FRESHMAN AT AUSTEN UNIVERSITY, TREASURER OF DELTA LAMBDA EPSILON)

MARIANNE : FOR THE RECORD, CATHERINE, I STAND BEHIND YOU AND YOUR TRUTH WHEN YOU SAY THAT ISABELLA THORPE WAS MURDERED. ALSO FOR THE RECORD, I'M NOT THE KILLER. I WOULD SOONER DIE THAN TURN ON ANOTHER WOMAN.

"I can't stand by any longer and allow Lizzy to take the fall for me. It was me. I'm the one you're looking for."

A brief pause followed, and then came the collective moment when everyone around the table—with the possible exception of Rushworth—realized that Marianne was referring to the color-dust bomb, not Isabella's murder.

Any confusion for these two occurrences could easily be forgiven due to the gravitas Marianne had given her confession. She stood tall, her chin high, eyes ablaze with the righteousness of what she was doing.

Beside her, Lizzy grimaced, motioning for her to stop. "Marianne, you don't have to . . ."

But Marianne would not be deterred. "It was noble of you to try to be my Sydney Carton, Elizabeth, but there comes a time when every woman must speak her truth."

With a sigh, Lizzy sank back into her chair and allowed her to continue.

In short time, Marianne confessed it all—how she had been the one to rig the color-dust bomb, how Lizzy figured out her plan and showed up early to the Kappa talent show to try to stop her, how it was all part of an ill-thought out but sincere protest against the Kappa's "highly transparent and superficial bid for attention under the guise of charitable work." Along with the color-dust bomb, she'd intended to unravel a banner that outlined the ways in which the Kappas could contribute to society if that was their true intention, though this part of her demonstration, at least, Lizzy managed to stop—and all for the best, since it was the part that pointed to Marianne as the perpetrator.

In hindsight, Marianne realized she hadn't taken into consideration the consequences of her actions, like the potential loss of her scholarship to the university, which would make receiving her college education (and gaining the ability to promote world change) much more difficult. (But not, Marianne insisted, impossible, since college education was an opportunity, not a right, and they should all remember just how privileged they were.)

"Lizzy convinced me not to speak up since the color-dust bomb in and of itself wasn't enough evidence to point to any one of us. But, when I realized she had become a suspect, I knew I couldn't sit by in silence any longer." Marianne looked to Lizzy, nodding. "Thank you for prioritizing female friendship. But I'll take the consequences for my actions, whatever they might be."

It was such an impassioned speech that no one had the heart to tell her nobody really cared. "Thank you for your honesty," Caty said at last, trying to give the situation as much weight as Marianne seemed to think it deserved.

Rushworth motioned between Marianne and Lizzy with his fork, once again empty after finishing Caty's chicken. "So does that make the red-head a suspect now? Since you thought the brunette did it because of the color-bomb thingy before?"

Caty side-eyed him, a little taken aback that he'd been able to follow the entire exchange even that well. It was possible that she was underestimating the Theta bro a little too much, that there was a sharp mind at play underneath all that boorishness.

As if to deflect this exact train of thought, Rushworth pounded his chest and let out a long, vociferous belch. It was either completely disgusting, or completely genius. (Or quite possibly both.)

Caty returned her thoughts to the question at hand, seeing that both Marianne and Lizzy were watching her with interest. She had a hard time believing that anyone who could feel that guilty about a color-dust bomb was capable of murder. Then again, maybe Marianne, too, was putting on a show to distract from her crime. Though judging by Lizzy's exasperation during her confession, if Marianne was acting, it was a part she played consistently.

Still, Caty had better at least dot the i's and check the t's. "Were you at Box Hill on Initiation Night?"

Marianne nodded. "Yes. But I was with Lizzy and Nora the entire time. Which means Lizzy couldn't have done it either."

"Unless they all did it together," Karoline said, though her sulkiness made clear that she didn't really believe it.

It had been entirely too long since the last time John spoke up— or so he seemed to feel, since suddenly, quite out of the blue, he scraped back his chair, balling up his napkin and throwing it onto the table. "This whole investigation is a joke! Why are we even looking at people who clearly had nothing to do with it—like me and the mentally unstable ginger—" He jerked a thumb toward Marianne, in case there was any uncertainty to whom he was referencing, then barreled straight over her outraged sputter. "And you haven't even brought up the business major. Not that I'm saying Isabella was murdered, but if she WAS murdered, he's the first person I'd be looking at."

As usual, it was difficult to untangle the mess of John Thorpe's thought process, but this time Caty found herself even more confused than usual. "Business major? What business major?"

"From the email." This was said matter-of-factly, even a little superciliously, as if John couldn't believe how stupid she was being.

"What email?"

"The email from Isabella to..." All at once, John seemed to piece together that he'd made a colossal blunder. Caty watched as the color actually drained from his face, like he was a cartoon character.

"Um," he said after a long pause. "Never mind."

Caty *did* mind, however, and so did those at the rest of the table, and soon John was peer pressured into confessing the truth of it. "Sometimes James would leave his laptop unlocked, and somehow or another I figured out his password to his email account," John confessed finally after his mental powers—be they what they were—had been taxed to their utmost limit. "So after Isabella broke up with him, I kind of … read the email."

Stealing passwords and snooping on private conversations? That seemed to be something of a Thorpe family trait, Caty thought wryly, remembering her own encounter with Isabella breaking into her phone to text Tilney. "What did it say?"

"I think he should do us one better," Tilney insisted. "I'm assuming you still remember James's password." He motioned toward John's phone, lying face-up on the tabletop. "Read it for us."

FROM THE FILES OF CATY MORLAND:
[EMAIL FROM ISABELLA TO JAMES MORLAND]
FROM: IZZYBELLY@AU.EDU
TO: JMOR5@LSU.EDU
SUBJECT: SOOOOO…
MESSAGE:

DEAREST JAMES,

So, YOU PROBABLY FELT THIS COMING, BUT I THINK IT'S TIME WE PART WAYS. YOU HAVE BEEN A GREAT FIRST LOVE, BUT AS WE BOTH KNOW, THOSE HARDLY EVER LAST, AND ANYWAY NOW YOU'LL BE FREE TO DATE ALL THOSE LSU GIRLS I'M SURE YOU'VE BEEN FIGHTING OFF WITH A STICK. GEAUX TIGERS! ;)

YOU WERE A GREAT FIRST LOVE. LIKE, THE BEST. I WILL ALWAYS REMEMBER YOU AND I'M SURE YOU'LL ALWAYS REMEMBER ME. TRY NOT TO PINE AFTER ME TOO LONG THOUGH, HAHA.

PLEASE DON'T THINK THIS HAS ANYTHING TO DO WITH YOU. THE DISTANCE WAS JUST A LITTLE TOO MUCH. SO MUCH DRIVING BACK

AND FORTH. AND IF I'M BEING HONEST, THERE IS SOMEBODY ELSE. HE'S AT AU WITH ME, SO IT MAKES MORE SENSE, AND HE'S A BUSINESS MAJOR AND A THETA, SO WE'LL HAVE MORE IN COMMON. PLUS HIS FAMILY IS TOTALLY OLD SCHOOL.

ANYWAY, HOPEFULLY WE CAN STILL BE FRIENDS. FOR REAL THOUGH. A PART OF ME WILL ALWAYS LOVE YOU. WHO KNOWS? MAYBE WE'LL BE LIKE *THE NOTEBOOK* AND FIND EACH OTHER AGAIN DOWN THE ROAD. AFTER YOU GROW A BEARD AND BUILD ME A HOUSE, HAHA. BUT FOR NOW, ADIEU, MY JAMES.

LOVE,

ISABELLA

❧ 11 ❧

Caty took a moment to process this new information. If Isabella had been telling the truth—always a big if, admittedly—then she'd had a secret Theta boyfriend who nobody knew about, and who had never come forward after her untimely death.

This information seemed to be sinking in with the Thetas around the table, as well. Hoping to catch them before they could school their expressions, Caty looked at Rushworth, Darcy, and Frank each in turn, studying their suddenly nervous faces.

"What's your major again, Rushworth?" Caty asked, not bothering to sweeten it; they all knew why she was asking, even Rushworth.

"Business," Rushworth gulped, and Darcy and Frank didn't wait to be called out by name before confirming they were the same.

"That could be virtually any Theta," Frank pointed out. "We're all business majors."

"True," Caty conceded, "but Isabella mentioned the family being 'old school'—the same term she used when she was putting the three of you on her Hit-It list."

There could be little arguing with that; for once the table was completely silent. "Now, whoever this mystery man was, he wanted Isabella to keep the relationship a secret for some unknown reason, because I was her best friend, and I never heard a peep out of her—and we all know Isabella would have been shouting that from the rooftops if she could have. Whoever it was must not have wanted anyone else to know about the relationship—and maybe they had to make sure nobody ever found out.

"So," Caty turned her attention first to Frank. "Where were you Initiation Night?"

"At Jane's house."

Marianne furrowed her brow. "But Jane was at Box Hill—that's where Isabella gave her the diary."

Frank nodded. "We were going to go together, make our big debut as a couple, but my aunt had just passed away and I didn't really feel up to partying. But Jane had to go since she was a new Initiate, and I didn't really feel like being by myself at my aunt's house or the empty Theta house, so I waited for her there." After a beat, he added, "Miss Bates made me brownies. From scratch."

Interesting that Frank hadn't gone to be with his father during his time of mourning, but from everything he'd mentioned so far, it seemed clear there was some distance in that relationship. And anyway, who didn't love Miss Bates's homemade brownies?

The story checked out, so Caty looked next to Rushworth. "And you?"

"Oh, I was there for sure." Rushworth said this without any guilt or trepidation, maybe even a little pride. "I was right in the thick of it for most of it—I'm sure we could find people to vouch for seeing me. Then I passed out around—" He scratched his jawline, right under his ear. "10?"

"10:30," Tilney confirmed for him. He, like everyone else, had seen the video posted to social media of Rushworth finally having one-too-many and timbering straight onto the dessert table.

"10:30," Rushworth repeated with a nod before looking to Caty. "When was Isabella killed again?"

"They think around midnight."

"Oh, great!" Seeing the looks around the table, Rushworth amended, "Not for her, obviously. But my alibi checks out."

So it seemed—though Caty would need to verify just how unconscious Rushworth had been for the rest of the night. "What about you, Darcy?" Caty turned her focus to the Theta president, who met her gaze coolly. "Can anyone vouch for your whereabouts that night on Box Hill?"

"No." At Marianne's dramatic gasp, Darcy grimaced and continued, "Because I wasn't there that night. I stayed home to FaceTime with my sister."

"Ooh, Guan-yin!" Karoline cooed. "I love her."

Caty and Tilney exchanged a glance. As far as alibis went, it was a strange one. "You stayed home from the biggest party of the year to FaceTime with your sister?" Caty echoed, not bothering to hide her skepticism.

"Yes."

"This isn't twenty questions, Darcy. You're going to have to give us a little more than that." Caty raised an eyebrow. "Or should we get in touch with Guan-yin to see why you needed to talk that night, of all nights?"

Darcy blinked at her—a long, slow, deliberate action. It was clear he was not used to being second-guessed and having his actions called into questions. "She was having a hard time." He raised his hand before Caty or Karoline could comment further. "And that's all I'm going to say on the subject, murder investigation or no."

His tone was final, authoritative. Caty wondered for one fleeting second what it must be like to wield that much easy power. If it had been Darcy investigating this murder, the culprit would likely have already turned himself in, and apologized for any inconvenience.

But that wasn't a particularly helpful train of thought, so Caty turned her attention to the Kappa vice-president. "Where were you that night, Karoline?"

Something—small, furtive, and fearful—darted through Karoline's eyes. "I stayed home that night. I had…homework to do."

Complete and utter silence fell over the table. If tumbleweeds had populated the dining room of the Pi Kappa Sigma House, one would have likely blown through at that very moment. As it was, Frank could not quite seem to stop himself from coughing to punctuate the awkward pause.

Karoline's enhanced green eyes flickered to Darcy, then back to the top of her plate. "It was going to be a lame party anyway, full of wannabes and charity bids. No offense." It remained unclear who this statement was directed toward, so no one entirely knew who was meant to remain unoffended. "And, you know. I was worried about my shoes. Elton felt the same. We decided to update our profile pics, see?"

Karoline produced her phone, showing Caty a long string of photo thumbnails of her and Elton posing in various positions, all of them dramatic and expertly lit. "We were trying to get just the right picture to go Instagram official," she explained, with a forced little laugh. "Turns out it also came in handy for a murder investigation alibi."

Something about her story sounded a little too rehearsed, which was odd since it was such an obviously bad alibi. As if echoing Caty's thoughts, Lizzy said aloud, "I'm confused, Karoline —which is it? You were doing your homework, you thought the party would be lame, or you wanted to update your profile picture?"

"D, Bennet. All of the above."

Lizzy opened her mouth, the gleam in her eye suggesting she had a ready retort. But before things could escalate between the two of them again, Caty hmmed loudly. "That's weird. The time stamps for these pictures end around 9:00—well before Isabella would have been murdered."

Karoline wetted her lips. "Oh?"

Caty handed back her phone. "I'm afraid this doesn't add up to much, in terms of alibi. Can Elton vouch that you were with him through the duration of the party?"

"Probably."

Even those at the table who were not so criminally inclined exchanged glances at this. "Probably?" Tilney prodded.

"I mean, I wasn't in his line of sight the whole time. I, like, went to the bathroom, or whatever."

"For an hour?" At Karoline's slow, deliberate blink, Caty explained, "I spoke to Elton earlier this week. He said you left for about an hour. Were you in the bathroom that whole time?"

Rushworth whistled low under his breath. "I've been there before."

Karoline wrinkled her nose in distaste. "God. That's obviously not what I meant. Y'all are disgusting." Another darted glance to Darcy. "I must have forgotten. I went out."

"To do what?"

"I...forgot."

"You forgot that you forgot you went out?" Tilney deadpanned.

Karoline huffed a frustrated breath, her accent getting a little more Mississippi twang to it as her irritation mounted. "Look, it's obviously not me, okay? I know we all have to pretend that we care she died, but Isabella was so far beneath me that I barely even noticed she existed. Believe me, I had way bigger fish to fry that night."

Silence. Caty wanted to probe further, but she was afraid she might push Karoline too far in the wrong direction and the older girl would just clam up altogether.

Luckily, Lizzy Bennet could always be counted on to push Karoline's buttons in just the right way. "Was there, like, a big purse sale or something that night?"

"Screw you, Bennet. I don't need markdowns, not like some people." Karoline's voice was a savage twang now. She shook her head. "I just wish I could be in the room when you hear the news."

"Karoline," Darcy said sharply—and Caty noticed for the first time that his jaw was clenched, his knuckles white on the tabletop.

Lizzy looked back and forth between them, no longer amused. "What is going on?"

"Oh, she's gonna find out soon enough anyway, and it's already done." Karoline tried for defiant with Darcy, but didn't quite manage it, reverting to batting her lashes and pouting a little. "I'm sorry, but you know how much she aggravates me."

Darcy said nothing, just fumed silently.

Caty, too, looked between the two, musing. "So I'm guessing you weren't talking to your sister, Darcy?"

"I did talk to my sister." It sounded like it was very important to Darcy that it was clear he hadn't been lying, at least not entirely. "And I also did…something else that night."

Karoline abruptly reached forward, pouring herself a healthy glass of the rum. "We staged an intervention. For my brother, Charlie." Catching Lizzy's eyes with what could only be described as a victorious gleam in her own, she continued, "It was obvious that Charlie had stumbled into some bad company around these parts. So we convinced him—and my parents—to let him finish out the semester in Paris."

"Paris," Lizzy repeated dumbly, as if she didn't quite understand the word. It was the first time Caty had ever heard the other girl anything but sharp and vivacious, the brightest and cleverest person in the room.

Marianne, too, looked visibly affected by this news. "He hasn't said anything to Nora about it."

So that was the reason for the upset. Caty remembered, vaguely, that Marianne and Lizzy had mentioned something about Nora and Charlie, which was part of why Karoline had run Nora and Lizzy out of the Kappas. Caty couldn't remember if they'd said they were dating or maybe just liked each other; either way, it apparently hadn't been serious enough for him to tell her he was moving to France, judging by the expression on Marianne's face. (That had to suck.)

"I'm sure he'll shoot off a text once he gets settled." Karoline drained her glass. "Jetlag can be such a bitch."

"But—" Marianne started again, before Lizzy clamped a hand down on her arm, and the two sat mutely, staring ahead—Marianne blinking back tears, Lizzy stone-faced and seething.

πκΣ

A pregnant pause followed, after which Caty at least cleared her throat. "Looks like Darcy, Rushworth, Frank, and Karoline all have alibis." She looked to John, who shifted uncomfortably. "That just leaves you, John. So where were you the night Isabella was killed?"

A long moment of silence followed. Then, sighing, John met her gaze. "Sorry, babe. This is gonna hurt you more than it hurts me."

FROM THE FILES OF CATY MORLAND:

[TWEETS RETRIEVED FROM JOHN THORPE'S TWITTER ACCOUNT - @TIGERBRO69]

@TIGERBRO69: HOT KAPPA ASIAN KEEPS BLOWING ME OFF INSTEAD OF JUST BLOWING ME #DISAPPOINTED #WHYDONICEGUYSALWAYSFINISHLAST

@TIGERBRO69: HOT KAPPA ASIAN IS A DIRTY LITTLE TEASE - WISH SHE WAS DIRTIER THO *[EGGPLANT, PEACH EMOJI]* #AMIRIGHT #ASIANFETISH

@TIGERBRO69: @MALALA I BET YOUR FARTS STILL SMELL LIKE MINE THO

C aty was at first too taken aback to protest against the pouty, reformed bad-boy look John was trying (and failing) to pull off; but then, once that moment had passed, she forced herself to stay silent, wondering if maybe John truly had something of importance to tell her. A confession would be nice, but she'd even settle for a helpful tidbit of information about Isabella that could help pull the entire mystery into focus.

By now, John realized he had the attention of the entire room and was clearly relishing it, giving a melodramatic sigh. Underneath the performance, though, Caty thought it might actually be difficult for him to talk about what happened to Isabella—he was her brother, after all, and that had to mean something, even to a creep like John Thorpe.

And then, he opened his mouth. "Look, this isn't gonna be easy to hear, babe. You know we had something special. But you were playing too many games. I had to move on."

Caty once again exercised all of her willpower to bite her tongue. "Explain, please."

He did, taking no little joy in detailing his exploits of that night. He even had pictorial proof, in various Instagram posts he'd made

—one, a picture of himself and some of his fraternity brothers dressed in Greek togas, heading to a massive fraternity party; another at the party, with one arm around a pretty blonde girl who looked like she was trying her best to lean as far away from him as possible, and the other around a pretty, plump girl, toward whom his back was angled; a selfie with him standing outside a dorm room, pointing to a name on the door—Olivia—his body blocking another name on the door, except for the first letter, "M"; and one final selfie of him in a girl's bed, smirking at the camera with mussed hair and kiss-swollen lips, the faint curve of a girl's shoulder visible in the shot.

John tucked his phone away, but not before gauging the reaction of the room; he was clearly hoping some of the Theta brothers would be impressed by his conquest. "I'm sorry you had to see that, Catherine. But you have to understand—Olivia Morton. She's one of the hottest girls in the school. And, you know, blonde, so." He made a *what are you gonna do?* gesture.

Caty suppressed an eyeroll. "So you were at the fraternity party, and then you went back to Olivia's room and fooled around with her?"

"If by 'fooled around' you mean 'sex,' then, yeah."

"What time did you go to the party, when did you leave with Olivia, and when did you return to your dorm?"

"I went to the party around 9, left around midnight with my lady friend, and got back around ten the next morning." He winked at Caty. "Let's just say, there was a standing ovation to my first performance, if you know what I mean."

Caty ignored him, thinking through the times. If others corroborated his story, there was no way John could have driven to Highbury and killed Isabella. Already his posts on his Instagram seemed to more or less confirm the times he'd been describing. So why did it seem like such a bullshit story?

"Olivia Morton," Tilney spoke up, absorbed in his own phone that cast a faint bluish-tinge on his glasses. "From Shreveport, right?"

"I guess so."

Tilney tilted his head, amused. "Weird. If she had such a great night with you, why did she unfollow you on Instagram?"

Tipsy Emma seemed to have really gotten into the spirit of the night, scraping back her chair so she could look over Tilney's shoulder at the phone. "Ooh, liar liar pants on fire! No one unfollows someone after a night of mind-blowing sex." She took the phone from Tilney and began scrolling herself. "Her biceps are next-level, though. I wonder what arm workout she uses…?"

Everyone at the table once again looked to John with renewed interest—not in response to the question about the arm workout, which it seemed unlikely he would know, but in response to him allegedly lying about sleeping with Olivia. If true, it didn't exactly make him a murderer, but it certainly didn't make him a saint.

Caty leveled John with her gaze, pleased to see he looked nervous by this sudden turn in the conversation. "Interesting. Why would Olivia unfollow you if the two of you had such a great time, John?"

He snorted. "I dunno. Who can understand women, am I right?" This time anticipating the nudge, Frank leaned away from his elbow.

"Anyone who isn't an idiot," Marianne spoke up hotly.

"Ooh!" Lizzy, too, was scrolling through her phone, as well, apparently joining Tilney on his deep dive through Instagram. "On Olivia's feed, she's posing with her roommate in the dorm room, each of them in their respective beds. Olivia is on the camera's left side, the other girl is on the right." She scrolled a little further. "Then, if you look at John's morning-after picture, you can see the sun is streaming onto his face from a window just above him on the right-hand side."

Rushworth frowned at her. "Huh?"

Far quicker on the uptake, Tilney looked past Darcy at Lizzy, giving her a look of respect. "Well-spotted."

"Either John and Olivia slept together in her roommate's bed for some unknown reason," Lizzy explained, "or, much more likely, John slept with the roommate and tried to make it look like he slept with Olivia." As an afterthought, she added, "Ew."

A moment passed as the table processed this. Caty waited for John to deny it, but even he seemed to realize this was far too scummy to argue his way out of. "Mary Musgrove," he said finally, without the usual John Thorpe bluster. "I may have gotten them a little confused—I'd had a lot to drink that night."

"What a prince." This from Marianne. "Expecting every woman you meet to conform to society's standards of beauty when *you* can't even meet the bare minimum for its standards of decency."

Darcy had thus far kept himself out of most of the fray, though even he could not keep himself from speaking up, "This is what you were doing the morning after your sister had been killed?"

John stared down at the table. "I didn't know what had happened to Isabella then. By the time I did…" But apparently he saw no point in completing that sentence, no point in justifying what must have been one of the lowest points of his entire life.

For a moment, Caty could almost feel sorry for him. No wonder John had to bluster about Isabella's death being an accident. For his sister to have a tragic accident while he was off being a complete asshole to someone else's sister must be terrible enough; but if Isabella was being murdered while all of that was happening… even John Thorpe couldn't be immune to that.

Knightley surprised everyone by clearing his throat. "You said you were at a party down at LSU that night. Was Caty's brother with you—James?"

John looked up, blinking, clearly taken aback by the question. "No. He stayed back at the dorm—too bummed over Bella to come out. I told him the best way to get over one girl was to get under another…" But he lost steam halfway into the sentiment, his heart clearly not in it.

A trickle of unease ran down Caty's spine. She looked to Knightley questioningly. "Why do you want to know?"

Knightley shook his head—more to himself, it seemed, than to her. "I can't believe I'm doing this," he said at last, rubbing at the bridge of his nose, "But there's an obvious suspect who isn't here tonight. And I'd like to know why."

A long moment of silence followed. "Who?" said Rushworth at last, looking around the room.

"James Morland, Caty's brother."

From the Files of Caty Morland:

INTERVIEWEE: James Morland

JAMES: Look, I don't care what she did or didn't do to me. She didn't deserve *THAT*.

❦ 13 ❧

When Caty was in first grade, she and James used to ride the bus together back and forth from school, though of course, James wouldn't sit next to her, because he was in fourth grade and fourth graders didn't ride with babies. Unless they already knew the Morland siblings, no one riding the bus would have had any reason to assume they were family—not James with his dishwater blond hair and blue eyes, and Caty with her long black hair and dark brown eyes. When the bus came to their stop, he wouldn't acknowledge her, just silently follow her onto the street, where he'd usually walk a pace or two behind her until they got home.

It didn't bother Caty. She didn't take it personally. She didn't think about it, really. Most days she was too busy worrying about if her best friend Missy liked her other best friend Grace better to care what James got up to at the back of the bus.

Until one day when one of the third graders, Maggie, got mad that Caty accidentally stepped on her backpack and threatened to hit her. Caty, who had spent most of her elementary school life being invisible, had never encountered such hostility, and blurted the first thing that came to her mind: "You better not, or my brother will beat you up!"

James had never before done anything that suggested he would ever be this violent, or this chivalrous, but Caty nonetheless stuck to her guns, even after Maggie scoffed that Caty didn't even have a brother. "Yes, I do—he's right there."

Caty pointed to James, and Maggie snorted. "That's not your brother. He's not Chinese."

Neither was Caty, she could have pointed out, but that hardly seemed the point. Determined to prove James was her brother, Caty waved, trying to get his attention. "James! James!"

There was a moment when he looked up, saw her motioning to him—a moment when Caty could tell he'd noticed her, and could tell, too, that he saw the attention all this commotion was attracting. Their gazes met. Then came the moment when she saw James decide to ignore her, looking away to keep talking to his friends.

Caty cried the rest of the bus ride home—silent tears, not her usual hysterics that she'd use to get her way with her parents. This sign of genuine distress seemed to mollify Maggie, who left her alone after that.

When they got to their bus stop, James tried to say something to Caty, but this time she was the one to make sure to walk a pace ahead of *him*, and he didn't say anything else to her about it once they got home.

But the next day on the bus, James sat next to Caty on the ride to school. They didn't say a word to each other all the way there. In fact, they never spoke about the incident after that, and it never happened again during all the years they went to school together. But no one on the school bus ever questioned if he was her brother again, and for that matter, neither did Caty.

Now, she realized as Knightley pointed to the elephant in the room she had been trying her best to ignore, it was her turn to return the favor. "James didn't have anything to do with Isabella's death. He's devastated."

Those were her mother's words, actually—Caty had spoken only briefly to James on the phone, and it had been a perfunctory exchange, in which she had obtained dates, times, locations, and other facts about his relationship with Isabella. There had been no discussion of feelings, on either end. She hadn't been home since that night on Box Hill, even though her mother had been calling and texting nonstop. Caty couldn't bring herself to answer, and she returned the texts at times she knew her mom wouldn't be able to engage. Her week had been full of interviews, scrambling to gather clues and suspects, living and breathing Isabella's murder. If she went home, saw her father's worry, James's sadness, heard her mother's, "Oh, Caty," that would be it. She wouldn't be able to keep going.

"You think someone couldn't be devastated after committing a murder?" Knightley held up a hand, warding off Caty's protest. "You brought all of us here tonight under the assumption that Isabella was murdered, told us all why we could be suspects—some of us for reasons, frankly, that just don't make any sense. So I think we all deserve to know why the most obvious suspect isn't here tonight."

Rage, unexpected, boiled in the pit of Caty's stomach, lodging somewhere in her throat. Who was the detective here, again? "Because he didn't do it. I know him. He isn't capable of it."

"But you said so yourself—everyone is capable of murder under the right circumstances."

"James did get dumped by Isabella just a few days before she was murdered," Frank chimed in. "That letter you read was pretty harsh—and embarrassing."

Tilney grimaced a silent apology at Caty. "Plus he stayed at the dorms that night instead of going to the party at LSU. So, no alibi. He could have driven to Highbury and back without anyone noticing."

Unbelievable. Just unbelievable. If any of them actually knew James, they would realize how pointless this conversation was when they should be focusing on who the real murderer could be. Sure, it was a little suspicious that James hadn't gone to the party, and she could see how they might connect a flimsy motive from that letter, but...but...

"Look—" Caty started to say, but she was saved the necessity of having to come up with a way to finish that sentence as the doorknob to the dining room rattled.

For a brief, fleeting moment the party guests exchanged startled, bewildered looks, before the door opened, revealing a rain-soaked, red-faced Mrs. Norris. "What the devil is going on here?" she boomed, glaring at the occupants of the table.

FROM THE FILES OF CATY MORLAND:
  [EXCERPT OF EMAIL SENT TO AUSTEN UNIVERSITY STUDENTS]

...ALL UNIVERSITY-AFFILIATED EVENTS WILL BE SUSPENDED UNTIL FURTHER NOTICE. BUILDINGS ON UNIVERSITY CAMPUS WILL BE CLOSED UNTIL FURTHER NOTICE. THIS INCLUDES GREEK ROW, WHICH WILL CEASE ALL ACTIVITIES IMMEDIATELY, EVEN IF THEY HAVE BEEN PREVIOUSLY APPROVED. ANY STUDENTS FOUND IN VIOLATION OF THIS MAY BE SUBJECT TO DISCIPLINARY ACTION, INCLUDING BUT NOT LIMITED TO SUSPENSION, EXPULSION, AND LEGAL PROSECUTION.
  SINCERELY,
  PRESIDENT DE BOURGH

❦ 14 ❧

For a sorority that so prided itself on its charm and flair, Barbara Norris had always seemed an odd choice to be appointed as house mother to the Kappas, being in possession of neither of these qualities. Looking at the woman in question now—appearing in the doorway of the dining room like some grim, disproving Poltergeist, the shadows highlighting her sharp, hawk-like features—Caty suddenly understood. The Emmas and Karolines were the princesses of the Kappa house, and Norris was the ogre meant to scare away anything untoward from breaching the castle. She would not want to be the thing, Caty thought with a shudder, that had to go into battle against such a force.

Mrs. Norris's yellowish eyes took in the occupants of the room, her mouth pursed tight against her quivering rage. "Are you out of your minds? Not only is the Kappa house closed, but there is an active tornado warning." Lest anyone mistake her words for concern, she added, "You do realize the university would be liable if anything were to happen?" She was really on a roll now, buoyed by her own righteous indignation. And don't give me any hogwash about not knowing—the whole lot of you are addicted to all that useless technology, so I know you got the alerts."

In one stealth motion, Tilney slid the bottle of rum off the table and into his lap—but not fast enough to escape Norris's gaze, amplified by her huge glasses. "Alcohol!" This, as if it were cocaine—and maybe in Norris's view, it really was one and the same. "Good God in heaven. What have I done to be burdened with such a heavy load...?"

"Mrs. Norris." Emma, who had not but a few moments before been giggly, giddily tipsy, now seemed remarkably sober. Her voice carried an unexpected ring of authority to it—and her accent, Caty noticed, had thickened considerably in addressing the older woman. "I am so sorry if we gave you a fright. We were holding a meeting about outreach to our fellow students during these trying times, when the weather overtook us and we became trapped in the house. Please believe it was no one's intention to break any rules."

Caty noticed that Emma didn't mention anything about the rum —as if by ignoring it completely, she could just make it disappear. How very Southern of her.

A great war seemed to be playing out across Mrs. Norris's face. On the one hand, so many rules had been broken, and she was nothing if not for her rules. But on the other hand, Mrs. Norris seemed to respond intuitively to authority, and there was no one more sure of being right and in control than Emma Woodhouse.

"I should report this to President de Bourgh," Mrs. Norris said at last, but it was clear from her tone that this was an idle threat, that she was simply waiting to be further mollified, and a collective sigh of relief emanated from the occupants of the table.

"Now, Mrs. Norris, I'm sure there's no need for that. Why don't you pull up a chair...?"

As Emma continued to smooth things over with the house ogre, Caty felt her mind begin to race again. James. They thought James had killed Isabella. Of course she wasn't so stupid that the thought had never crossed her mind, but she knew it couldn't be true.

Only now, she wondered how she could have been so certain. Caty knew James, she knew he wasn't capable of this sort of thing... but how many true-crime specials had she listened to, watched, read, where the murderer's relatives said the same thing? *"I never would have suspected so and so, he seemed like such a nice guy,"* etcetera, etcetera. As a distant, safe spectator, how Caty had scoffed at their naivety. *Anybody* could be capable of murder. She knew that. And yet, she couldn't quite believe it, not when that anybody was somebody to her.

No. Not James. This wasn't just blind loyalty; Caty felt it in her gut. There had to be something missing, some avenue she hadn't yet fully explored . . .

The diary. Unbidden, Caty's thoughts returned to Marla Bertram's journal, the thing that had started it all. Was she just being obstinate, or was there a reason she kept circling back to it? She felt as though she'd exhausted every possibility tonight at the dinner, but something—a hunch, intuition?—told her not to give up so easily.

Her eyes landed on Mrs. Norris, still hovering, not taking the chair that Knightley had fetched for her at Emma's command, though she had taken a few concessionary steps into the room. There was no denying the woman was intimidating, and as Tilney had pointed out earlier, no one seemed to doubt that she could be capable of murdering Isabella. She had a motive, too, if she'd known that Isabella had the diary and was worried that something in there might cause harm to Marla Bertram. Already Mrs. Norris had broken into Caty's and Isabella's room to try to find the diary; what else might she be capable of?

Caty had been operating under the assumption that Mrs. Norris couldn't have been there that night on Box Hill. But what if that wasn't true?

And suddenly, just like that, it fell into place.

As if in a trance, Caty rose to her feet, feeling a calm determination overcome her as she advanced toward the older woman. At first, her progress went unnoticed, as the others tried to wheedle Mrs. Norris into the empty chair and she resisted, clearly enjoying all the attention.

"No, I couldn't possibly… if anyone found out that I'd turned a blind eye—"

She stopped as she noticed Caty, now standing directly in front of her. For a brief moment, their gazes met.

Then Caty looked back at the table, triumphant. "We were wrong," she explained, "she could have climbed to the top of Box Hill."

And to demonstrate her point, she kicked the cane out of Mrs. Norris's hands.

Caty beamed at this, her *pièce de résistance*, her Poirot moment, ready to explain how she had so cleverly deduced it all—

—until Mrs. Norris, screamed in agony that could not be feigned as she crumpled to the ground like a marionette with severed strings.

For a moment, Caty could only stare at her, horrified, before looking up to see a table-full of equally horrified faces looking back at her. "Whoops...?"

VOLUME THREE

"Indeed, I am very sorry to be right in this instance. I would much rather have been merry than wise."

Jane Austen, *Emma*

Locked in the den on the ground floor of the Pi Kappa Sigma house, Caty had been doing a lot of soul-searching. Kicking out Mrs. Norris's cane had been an admittedly low point in a night of missteps and self-revelations that were less than flattering. She had been so quick, so desperate, to jump to certain conclusions, to force the clues to add up to some version of Isabella's death that would be palatable to her. In actuality, there were two possibilities that she hadn't allowed herself to fully consider, which in all likelihood were the most plausible options.

The first, that James had something to do with Isabella's death. Despite his terrible taste in music and the truly horrific-smelling farts that she had been forced to endure in her lifetime, Caty loved James. Loved him so much that even though she had watched all the true-crime shows and listened to all the podcasts and knew that the boyfriend was always the first and most logical suspect, she hadn't ever once truly considered him as a possibility.

She did so now, texting the question with trembling hands and tear-filled eyes, afraid that he might be angry or hurt. More afraid that he might be guilty. *WHERE WERE YOU THAT NIGHT?* Short, simple, to the point. She knew she didn't need to elaborate on which night was the night in question. Quite possibly James had been waiting all along for her to ask.

As she waited in tense, knee-jiggling anticipation for what his response might be, Caty allowed herself to think through—for the first time—that other possibility she had not been allowing herself to face: that Isabella's death had been nothing but a terrible accident.

Strange as it might seem, in some ways this prospect was worse than the thought of James being guilty. Not because Caty wanted him to have anything to do with it, but because if everyone was right, if Isabella had just taken a wrong turn that night, gotten lost in the fog...then it was all just so pointless. All of those hours interviewing, following various leads, sifting through clues and bread-crumbs, would have been rendered meaningless, because that's what Isabella's death would be. There would be no one to blame. No one who could explain to Caty why it had happened.

Finding out the reason Isabella had been murdered might be horrifying, might be enraging, might be devastating, but at least she would have a reason. Something to help it make sense.

The door creaked open and Emma poked in her head, not proceeding any further into the room. Doubtless, she was afraid Caty might randomly attack her, like she had Mrs. Norris. Caty couldn't honestly say at this point that the fear was unwarranted. She had not begun the evening thinking she would be getting into a physical altercation with anyone, least of all the Kappa House Mother; she could no longer say for certain just what she was capable of.

"So..." Emma spoke in her usual brisk, forthright tone, though for the first time Caty thought she detected the undercurrent of something that sounded very much like uncertainty. "Mrs. Norris has agreed to not press any charges. But the group has taken a vote, and we think it would be best if you stay, um, *contained* in here until the tornado warning is over, and we can all go home."

Caty nodded, swallowing. "Okay."

A moment's hesitation; it seemed as though Emma had been

anticipating more of a fight, and didn't quite know what to do with Caty's acquiescence. "Can I bring you anything?" she asked finally.

Caty supposed it would probably be in bad taste to ask for a helping of the dessert. She'd really been looking forward to the trifle. "No, thanks."

"Okay." Emma paused in the doorway, biting her lower lip. "I'm sorry, Caty. I should have never encouraged this. It wasn't very good mentoring on my part."

Mentoring? The word took Caty aback. She had thought all this time that Emma was just trying to be her friend. But it made more sense that the popular, beautiful upperclassman would have only taken her on as a project.

Caty was not so very good at reading people, she was beginning to discover.

Emma pulled the door to the den shut. The lock clicked after her, a cringing reminder of Caty's dangerousness, her deviance.

Left alone with her thoughts, Caty was forced to return to the unpleasant question of just *why* she'd been so certain Isabella had been murdered. Something about the way Isabella had looked, lying there on the forest floor...

But not even the police had been able to determine much from the crime scene in the chaos that had followed finding Isabella's body, with so many drunken undergraduates trampling over the area where they thought Isabella must have fallen from. Caty couldn't even really be confident now of what she'd actually seen, because she'd been drunk and distressed, and most likely she'd been in shock from discovering the dead body of her best friend.

Kind of best friend. One-time best friend. They hadn't even been speaking anymore the night Isabella died. Afterward, Caty had consoled herself with the knowledge that they would have made up, eventually. But now she wondered if that were true. As much as she hoped they could have patched things up, Caty seriously doubted she could stay close with someone who had dumped James in such a callous way.

Truthfully, they might not have even been friends when all was said and done, and here she was, fighting tooth and nail to find Isabella's murderer. Trying to prove said murderer even existed.

Caty's phone pinged, a thankful reprieve from her train of thoughts, until she remembered. *James.* Feeling a little sick to her stomach, she brought the screen eye-level, surprised to see that instead of her brother's name, she had a new message from her mom.

JAMES ASKED ME TO LET YOU KNOW HE WAS HERE LAST SATURDAY NIGHT. THAT NIGHT HE WAS FEELING PRETTY LOW SO HE WANTED TO BE WITH ME AND DAD AND THE GIRLS. I'M SUPPOSED TO CONFIRM THAT HE SPENT THE NIGHT.

As she'd suspected, James had understood the motive behind her text and what it was she'd really been asking him. He'd also watched enough true crime with Caty to know his story would be way more plausible with an alibi, which he had helpfully provided without her having to prompt.

Caty felt a sagging relief overtake her. All the tension that had been coiling in her spine suddenly dissipated, leaving her slumped and exhausted in her chair. It wasn't James. It couldn't have been James. Thank the Lord he'd decided to go home that night instead of staying cooped up alone in his dorm. It might have been harder to believe him, then, no matter how much she might have wanted to.

That was the problem with getting involved with murder, she was beginning to realize. Isabella's death wasn't some isolated, insulated thing. It touched everything around it, and everyone within reaching distance. It tainted one's vision of people, casting the most sordid light on their motivations, their behaviors.

Caty still wanted to find Isabella's murderer, of course, but she understood now what that would really mean. It would change everything. It would change *her.* Every person in that room would be forever altered tonight, the innocent and the guilty.

As much of a painful self-reflection as this was, Caty still could not entirely quell the voice in her head that reminded her that this was the point in the true-crime reenactments when the tenacious detective would look out the window, staring at the rain as they puzzled through the mystery.

The thought was so absurd that Caty half-stifled a giggle, wondering if she really had lost touch with reality tonight. Even so, the allure of adhering to genre convention proved to be too tempting for our young heroine to resist, and she moved to the window, tilting the blinds so she could peer out at the night.

Beyond the ghost-like apparition of her own reflection in the pane, Caty saw the storm-battered backyard of the Kappa house. Sticks, leaves, and Spanish moss had been scattered across the normally pristine lawn, and the limb-sized branches of the massive oaks swayed ominously against the still-robust gusts of wind. Through the sleeting rain, Caty spotted the cottage that Mrs. Norris lived in, the windows darkened, though a thin twist of smoke escaped the chimney.

It took a moment for that picture to strike Caty as being decidedly odd. Mrs. Norris was in the main house now, so it made sense that she would have turned out her lights, but when she'd stumbled across the dinner party, she'd seemed astounded to find them all there. Wouldn't Mrs. Norris have seen the lights from her windows, and wouldn't they in turn have noticed the lights were on in the cottage?

Perhaps the dark and stormy night had kept them from spotting each other, but Caty couldn't shake the image of Norris sitting in her darkened cottage, watching them lit up in the main house windows. Plotting.

Mrs. Norris wasn't actually an ogre, she knew that. There was no reason to imagine her lurking in the dark.

But then Caty remembered another figure, hiding in the shadows: whoever had been creeping in the hallway that night, listening as Caty looked through Isabella's things. It was possible it was someone from the dinner party, but less likely, since they were such a small group, and someone was sure to be noticed if they suddenly went missing. It made more sense for it to have been Mrs. Norris, who no one knew was in the house.

There was only one reason Caty could fathom for Mrs. Norris to be snooping through the house at night. Only one reason Mrs. Norris had also done so seven weeks before, when Isabella was still alive.

Marla Bertram's diary.

Caty knew how the faces at the table would look if she brought up the diary yet again— Emma's worry, Tilney's skepticism, Knightley's irritation. She knew she was like a dog with a bone about the diary, that she just couldn't seem to let it go. But it had disappeared from her possession; it had been stolen from Jane Fairfax; and now, Caty was willing to bet her entire reputation on it, it was in Mrs. Norris's cottage.

Of course, there was only really one way to find out.

Pushing up the window, Caty hoisted herself outside and into the tempestuous winds and pelting rain.

FROM THE FILES OF CATY MORLAND:

INTERVIEWEE: BARBARA NORRIS (HOUSE MOTHER OF THE PI KAPPA SIGMAS)

MRS. NORRIS: OF COURSE I DIDN'T BREAK INTO ANYONE'S ROOM. THAT'S AN ABSURD ACCUSATION. I'VE SLAVED AWAY AS THE HOUSE MOTHER FOR THE KAPPAS FOR MONTHS, AND BEFORE THAT I WAS A FAITHFUL EMPLOYEE TO REVEREND THOMAS AND HIS FAMILY. NEVER THE WHIFF OF ANY SCANDAL, YOU CAN BELIEVE THAT.

CATY: WELL, THERE HAVE BEEN SOME RUMORS . . .

MRS. NORRIS: WHAT RUMORS?

CATY: ABOUT MARLA BERTRAM, AND WHY SHE LEFT THE KAPPAS THE WAY SHE DID.

MRS. NORRIS: FLAGRANT LIES, ALL OF THEM. I'LL TELL YOU WHAT IT IS—PEOPLE WHO ARE JEALOUS OF REVEREND THOMAS'S FAMILY AND WANT TO SEE THEM TAKEN DOWN A PEG OR TWO. THERE'S ABSOLUTELY NO PROOF THAT ANYTHING EVEN REMOTELY UNTOWARD HAPPENED.

CATY: BUT IF THERE WAS PROOF—

MRS. NORRIS: THERE ISN'T. BECAUSE THERE'S NOTHING TO

PROVE. AND THE SOONER PEOPLE STOP SNIFFING AROUND AND SPREADING RUMORS, THE BETTER WE'LL ALL BE.

CATY: 'SPREADING RUMORS.' YOU MEAN, LIKE ISABELLA THORPE WAS?

MRS. NORRIS: I WOULD BE VERY CAREFUL IF I WERE YOU, MISS MORLAND. YOU WOULDN'T WANT TO MAKE AN ENEMY OUT OF ME.

$$ 2 $$

It wasn't until Caty was outside in the heavy, battering winds, with the tree branches swaying precariously overhead, that she realized there was no guarantee that the cottage was unlocked. She'd just escaped from a window on the bottom floor of the main house, but—like many other Southern houses built in potential flood zones—the Kappa house was elevated a few feet off the ground, meaning that she wouldn't be able to climb back in from the outside. She may very well have just trapped herself outdoors during a tornado warning.

Unfortunately for Caty, Mrs. Norris had had the foresight to lock her door before she ventured over to the main house. More fortunately for our heroine, Mrs. Norris had a standard pin cylinder locking mechanism on her door. It was not luck, but preparation and foresight, that young Caty had opted to spend her 18th birthday money on a lock-picking set, then spent most of the summer before freshman year watching as many online videos and tutorials as she could find. (A future private detective must always be prepared for these kinds of circumstances, naturally.) However, it *was* pure luck that the lock was a pin cylinder, since Caty was hit or miss with warded locks—a small kindness that the notoriously miserly Mrs. Norris had doubtless not intended.

Inside the one-room cottage, the living room/kitchen combination was dark and still, with no evidence that anyone had recently been inside, save be for the embers of a fire that looked as if it had been recently put out.

Caty hurried across the room, staring at the remains in the fireplace. Most of the pages of a book had been burned away, though the leather cover remained, warped from the heat but still distinctive. *Property of Marla Bertram.*

It was both astonishing and exactly what Caty had expected to find. For a moment, she could only stare at the sight stupidly, before she grabbed the fire poker and attempted to remove what remained of the diary. Discarded on the floor, the skeleton of the diary was too hot to touch, but Caty snapped a few quick pictures, just to have photographic proof of what she'd found.

While she waited for the diary to cool enough that she could ascertain if any of the writing had been salvaged, Caty tried to calm her mind of its frantic repetition of *Holy shit! Holy shit!* by thinking what A.W. Radcliffe would do in her position.

The answer came in Radcliffe's cool, clear, podcast-friendly voice: She should search the room, of course. Find other pieces of evidence that might link Mrs. Norris to Isabella.

Caty started with the desk tucked into the corner of the room. In *The Mysteries of Udolpho*, people were always hiding things in the wall or under loose floorboards, but somehow, it was hard to believe Mrs. Norris had that much imagination. She'd burned a stolen diary that linked her to the death of an undergraduate in her own living room, after all; and since she didn't strike Caty as being particularly stupid, it must be that she was simply too arrogant to think anyone might suspect her.

Alas, the contents of the desk proved to be uninspiring. No muddy shoes that would suggest Norris had been at Box Hill the night Isabella died, or ransom notes from Isabella. Those would have been helpful, but maybe—Caty reflected wistfully—it would have been a little too on the nose. She would have settled for something a little more obscure but nonetheless helpful, but all she found were neatly boxed stationary supplies, a packet of receipts for Kappa-related activities, and a cell phone.

Disappointing. Regardless, Caty snapped pictures of the drawers just in case there was anything she'd missed, then circled back to the diary, now cool enough to carefully prod. This, too, proved to be a disappointment. Aside from the shriveled, charred cover, not much remained of Marla Bertram's journal. Whatever secrets that she'd recorded so carefully in code were forever lost now.

What remained behind was a new certainty for Caty—that her instincts, though at times misguided, had ultimately been correct. Marla Bertram's diary was at the root of Isabella's murder, only it hadn't been Knightley covering his tracks. It was Mrs. Norris. She must have stolen the diary from Jane at the coffee shop.

And once Caty realized this must be true, other certainties began to register in her mind. That Isabella had been spreading rumors about Marla Bertram (to Jane, and likely others) that suggested she might have very well known about the diary hidden in Caty's things. Whether she'd managed to crack the code or not, Isabella had made people believe that she knew all of Marla's deepest, darkest secrets. And there was one person who was desperate enough to protect Marla, desperate enough to find the diary, that she'd broken into Caty's and Isabella's room at least once. Which meant she might have been desperate enough to steal Jane's bag at the Crescent.

Desperate enough to kill Isabella to make sure all the diaries' secrets died with her.

As the thought crossed her mind, Caty looked up to see the woman in question, standing silhouetted in the doorway of the cottage. For a moment, the two stared at one another.

Slipping into the room, Mrs. Norris closed the door behind her, and locked it.

FROM THE FILES OF CATY MORLAND:

[Excerpt from The Mysteries of Udolpho, *Season 1, Episode 9, "Behind the Veil"]*

"We have this idea that the truth will set us free, and sometimes it can. But sometimes the truth is so jarring, so horrible, so unbelievable, that we must always go into a quest for the truth knowing that we risk our innocence, our sanity, maybe even our very lives." -A.W. Radcliffe

$$\text{☙ 3 ❧}$$

"**M**iss Morland. You will hand over that phone to me immediately."

Mrs. Norris held out her palm, her tone brisk and expectant, as if there was not a scenario she could imagine where Caty would not obey her.

Caty remained rooted to her spot, phone clutched in her increasingly sweaty hands. There was no way she was going to hand over the only evidence she had, but she feared the combination of the dark night, the crackling flames, and Norris's sharp, demanding face in the flickering shadows, would somehow overpower her common sense.

She had always been considered one of the good kids in school —never got detention, never talked back to a teacher, never cheated on a test. As a young girl she had responded with aptitude to the rules of polite society. *Share with others. Respect your elders. Don't talk back.* Caty wondered now, fleetingly, if that was an innate part of her personality as she'd always believed—this willingness to please—or if it had something to do with the psychology of being adopted, the fear of being sent away for being bad.

This musing was a bit off-topic, Caty knew as she stared Norris down, but there might be something to it. The point being, every-thing in her quailed against the idea of breaking a rule, thwarting authority, being disobedient. Despite all her recent bravado in charging ahead to solve Isabella's murder (and yes, even in spite of her gratuitous eye-liner in the past week), Caty knew at her core that she was no rebel. She was a people pleaser. She was a good girl.

"Actually, I won't, Mrs. Norris." The taunting, irreverent tone that came out in Caty's voice was one she didn't at first recognize—and then all at once, she realized she was channeling Isabella. "I think the police will be interested in your little impromptu fire."

Mrs. Norris took a step toward her. "I doubt they'll care."

"Well, they're already on their way, so we'll ask them once they get here." A lie, that, but Caty needed to buy some leverage.

It worked, too, since Mrs. Norris stopped in her tracks. For a long moment, they regarded each other. "I think you're bluffing."

"Let's wait it out and see."

Another long silence. "I don't know what you think this is proof of," Mrs. Norris said at last, motioning toward the scorched diary, "but I had nothing to do with Isabella's death."

A chill coursed through Caty. "Funny that you should jump straight to that, Mrs. Norris."

"I know all about your pathetic little investigation. If you can even call it that. For all your poking and prodding and digging around, you still have no idea what kind of girl your little friend was."

"And what kind of girl was that?"

"Trouble," Mrs. Norris spat. "Did you know she was trying to blackmail me with Marla's diary? To keep herself in the sorority. That's right—Isabella went through your things and stole the diary, then began photocopying pages and sending them to me. She wasn't just disloyal to the Kappas, she betrayed your trust. What kind of 'friend' is that, Catherine?"

Caty remained silent.

"No, I didn't kill her, but I'm not surprised someone did. She would have kept on with those same games all her life; it was just a matter of time until she crossed someone who didn't want to play."

Surprisingly, Caty found she believed Norris. What point was there in lying now? It was just the two of them, all alone. The empty cottage, the howling wind. No one to hear her scream.

At the thought, Caty swallowed. "She's not the only opportunistic one," she reminded Norris—in part, to distract the older woman from coming to the same realization about how isolated they were. "If you didn't kill Isabella, how did you get the diary?" She knew that Jane Fairfax had been holding onto it, of course, but she wanted to see if Mrs. Norris would own up to this. "And what's in there that you were so desperate to hide?"

A beat, and then Mrs. Norris smiled. It was the first time she'd ever seen such an expression on the older woman's face, Caty realized with a shudder, and it did not suit her.

"I don't think the police are coming, Catherine. Are they?"

There was not enough distance between them, Caty realized. They were too close and the Kappa house was too far away and the wind was too loud.

"Maybe not right away. But I imagine they'll want to ask you some questions after they've seen this."

Caty held up her phone, which she had been holding at her side, camera facing out. Someone from her generation probably would have noticed the small, furtive movements of her thumb across the screen when Norris first entered the room, but Mrs. Norris, as previously established, was a Luddite. Even now, she scoffed at Caty, not understanding. "Oh, I'll be destroying the phone before anyone sees those pictures."

Caty smirked back. "That won't help, I'm afraid. I've been livestreaming our conversation." And she'd tagged Tilney to make sure he'd get the notification, though this seemed too complex a process to try to explain to Mrs. Norris, who was already frowning at the term 'livestreaming,' clearly not understanding its implications. "It means that I've been broadcasting this to anyone who's on my feed." She checked the screen, quickly. "So far it only has 11 views, but I'm sure that'll pick up once the word gets out that you had something to do with Isabella's death. Ooh, now we're up to thirteen. Seventeen. Twenty-one!" She angled the screen to her face.

"For the record, the evidence that Mrs. Norris was talking about destroying were the pictures on my phone of Marla Bertram's missing diary—or what remained of it after Mrs. Norris tried to burn it."

As Mrs. Norris gaped at her, Caty pointed the camera again at her face. "Not bad for some useless technology, huh, Barb?"

Mrs. Norris's complexion had purpled with indignant rage. "You foolish girl, you—" But alas, before she could finish the sentiment, the door burst open and Knightley and Darcy flanked Mrs. Norris on either side as Emma and Tilney rushed over to Caty.

"Oh my god, are you okay?" Emma asked, even as a grinning Tilney peered into Caty's still-streaming camera. "And that's how you make technology ya bitch!"

FROM THE FILES OF CATY MORLAND:

[EXCERPT FROM THE COMMENTS ON CATY'S LIVESTREAM VIDEO]

LIZZYB - @MRCOLLINS YOU MIGHT BE INTERESTED IN THIS...

MRCOLLINS - ON BEHALF OF PRESIDENT DE BOURGH, I WOULD ASK THAT ALL REMAINING MEMBERS OF THE STUDENT BODY AND THE PUBLIC REFRAIN FROM WATCHING OR COMMENTING ON THIS VIDEO. WE MUST LET THIS INCIDENT AND ALL INVOLVED RECEIVE DUE PROCESS FROM THE LAW.

LOULOUM - OMG!!! I KNEW IT!!! NORRIS IS A PSYCHO [KNIFE EMOJI]

LOULOUM - P.S. CATY DO YOU KNOW THE PAGES FOR BIOLOGY HW? [KISS EMOJI]

YATESY - SHOCKING TURN OF EVENTS. SHOCKING. BUT, DISTRACTED BY THE SNACK WHO SHOWED UP AT THE END? WHO IS THAT? [FOX EMOJI, WINKY-FACE EMOJI]

[...]

SHEPHERD&SHEPHERD - ON BEHALF OF MY CLIENT, THE HIGHLY ACCLAIMED AND RESPECTED REVEREND THOMAS BERTRAM, WE WOULD LIKE TO CLARIFY THAT BARBARA NORRIS IS A FORMER EMPLOYEE OF THE BERTRAM FAMILY AND HAS NO PRESENT TIES TO REVEREND THOMAS OR ANY OF HIS AFFILIATES . . .

❧ 4 ❧

As the police would be unable to arrive before the tornado warning ended, Mrs. Norris was secured in the window-less cellar, promising—rather predictably—that they hadn't heard the last of her. "Reverend Thomas's lawyer will make short work of this mess, you'll see!" she vowed, and Caty for one had been glad for the satisfying click of the lock on the door.

In truth, she had no idea how a livestreamed confession would hold up in court, or whether there was any further evidence to connect Mrs. Norris to Isabella. Luckily, they had at least one guarantee that Mrs. Norris wouldn't be able to completely finagle her way out of any consequences.

"I shared your livestream on my feed," Lizzy told Caty, after complimenting her on her quick thinking. "And one of my followers is Mr. Collins, President de Bourgh's assistant." She showed Caty the message he'd sent her, his nervous energy radiating through the screen as, in as formal language as possible, he distanced the university from any of Mrs. Norris's actions and claimed they were not a reflection of the Austen University faculty, staff, or alumni. "Sounds like she'll be needing to look for another job next semester," Lizzy summarized with a grin.

That was relieving to hear, but Caty couldn't dwell on it for too long. There were bigger crawfish to boil, with Isabella's murderer still unnamed and the tornado warning about to expire. Caty's intuition told her that if the party disbanded, she would forever lose her chance to figure out who here had been responsible for Isabella's death.

And intuition, Caty was beginning to learn, was something not to ignore, even if it occasionally took one down a wrong turn.

While the others updated their pages as the story began circulating around campus, claiming dibs on their connection to the scandal, Caty pulled Tilney aside. "I need your help."

"For you, V.M.? Literally anything."

Caty grinned. "I'll hold you to that. But for now, I just need you to listen to me spitball some ideas and tell me if I'm sounding too Reddit."

"Done."

"Isabella was blackmailing Mrs. Norris with Marla's diary. We know that now. On the night she was killed, Isabella gave the diary to Jane, presumably because she was afraid someone was going to take it from her. Was she just covering her tracks, or did she know someone was coming for it that night? It couldn't have been Norris, because, as we all saw, she couldn't have climbed to the top of Box Hill without her cane. So that means . . . ."

"Mrs. Norris had an accomplice."

Caty took a moment to ruminate over it as well. It was the only thing that made sense, but she couldn't imagine who else would be so devoted to the Bertram family that they would resort to murder to get back a diary. And why did they kill Isabella without making sure they got hold of the diary first?

That part didn't make much sense, no matter how Caty tried to look at it. If the diary had been wrenched from Isabella's hands before she toppled over the edge, that would have been one thing. But it was in Jane's safe, unwitting possession, and it hadn't been stolen from her until almost a week later.

It was possible, Caty supposed, that someone had seen the transaction between the two girls and banked on being able to take the diary from Jane at a later date, but that seemed like a risky gamble to take if whatever was in Marla's diary had been worth killing over. Plus, why kill Isabella at all if she no longer had the diary to blackmail Mrs. Norris with?

They were interrupted by the approach of a sheepish Emma, holding out a dish of trifle to Caty. "I saved this for you. From before." She faltered, clearly out of her element. "I'm sorry I didn't believe you. And that we, you know. Locked you in a room."

"Ineffectively locked her in a room," Tilney corrected, though he, too, looked contrite.

Caty could have reminded them that the reason for this punishment had been her kicking out a cane from underneath a disabled woman, but a new idea was dawning on her, and maybe it wouldn't hurt for Emma to feel like she owed her one.

"Thanks," she said, accepting the gift of the trifle. "While I have you, do you know if anyone here tonight was close to Marla Bertram? Anyone who might have had an interest in helping Mrs. Norris get her diary back?" Seeing some hesitation in Emma's eyes, Caty hastened to add, "I only ask because you're so connected. You know everything about everyone."

Pleased to be deferred to as the social expert, Emma looked around the room surreptitiously. "Well, she and Rushworth had a little fling sophomore year. I don't think it was serious, though, and anyway, Marla cheated on him, so I'm not sure there'd be too much loyalty there."

Possibly. But in all this time of talking about Marla Bertram's diary, Rushworth hadn't once owned up to the fact that he used to date her. That seemed . . . curious.

"She and Karoline knew each other through the sorority, of course, but there was no love lost there. Marla made a pass at Karoline's brother, Charlie, and . . . well. Karoline's always been a little protective."

That seemed like an understatement, considering Marla was now the second person to be named as Karoline's enemy for trying to fraternize with Charlie, the first being Nora, Marianne's sister.

Emma cleared her throat, shifting a little. "And Knightley is pretty close with Eddie, Marla's brother." She hastened to add, "But I don't think he spent that much time with Marla. Not that I knew of, anyway."

Knightley. Somehow it always circled back to him. Strange that he, too, should fail to mention his connection to the Bertram family when Caty had spent all night talking about Marla's missing diary. With her track record of falsely accusing Knightley, though, she didn't want to jump to any conclusions.

Luckily Tilney seemed to feel no such compunction. "V.M.," he said slowly, "remember that letter that Isabella sent to James, where she said she was dating a Theta business major. Did she ever say he was an undergraduate?"

"No," Caty said, as the wheels began to turn in her mind. "No, she didn't."

"And remember how Knightley wrote that email to Anne about dating an undergraduate? You assumed he meant Jane Fairfax, but what if he meant Isabella?"

As Emma made a sort of whirring noise of protest, Caty spoke over her, not wanting to lose the train of thought as it started to take on steam. "What if Knightley knew, through Mrs. Norris, that Isabella had gotten hold of the diary? And he thought dating her would be the best way to coerce her to give it back."

"He'd want to keep it secret, because he wouldn't want anyone finding out that he was dating Isabella. Using her."

"Because Marla's diary would incriminate Knightley, if it got into the wrong hands. He would lose his job as a GRA, maybe even lose his place in his master's program. So Norris persuaded him to get it back from Isabella."

Caty was having difficulty breathing, it was all coming together so fast. "He confronted her that night, but Isabella was one step ahead of him. She'd given the diary to Jane. That must have been frustrating to Knightley, with all the effort he'd put in. They argued. And then—"

"No."

Tilney and Caty had gotten so caught up in their makeshift reenactment that they had all but forgotten Emma was there. Looking at her now, Caty saw the usually sun-kissed blonde had turned quite an alarming shade of white. "It's not possible."

This was not going to be pleasant. "In a way," Caty tried, "it's better for us to look at Knightley if he has nothing to hide, so we can clear him . . ."

The look on Emma's face brought a whimpering end to that particular attempt at comfort. "If we're investigating Knightley, then I'm not a part of this anymore. He didn't. Do it." Emma shook her head, a violent refusal. "He's the kindest, most decent...He isn't capable of it."

"He's the most viable suspect we have now," Caty told her as gently as possible. "It all fits. Nobody else makes sense."

"That isn't true." Emma raked a hand through her hair, leaving it uncharacteristically disheveled. This, combined with the intensity of her eyes, proved a rather unsettling picture. "There are a ton of other people we should be looking at. Did y'all know Rushworth got a DUI two summers ago? What if Isabella found out about that and was blackmailing him, so he decided to kill her?"

"Well, Rushworth posted his mugshots as his Facebook profile picture, so I don't think he's hiding that whole thing," Tilney pointed out, "which would make blackmail pretty difficult."

"Okay. What about Robert Martin?"

"Who's Robert Martin?" asked Caty.

"I'm glad you ask. During a Rush event fall semester, he had to be reprimanded because he showed up stinking like pot." Emma looked back and forth between them, triumphant. "*And*, he's poor."

"Being poor isn't a crime, Emma," said Tilney. "And—this should go without saying, but I'm gonna say it anyway—it doesn't mean you're a murderer."

Emma glared down his flippancy. "I know that. But think about it. A known connection to illegal substances. Everyone knows that marijuana is a gateway drug. Maybe over Christmas break, Robert became addicted to cocaine or heroin or something, and killing Isabella was the only way to get his fix."

"How, exactly? Did Isabella have access to cocaine or heroin?"

"Maybe. We don't know everything about her, do we?"

Another long silence, more meaningful glances between Caty and Tilney, until at last Emma snapped, "Look, it might be farfetched, but I don't see why these ideas are any more ridiculous than saying Knightley is a killer. Y'all have targeted him for some reason but I'm telling you, it doesn't make any sense. He isn't capable of murder—and even if he was, Isabella isn't his type. Knightley. Didn't. Do it."

Caty could see there would be no persuading her otherwise. She took in a deep breath, deciding to gamble. "Then prove it."

Emma blinked at her, dumbfounded. "What?"

"Prove it. You and Knightley are close. If there's anyone he'd confess to, it would be you. So ask him. Point blank."

Emma laughed, but it sounded weak. "Just march in there in front of everyone and ask him, hey Knightley, kill anyone lately?"

"Not in front of everyone. Tilney is very good at providing distractions."

Tilney nodded in confirmation of this.

Caty advanced on Emma, compelling the much taller girl to fall back a step. "Put your money where your mouth is, Emma. If you're so sure Knightley didn't kill anyone, then ask."

A lengthy moment followed, during which Caty held her breath, waiting to see how Emma would respond. At long last, the Kappa president raised her chin a little, then nodded. "Fine." She started to leave, then turned back to snatch the dish of trifle from Caty's hands. "This dessert is for people who believe in their friends," she snapped, and stormed out of the room.

FROM THE FILES OF CATY MORLAND:

[INSTAGRAM POST FROM EMMA WOODHOUSE TO GEORGE KNIGHTLEY]

@SIRKNIGHTLEY HAPPY BIRTHDAY TO ONE OF THE MOST INFURI-ATING, AND ONE OF THE VERY BEST, PEOPLE I GET TO CALL 'FRIEND.' I KNOW YOU WON'T SEE THIS FOR AT LEAST ANOTHER WEEK BECAUSE

YOU NEVER CHECK YOUR INSTAGRAM (!!!!) BUT PLEASE USE THIS AS AN EXCUSE TO SHUT WHATEVER TEDIOUS DOCUMENT YOU'RE WORKING ON AND HAVE A PIECE OF THE EXCELLENT KETO-FRIENDLY ANGEL FOOD CAKE I MADE YOU THAT YOU PROBABLY HAVEN'T TOUCHED YET. XOXO, ALWAYS

5

B ack in the dining room, the excited buzz around capturing Mrs. Norris had died down, boredom and antsiness taking its place. Rushworth and John Thorpe had cleared the table to set up a makeshift paper-football tournament, Marianne was doing yoga in the corner, and Darcy seemed to be typing out a long, involved email on his phone, ignoring Karoline's attempts to divert his attention.

Out of sheer desperation, it seemed, Karoline called across the room to Lizzy. "Want to walk around the room with me?" Lest anyone mistake her offer for an olive branch, she quickly added, "That was a really heavy meal, and you look like you could do with a metabolism boost."

Lizzy, who had somehow managed to stash a small paperback in one of her dress pockets, didn't bother to look up from the book, just flipped Karoline the bird.

"How much longer until this tornado warning is over?" Frank groaned, his knee jackhammering with pent-up energy. "I can't stand being cooped up!" In response, Jane rubbed his back sympathetically.

It was the perfect time for a Tilney intervention, Caty thought as she slipped back into the room, making eye contact with Emma. Emma glared back at her a moment before nodding. She was ready.

Tilney sidled up to the table where Rushworth and John were playing, pretending to show interest in the game. "Great idea, guys. I love ... sports and things." He paused, letting a moment pass before clearing his throat and tugging at his collar. "That's weird…"

But as bored as everyone was, they all seemed too preoccupied with their individual pastimes to have noticed. Caty made a hand motion at Tilney, indicating he should crank it up a notch.

He coughed again, much louder this time—the sort of abrasive, guttural cough that old men seemed to love doing in public spaces. That got more attention. "Are you sick?" asked Marianne, visibly recoiling, even though she was sitting across the room.

"My throat feels strange. Tight." Tilney rubbed at the offending body part, coughing again. He looked to Emma imploringly. "Was there honey in the trifle?"

Emma alone out of everyone in the room looked deeply unconcerned. "Mm-hmm."

"That would explain it." Another cough from Tilney, then some raspy, struggled breathing. "I'm allergic. Not deadly allergic, but enough that people should definitely be concerned . . ."

As people clustered around Tilney, asking what they could do, Rushworth surprised everyone by pushing his way to the front. "Let me help. I'm pre-med."

"You're pre-med?" Tilney repeated dubiously, then remembered he was supposed to be hyperventilating and doubled down on the act.

As all of this happened, Caty watched Emma follow her cue, taking Knightley and leading him by the hand toward the hallway. Caty heard her say something about getting an EpiPen from upstairs as they disappeared from the room.

After waiting a few seconds, Caty silently slipped out after them.

❧ 6 ❧

Caty followed a cautious distance behind Emma and Knightley, grateful that she knew what stairs and floor-boards to avoid in order to minimize creaking—no small feat in such an old, Southern house. Seeing the direction they were heading, she assumed Emma was taking Knightley to her room.

Sure enough, there was a light coming from Emma's bedroom. The door had been left accommodatingly open, allowing Caty to hear bits of conversation. She paused at the doorway, peering through the crack at the hinges, to see Knightley and Emma sitting on the floor, a plastic tub open between them, many of its contents strewn across the rug.

". . . remember there being a First Aid kit somewhere," Emma was saying.

Worried that Knightley might look up and spot her, Caty forced herself to step back, so she could no longer see, but only hear what they were saying.

Emma seemed to have committed to the pretense of searching for an EpiPen, and for a moment, there was only a quiet shuffling as they looked through the tub. Caty hoped Emma was using this time to steel herself, not losing her nerve altogether. It wasn't that Caty expected Knightley to give a full, torrid Agatha Christie-style confession, but if he admitted to any one of the things connecting him to Isabella or Marla or even Mrs. Norris, she might have a chance of proving the rest. And if Knightley was going to bare his soul to anybody, it would be Emma.

"It doesn't seem like it's here." This from Knightley. "We should probably go back downstairs, call an ambulance…"

He grunted, as if shifting to rise to his feet. Caty fell back a step, knowing she'd have to beat a hasty retreat before Knightley caught her spying in the hallway.

But Emma's voice caught her, holding her in place. "Who was that email about?" A brief pause. "The one you sent to Anne."

Well-played, Emma. Knightley might not own up to killing Isabella, but maybe he would admit that his inquiry to Anne about dating an undergraduate had been about her. And after that, it would just take connecting a few more dots.

A longer silence followed, before Knightley at last said, "I think you already know." He took in a rushing gasp of air, then laughed, sounding almost relieved that the cat was finally out of the bag. "I've been wanting to tell you for so long—"

This was it! Caty could not believe it, and yet she had somehow also known it all along. Knightley was going to confess to everything.

"No, don't!" This entreaty from Emma. "I changed my mind. I don't want to know."

Emma! Caty could have strangled her pretty, foolish friend. They were so close. Emma knew what it would mean to them, to Isabella, to get this confession, to be able to take it to the police and see justice served. Only…

Only, she loved him.

Caty realized it now, for the first time, hearing the pain in Emma's voice at the thought of Knightley being a murderer. She loved him, and she didn't want it to be true.

Knightley sounded chastened. "If you don't want me to say it, that's your choice, Emma, and I'll respect that. I just hope I won't lose your friendship."

"Never." A brief moment of hesitation, then Emma's voice, resolute. "I'm sorry. Whatever you have to say to me, I'll listen. And I swear to you, I'll do whatever I can to help you. I'm sure Daddy knows a good attorney."

"Attorney? I don't think it's that serious. I've already turned in my resignation."

"That's not going to be enough, Knightley. You need to prepare yourself for the consequences."

"It's stupid, I know. I only had a few more months to go—I should have just bided my time. But when I heard that Isabella died at that stupid party, all I could think of was, what if that had been you? And I realized I couldn't wait any longer to tell you that I . . . I love you."

Wait—what?

"What?" Emma echoed aloud, sounding just as stunned by this declaration as Caty felt.

"I don't expect you to . . . you don't need to feel the same way. I just needed you to know, to hear from me why I needed to step down as GRA and focus on my studies."

"Well, of course I feel the same way."

"You do?"

"Yes!" Emma laughed, relieved as a prisoner who'd received pardon just minutes before execution. "My God, Knightley. I thought you were a *murderer* and I still loved you."

A beat as Knightley processed this. "You what...?"

Caty left the two lovebirds to sort it out among themselves. It all made perfect sense now. The dots had been connected, all right, but she'd been anticipating the wrong picture. The email had been about Emma, of course. Emma, who teased Knightley and deferred always to his advice, even if she resisted it at first, and who made sure he ate while he was writing his thesis. It could only have ever been her.

As all of Knightley's links to Isabella and Marla dissolved with this new knowledge, Caty felt unnervingly as though she were embroiled in a real-life game of chutes and ladders. Every time she thought she'd managed to climb to some new level, she found herself sliding back again to the start.

Think, Caty instructed herself. *Think.*

Her phone buzzed, causing Caty to jump. Fearing that Knightley and Emma would hear her, Caty hurried further down the hallway, waiting until she'd reached a small alcove above the back staircase before looking at the message.

It was from Tilney. *HELP. RUSHWORTH IS TALKING ABOUT GIVING ME CPR EVEN THOUGH I'M CONSCIOUS AND BREATHING.*

Caty typed a hasty response, letting him know that he was free to make a sudden and miraculous recovery without dubious medical intervention. When she finished, she sighed, glancing out the window at Norris's cottage—then did a double take as she realized there was someone, shrouded in darkness, trying the back door.

She'd always disliked the cartoon image of a lightbulb going on over someone's head when they had a realization, thinking the image was too unrealistic. Her own moment of sharp, rapid discovery felt more like a key turning in a lock, and suddenly opening a door that had been previously barred.

Caty looked down at her phone, then back out the window, seeing the mystery figure had managed to let themself inside Norris's cottage.

"Of course," she breathed, and raced down the darkened staircase.

FROM THE FILES OF CATY MORLAND:

[EXCERPT FROM A.W. RADCLIFFE INTERVIEW WITH THE PRETTY PERFECT MURDER PODCAST]

PPM: HOW DO YOU KNOW WHEN YOU'VE DONE ALL THE RESEARCH YOU CAN DO AND YOU'VE REACHED THE END OF THE MYSTERY?

RADCLIFFE: IT CAN BE TRICKY. BUT AT SOME POINT YOU

HAVE TO TAKE A STEP BACK, LOOK AT ALL THE PUZZLE PIECES YOU'VE BEEN GATHERING. ASK YOURSELF, AM I STARTING TO SEE THE PICTURE? ON THEIR OWN, THESE INDIVIDUAL ELEMENTS MAY NOT ADD UP TO ALL THAT MUCH, BUT WHAT DO THEY MAKE WHEN YOU PUT THEM ALL TOGETHER?

❧ 7 ❧

There were only a few minutes until the tornado warning would be over, and the police would be arriving to pick up Mrs. Norris once the threat had passed. Still, now that the murderer was almost certainly inside Mrs. Norris's cottage at that very moment, Caty wanted to be sure backup arrived as promptly as possible.

Before leaving the Kappa house to run across the yard and confront said murderer, whoever they might be, Caty paused under the awning over the back door, calling Detective Lucas.

The detective answered after the second ring, sounding almost as if she'd anticipated Caty's call; maybe the local police had notified her that Mrs. Norris was currently locked in the Kappa house cellar, a likely accessory to the crime. "Caty?"

"They're in the cottage behind the Kappa house," Caty said, then hung up before Detective Lucas could try to persuade her to stay away and let the police take care of things. That was Detective Lucas's job, to try to keep her safe; but there was no way Caty could come this close and not see for herself who it was, not look into the eyes of Isabella's killer and ask, simply, why?

Putting the phone on silent and slipping it into her pocket, Caty held an ineffectual arm over her head as she raced through the rain to the cottage. Outside, she braced herself, surprised to find that her hand was trembling as she reached forward to push open the door.

Caty did not know who she expected to find standing in the darkened living room, but she blinked in surprise when she saw who it was. "Oh," she said.

Frank Churchill stared back at her for a moment—startled at first, maybe even a little frightened, and then resigned. So much for the brutal killer she'd been anticipating.

For a moment, a long silence stretched out between them. Then Caty motioned to the phone in his hands, the one he'd retrieved from Mrs. Norris's desk. She'd been so frazzled by her earlier encounter with Norris that it hadn't properly registered with her how strange it was to find a brand-new, latest-model iPhone in the older woman's desk—she, who was always chiding people on their reliance on technology and didn't understand what livestreaming was.

Caty motioned to the phone now, to break the silence. "It's Isabella's, right? I didn't recognize it before, without the cover."

Frank nodded, looking down at the phone in his hands like he didn't quite know what to do with it, now that he had it. "I was just…" he tried, but trailed off as he seemed to realize it was futile. He sighed, running a hand over his face, before looking to Caty imploringly.

"It was an accident," he said, sounding like he was trying very hard not to cry.

πκΣ

Frank explained it all then, starting—as many stories do—from the very beginning. When he was four years old, his mother passed away. His parents had married straight out of high school, and Frank's father was still very much a boy himself when he got

married, became a father, and then a widower. After some deliberation between the two families, it was decided that Greg Weston
would join the military and further his education, while Frank would
be adopted by his great-aunt, Bernadette, and raised as Frank
Churchill.

Though he was known around campus for being affable, easygo-
ing, and infinitely likable, this moment had impacted young Frank in
a way that could never fully be outgrown. "You never forget being
given up," Frank said quietly, and though Caty very much wanted to
hate him, she felt a little shiver of acknowledgement at his words.

How Frank's life might have been different if he'd stayed with
his father is entirely a matter of conjecture, but more certain was
the impact that living under his Aunt Bernadette's rule had on his
life. She loved Frank—that was an unquestionable fact—but the way
Mrs. Churchill loved was through control. His entire life, she kept
strict watch over everything he did: what he ate, when he slept, who
his friends were, what sports he played, what clubs he joined, what
classes he took, what books he read. With Mrs. Churchill, it was not
a conversation, it was a decree.

By some miracle, Frank was able to persuade Aunt Bernadette
to allow him to study abroad in Austria. This accomplishment had
taken an infinite amount of persuasion, research, promises of daily
phone calls, access to his social media and emails—but the payoff
had been a small taste of freedom.

And then, of course, meeting Jane.

Switching schools to Austen University to be with Jane,
dreaming of a future with her, had felt like a monumental act of
rebellion for Frank, so accustomed to being pliant to his aunt's will.
But he knew it would take a careful amount of finessing to persuade
Aunt Bernadette to give Jane a chance and not reject her outright.
There were no second chances with Mrs. Churchill.

What Frank hadn't anticipated was how stressful it would all be.
How much pressure he'd be under from his aunt, who wanted him
around all the time after returning from his semester in Austria. She
seemed suspicious that something had changed in him, or maybe
she was just anxious about losing her long-held influence with him

spending more time with his father. Regardless, she was holding on tighter than ever. Between trying to keep her happy, adjusting to the new school, dealing with his father being so present in his life again, and maintaining his relationship with Jane, it got to be too much for Frank.

He knew if his aunt could just relax, things would be much easier. He tried sneaking some natural supplements into her daily rotation of pills—L-Theanine, chamomile, things like that—but nothing seemed to work.

Then he remembered that tipsy freshman pledge at the Theta party talking about how her sister was a Pharma rep and could get her any drug she wanted. Frank did some covert research and found out the girl's name was Isabella Thorpe.

When Frank first texted Isabella (the same night Caty had broken into Anne's room, looking for proof about Marla Bertram), she seemed giddy at the prospect of getting to talk to an upperclassman, and she was more than happy to help him get what he wanted. She'd been the one to suggest Alzaprone when he explained his problem with his great-aunt. Not wanting to limit the medication's relaxing effect on Mrs. Churchill to when he was physically present in New Orleans and could slip them into her pill purse, Frank cut the pills in half, shaved off their name-branding, and switched them out with the Aspirin on her nightstand for her frequent headaches. The results produced a sleepier, more relaxed version of Aunt Bernadette, making his time in New Orleans infinitely more manageable.

This bought him more freedom throughout the week, too, but by then, Aunt Bernadette wasn't Frank's only problem. In a quick escalation only over a few days of contact, Isabella had begun texting almost as often as his great-aunt used to, and Frank soon realized that she had interpreted their camaraderie in this deception as something more. He would have set the record straight, but he was afraid of getting cut off from his supply of Alzaprone, and of the scene that Isabella might make. If Mrs. Churchill would've needed some persuasion to come around to the idea of a Jane Fairfax, there was no amount of consoling that could ever reconcile her to an Isabella Thorpe, even if it was a relationship born of blackmail (not the first in the Churchill family).

Not to mention that if Jane ever found out about his texting with Isabella, he might lose her forever. And then what would all of this have been for?

But as time wore on, Isabella began to grow more and more insistent. That stunt at the talent show had been for his benefit; it was only because Isabella had such terrible aim that she'd hit Darcy in the face instead of Frank, who had been sitting right next to him. That was the night he realized that she had terribly misunderstood everything, but the damage had already been done. She'd dumped her boyfriend for him, and even though he'd never asked her to do so, Isabella held that as leverage over his head, along with an increasing list of demands. If he liked her, why didn't they ever see each other or meet up in public? He wasn't just using her for her pharma connections, was he? Because that would make him a Bad Guy, and Bad Guys did not get free access to trial prescriptions. Bad Guys should be outed, publicly, for using people. Never before had Frank's easy charm and affability been so terribly misplaced.

He tried to soften the blow by letting Isabella down easily; but by then, it was already too late. Unbeknownst to Frank, his aunt had taken to mixing what she believed to be Aspirin with her nightly glass of bourbon. The Alzaprone and alcohol would be an unwise combination for someone of any age, but with Aunt Bernadette's advanced years, combined with her other health problems, it proved to be lethal.

Frank was devastated by his great-aunt's death. As much of a pain as she could sometimes be, she was the woman who raised him, the person who cared for him when he'd been abandoned by everybody else. At first, he tried to convince himself that her death was from natural causes, but the more he read up on Alzaprone and alcohol-related deaths—especially with the elderly—the less likely he realized this was. He began to tailspin, panicking that somebody might find out what he'd done.

In many ways Frank had always been a lucky person, blessed by opportunity. Proof of this came when his great-uncle and father agreed that there wouldn't need to be an autopsy. Mrs. Churchill had been old, after all, and there was nothing so unnatural about her slipping away in her sleep one night. She was the sort of woman in life whose dignity would have been affronted by being cut open, weighted, and measured; it was better to let sleeping dogs lie.

It's possible that nobody would have ever learned the truth, if it hadn't been for Isabella. A day before his aunt died, Frank had mustered up the courage to end things with her for good. He tried to do it as gently as possible, not wanting to do anything that would encourage her to make a big dramatic scene—anything that might get back to Jane. He figured someone like Isabella probably had a few irons in the fire, romantically speaking, but he still thought it best to be tactful and not burn any bridges. That was the Frank Churchill way, after all.

He thought he'd succeeded, too, until he received the text message from Isabella, informing him that she knew what he'd done to Aunt Bernadette. She had been doing her own research on Alzaprone, which she wouldn't hesitate to share unless he agreed to meet with her that night—Initiation Night, on Box Hill. It might get Isabella into some trouble to admit her part in giving him the contraband Alzaprone, but it seemed to be a gamble she was willing to take to make sure she got what she was owed. Frank was going to be her big cash cow, one way or another, it seemed.

It seemed a bit too convenient, but honestly, Isabella's death was just as much of an accident as his aunt's. They found a secluded spot, away from the party, and he tried to deny everything, to flatter her, to talk some sense into her—but nothing worked. Isabella was determined to take him down, it seemed, or to die trying.

Things escalated until they were shouting at each other. She shoved him. He shoved her back. The ground was muddy, slippery, and in the fog they didn't realize how close to the edge they'd gotten. After righting herself, Isabella tried to storm off, promising she was going to ruin him, but her sense of direction must have gotten turned around in the heat of the argument, and she ended up walking straight over the edge.

Frank would never forget the sound of her scream. He called

out to her, but the music from the party was too loud, and he couldn't be sure if she was making any noise. He scrambled to the bottom of the ravine and found her, but by then it was too late.

Too late in more than one aspect, it turned out. Not only was Isabella dead, but their argument had had an audience. Mrs. Norris had been parked at the foot of the hill, concealed from the eyes of the other partygoers by some accommodating bushes, waiting to confront Isabella about Marla's missing diary.

Frank didn't know much more about the bad blood between Norris and Isabella, only that Isabella had apparently been black-mailing Mrs. Norris with the diary so she would vote her into the sorority. And, after what she'd seen, Mrs. Norris decided to pay it forward by blackmailing Frank for Isabella's murder. She'd reached the body before Frank could and taken Isabella's phone as insurance. Frank had a week to find Marla's diary and return it to Mrs. Norris before she went to the police.

In another coincidence that seemed too convenient to be true, the diary turned up in Jane's possession. Frank didn't know why Isabella had given it to her. Maybe Isabella had figured out about him and Jane (she did have a way of sniffing out a scandal) and it was another way of messing with him. Or maybe, since Isabella couldn't have foreseen an alliance between Frank and Mrs. Norris, she'd simply passed it off to Jane to buy some more time stalling the Kappa house mother.

Jane certainly didn't realize the significance of what she had, and Frank thought about just taking it from her room and hoping she wouldn't notice it was gone. But after word got out that Caty was claiming Isabella had been murdered, Frank worried it might draw too much notice if the diary went missing. Instead, he encouraged Jane to stop at the Crescent before delivering the diary to Detective Lucas, then made it look like her entire bookbag had been stolen.

It was a bit of a gamble, since there was no guarantee he'd be able to get it away from Jane before she handed it over to Charlotte —but then, Frank had always been unusually lucky. Payback, he secretly believed, for being abandoned by his father all those years before.

With the diary safely returned to Mrs. Norris, he'd thought he was in the clear. The only thing still hanging over his head was Isabella's phone, which Norris had refused to return, claiming she needed leverage. Frank had deleted Isabella's messages from his phone, but he doubted she'd done the same. So that night, with everyone distracted and Mrs. Norris locked up, he thought he might as well press his luck and erase the last remaining evidence.

It would just take a few minutes, he reasoned. A few minutes to pave the way for him and Jane. No one would even notice he was missing.

It wasn't like the movies, where the killer is caught and describes his deeds in gleeful, gory detail. There was nothing joyous about it, or even frightening—as Caty informed Detective Lucas and Detective Wentworth later. Nothing in Frank's manner was intimidating or menacing. He wasn't threatening her. He was just a dumb, scared boy, who had gotten in way over his head.

"I was so close," he concluded, raking a hand through his hair as he gave a rueful laugh. But when he looked up at Caty again, his eyes were full of tears. "I guess the police are on their way, aren't they? And you'll have to turn me in."

He said it as a statement, but there was a hint of a question in it. "Yes," Caty said to both, emphatically.

Frank looked down at his feet, nodding. "For what it's worth, I never meant to hurt anybody." A pause, and then he added with a trembling voice, "I know you don't owe me anything, but could you do me one favor? Could you not say anything to Jane? Let me explain it to her. I know she'll hear things, but—I want to be the one to explain how it happened."

Caty *didn't* owe him anything, but she nodded. It was not a role she would relish, telling Jane the truth about Frank, and the part he'd played in not one but two deaths.

Frank nodded, then glanced down at his watch. "It's 9:47. The tornado warning is over. Should be any minute now."

Caty certainly hoped so. She had kept up her vigil, as exhausting as it had been. She'd been told she was wrong in so many different ways, but it had always been there, that kernel of truth, buried underneath all the false starts and missed turns. It was gratifying, to know she'd been right, and vindicating. But she suddenly felt so tired, and ready for the storm to pass.

In the distance, over the rain and faint rumble of thunder, came the sound of sirens, fast-approaching.

FROM THE FILES OF CATY MORLAND:

[TEXTS RETRIEVED FROM ISABELLA'S PHONE]

FRANK: HEY ISABELLA, IT'S FRANK CHURCHILL. I DON'T KNOW IF YOU REMEMBER BUT WE MET BRIEFLY AT THE THETA PARTY A FEW WEEKS AGO.

ISABELLA: OH HEY I WAS A LITTLE TIPSY THAT NIGHT LOL

SHHH DON'T TELL HAHAHA

BUT YEAH I REMEMBER YOU

I'M SURPRISED YOU REMEMBER ME

LOWLY FRESHMAN ETC.

FRANK: WHO COULD FORGET AN ISABELLA THORPE? ;)

❧ 8 ☙

W as there anyone who did not know the whole of it before the week was through? The attendees of the dinner party agreed not to divulge Frank's name before the police could make an official statement, but trying to conceal news such as this was like trying to catch water with a sieve. Even with the best of intentions, it could not be accomplished, and soon the entire university was buzzing with the scandal.

One piece of good fortune for the now-unlucky Frank was that his family was rallying around him as they awaited his arraignment. "I left my son a long time ago," Professor Weston said in a prepared statement offered at a press conference. "It's one of the biggest regrets of my life. I will not make that mistake again."

It was uncertain how Frank would plead, though Tilney speculated with Caty over coffee at the Crescent (an almost daily ritual for them now) that his best bet would be getting tried for manslaughter. "If Frank can persuade the jury that both deaths were an accident, he might get off with just a few years' prison time—especially with his family's connections."

"Might?" Caty echoed, picking up on the uncertainty in the word as she scooped the dollop of whipped cream from his drink into her own mug. (He wasn't into "gratuitous sugar," which she'd struggled with at first, wondering how she could be best friends with someone with such clearly bad taste, until she realized his loss was her gain.)

"One accidental death is a bit of a stretch, but still plausible. Two, though?" He sighed, shaking his head. "To quote the General —" this was Tilney's nickname for his father—"'That must be the unluckiest son of a bitch in the state of Louisiana.'"

Caty considered this, thinking over what she knew of Frank—his manners, his charm. His possessiveness of Jane, and desperation to keep her, at whatever cost. He had fooled them all, including Caty, who had been looking for a murderer and never once thought to suspect him—at least, not seriously. Including Jane, who had loved him so much she had overlooked one too many red flags.

"He hadn't been sleeping, and he'd lost his appetite," a numb Jane confided to Caty, after asking Caty to meet her at the Crescent and fill in all the gaps in the story Frank had told her. "I thought he was just mourning his great-aunt. I guess he was, in a way…"

More promising in the development of their relationship were Emma and Knightley, who were happily dating, despite her having been semi-convinced that he was responsible for Isabella Thorpe's death. "I never believed it," Emma insisted, in defiance of all the evidence that suggested otherwise. And though Knightley may have had his suspicions to the contrary, it was ultimately much more amenable to maintaining their new-love bubble to just believe her.

Also (reluctantly) coming around to Knightley was Caty. Though she had suspected his involvement in any number of crimes, now that she had sat down and had several proper conversations with the grad student in question, she had to admit he seemed like a pretty decent guy. It was nice to know a few of those existed, although she herself had sworn off dating for the foreseeable future.

"So you can focus on your next mystery?" Detective Lucas asked her over their coffee meetup. (Really, the Crescent should be giving Caty a fee for how many customers she was bringing in, due to the newfound demand for meeting up and having coffee with her.)

Caty bristled, searching for teasing in Detective Lucas's tone, but there was none of that from the older woman. She had been supportive of Caty's interest in crime, answering all her questions and giving her advice on how to go about becoming a detective, should that be a path she decided she wanted to pursue in the future.

"I've decided to give mysteries a break, at least for the next few months," Caty returned. It was almost summer vacation, and she craved a real holiday—sleep, laying by the pool, reading books for fun. Tilney promised her that there would be plenty of the above when she visited him at his home in Northanger, after she put in her obligatory time in Baton Rouge to reassure her parents that she wasn't too psychologically damaged from the semester.

"What will you do instead?" Detective Lucas took a sip of her espresso, eyes mirthful over the rim of her cup. "I hear needlepoint is popular again."

Caty snorted at that, then sobered. "I actually thought I might try to find out who my birth parents are."

She had not said the words aloud to anyone, and she wasn't entirely certain why she'd chosen Detective Lucas to be her first confidante. But the detective's eyes were kind and interested, so Caty continued, "I thought I didn't care, but lately I've had this feeling like... I don't know how to explain it. Like I'm a heroine in the wrong story?" She shrugged, a little embarrassed at the metaphor. "I thought finding out more about my past might help."

Detective Lucas smiled a little ruefully, like maybe she understood. "So, moving on to genealogical mysteries instead."

Yes, Caty laughed in agreement, that was a good way to put it. It would be nice to get away from murder, at least for a little while. But once she had time to rest and recoup and truly mourn Isabella now that her murder was solved, Caty had some serious questions that would need to be answered about Marla Bertram's diary, and just what Mrs. Norris had been so desperate to hide.

Not that Caty was going looking for a new mystery, per se. But if one just fell into her lap, what was a girl to do?

πκΣ

Once the dust had cleared and the intense scrutiny from the world had at last faded, most of the dinner party guests from that fateful night (who had *not* been charged with murder) gathered together.

Caty Morland. Henry Tilney. Emma Woodhouse. George Knightley. Jay Rushworth. Fo-Hian Darcy. Karoline Bingley. Elizabeth Bennet. Marianne Dashwood.

Jane Fairfax couldn't make it, for the obvious reasons, as well as another more positive outcome. She would not be finishing her semester at Austen University, instead taking some time off to spend with family before going to a summer program in Ireland, recommended by an old professor from the conservatory. If Frank's case went to trial, and if she was called as a witness, she would have to return; but she refused to let this ruin her life. For a brief time it had revolved around Frank Churchill, but she was determined it no longer would.

To no one's surprise, John Thorpe hadn't answered any of Caty's texts, and he did not show up at the gathering at Box Hill. (He did, however, post another fart video at roughly the same time as the gathering, which felt like an appropriate contribution.)

Karoline had initially seemed as though she planned to follow suit (by ditching, not by posting a gas-related video) but someone— maybe Emma, but probably Darcy—had persuaded her to come along. She was glowering, irritated, but present.

And that mattered, Caty realized with an unexpected rush of emotion at the sight of all of them standing at the edge of Box Hill, where Isabella had fallen. They had been through something together that night, the lot of them. It didn't make them friends, exactly, but it bonded them in a way that was hard to define. (Though Tilney very much wanted to, dubbing them all "The Austen Murder Club"—t-shirts pending.)

Emma had purchased them each a hollyhock—the Kappa's

house flower—and she distributed these with her usual efficiency before linking up with Knightley once again.

Looking out over Highbury, they remembered Isabella. Caty and Emma recalled a few memories, Tilney quoted Henry David Thoreau, and Marianne followed up with a poem by Maya Angelou. Then they tossed their flowers over the edge.

"Goodbye, Isabella," a few called, while the others watched on in silence.

Isabella hadn't been the only life lost in recent weeks, of course. There was also Mrs. Churchill, and the other casualties of Frank's senseless actions: his family, his future, Jane.

Yet even now, it was hard to vilify him completely. He'd been selfish. He'd been stupid. And now, he would pay for it, and so would so many others.

Caty's grief was complicated as she looked down at the fallen hollyhocks. She knew that Isabella had been far from perfect. She could be selfish, manipulative, and oblivious to others' feelings. Chances were that, had she lived, she and Caty would no longer be friends—between Isabella dumping James, and breaking into Caty's phone, and stealing Marla Bertram's diary from under her pillow, and probably other things Caty didn't even know about.

But . . . *but*. None of that negated that Isabella was the very first friend Caty made at Austen University, when she was far from home and out of her element and most in need of companionship. She thought of the Isabella who curled up on the couch with her to watch *The Cases of Otranto* and discuss theories late into the night. The Isabella who linked her arm through Caty's during Rush week and urged her to laugh her way through it, because they were the coolest bitches there, dammit, and life was meant to be a great big goddam adventure. And she knew, no matter what else came afterward, that she would always miss her.

Grief was complicated, after all, and it wasn't only the perfect people in life who deserved to be loved.

As if sensing her conflicting emotions, Emma took Caty's arm. On her other side, Tilney's fingers intertwined with her own, giving her hand a reassuring squeeze.

They had lost so much, all of them, but look what they had gained.

Then Tilney was linking arms with Lizzy, and Marianne was joining on her other side as they descended the bumpy path down the hill. Behind them followed Karoline, Rushworth, Darcy, and Knightley, not holding onto each other, but showing a side-by-side solidarity.

This lasted for a few companionable moments. Then, fearing things had become just a little too sentimental, Caty impulsively broke ahead from the others and began running as fast as she could. "Last one to the bottom has to streak back up the hill!"

It was a very un-Caty-like thing to say, all things considered. But she thought Isabella just might approve.

THE END

ACKNOWLEDGMENTS

Thank you for reading this book! My journey to publication has been a long, arduous process, and there were many days where I thought no one would ever read anything I'd written. If you've come this far, that means the world to me.

Thank you for those who helped me get here. Thank you especially to my husband, Mike, who was the sounding board for this idea, the cheerleader who encouraged me to finish, and the dreamer who had the courage to bring Bayou Wolf Press into reality. This book would not exist without you.

Thank you to Johnny, for being cute and learning to sleep through the night so I could write sometimes.

Thank you to those who read early drafts of this and helped shape it into what it is now, including Sarah LaPolla, Kristina Gibby, Sarah Smith, Jennifer Rands, and Daphne Loukides.

Thank you to the friends, family, mentors, and teachers who have encouraged me and my writing over the years. Thank you also to all the wonderful adaptations I watched/read/listened to and thoughtful criticism I digested while writing my dissertation on Austen adaptations, which most certainly inspired this novel.

Thank you to my grandmother, Eileen, for introducing me to Jane Austen and encouraged a love of reading. Thank you also to *Wishbone* for engraining the plot of *Pride and Prejudice* into my mind.

Last but certainly not least, thanks to Jane Austen. Also, murder.

ABOUT THE AUTHOR

Elizabeth Gilliland teaches at the university level, putting as much Austen into her syllabus as she can get away with. In 2018, she earned her PhD from Louisiana State University, where she wrote her dissertation on Jane Austen adaptations and fever-dreamed this series in a caffeine-induced haze. She has worked as a ghost-writer, closed captioner, copywriter, beef jerky manufacturer, and a lot of other weird jobs in between. She is a proud member of the Jane Austen Society of North America, and excerpts of the Austen University series have won awards through JASNA and Jane Austen & Co/The Jane Austen Summer Program. She lives in Alabama with her husband and son.

BAYOU WOLF PRESS

Bayou Wolf Press is an independent publisher of quality fiction. If you enjoyed this book and would like to support us, the best thing you can do is leave a review on Amazon, Goodreads, or wherever you review books. If you'd like to learn more about our press, sign up for our newsletter, and stay informed on upcoming books, please visit our website.

www.bayouwolfpress.com

BOOK TWO: THE PORTRAITS
OF PEMBERLEY

Read on for a preview of the second book in the *Austen University Mysteries* series: *The Portraits of Pemberley*.

❧ I ❧

(THE PORTRAITS OF PEMBERLEY)

George Wickham was found (by a freshman of no real importance) on the campus square, tied up, spread-eagle, hungover, and completely naked.

While there were many at Austen University who felt the punishment fit the crime, there were also those who failed to see the poetic justice—among them, naturally, Wickham himself, along with the Austen University administration, including President de Bourgh.

And, as it was rapidly becoming clear to Elizabeth Bennet as she sat in the waiting room outside her office door, whatever President de Bourgh thought, so too thought her office assistant, Mr. Collins.

"You've made us quite upset, Miss Bennet," Collins informed her, glaring across his desk. "*Quite* upset."

Along with having his lips permanently attached to President de Bourgh's ass, Mr. Collins was, unfortunately, Lizzy's first cousin once removed. Up until recently, this relation had not seemed quite so unlucky, since it was at Mr. Collins's encouragement that Lizzy had applied to Austen University and gotten a full-tuition scholarship for academic achievement. Coming from a family with five daughters, Lizzy knew this was no small financial feat, and thus managed to hold her tongue at her distant cousin's strange habit of insisting on being called "Mr. Collins," even by his relatives.

Observing this sycophantic behavior in her cousin, however, Lizzy felt a twinge of worry about her genetic makeup. She'd already had her concerns from her mother's side, but now she had to worry about what unpleasant dormant lurkers might be hiding on her father's side, too.

"I'm sorry to hear that, Mr. Collins," Lizzy told him evenly, and could not help herself from adding, "*quite* sorry."

Collins's face furrowed with the effort of determining if he was being apologized to, or mocked. Fortunately before any permanent wrinkles could be set into motion, the intercom buzzed, and President de Bourgh's imperious voice sniped over the speaker. "Is she here?"

"I'll bring her straight in." Collins opened the office door and glared Lizzy into entering.

With her Southern flair for the dramatics, President de Bourgh kept the back of her office chair turned toward the door, waiting for Mr. Collins to come to stand behind the desk with his outraged glower, before slowly turning to face Lizzy.

Caren de Bourgh was precisely the sort of woman who looked as though she would never die, which was to say, she had the appearance of a hardy tangerine left out in the sun for just a bit too long. Her hair was dyed a deep black which nobody had believed to be her natural hair color for at least the last twenty years, and it was styled in a gravity-defying bouffant that betrayed her age more than any grays could. She had a penchant for wearing bright-colored shirts and distinctive pieces of jewelry, the bigger the better, that was perhaps matched only by her love of pralines, of which she always had a tin on-hand.

"Elizabeth Bennet," she drawled in her distinctly Charleston accent, "take a seat."

Lizzy did so, careful to keep her back straight and to only cross her legs at the ankles. These old Southern women had eyes like hawks, and took any sign of comfort or familiarity as an indication of bad moral character.

"I suppose you know why you're here?"

"I'm assuming it's because of my article."

"If you can even call it that." Mr. Collins's own mild accent always became much more pronounced in his boss's presence.

President de Bourgh retrieved the offending article from the *Juvenilia*—the weekly university publication—and placed it squarely in the middle of her desk. "Would you care to explain to me what this is?"

Lizzy observed where President de Bourgh's finger had landed. "I believe that's a penis, President de Bourgh."

A pixelated penis, but still it took a full minute for the furor to die down, with President de Bourgh loudly condemning Lizzy's forward, Yankee ways, and Mr. Collins following his boss in an awkward echo.

Lizzy waited for the commotion to die down before supplying, "I suppose you were referring to the article itself? It would have been strange if the school paper didn't cover the incident." Wickham's public display had been huge news across campus, after all— and hard to miss, with so many people posting pictures before security was able to cut him loose.

"We made it very clear to your faculty chair that nothing about the incident was meant to be broadcast through school media. Professor Palmer led me to understand that you were instructed not to write the article, but printed it anyway."

Lizzy raised an eyebrow. "I was advised not to, but 'instructed'? That sounds an awful lot like censorship."

"Your point being?"

Propriety be damned. Lizzy crossed her legs, taking pleasure in the little hitch of distaste on de Bourgh's upper lip. "Look, the article is out there. Can't undo it. No use crying over spilt milk—or loose nuts, as the case may be."

She'd hoped the phrasing might incur another outcry of moral outrage, but instead de Bourgh glared at her. Not so much a glare of dislike, although that emotion was certainly present in her steely blue gaze, but one of calculation. "You're awfully self-assured for someone so young. Pray tell, how does someone of your age get to be quite so confident?"

"Pray tell," Collins echoed with a sneer, until President de Bourgh waved a hand in his direction and he clapped his hand over his mouth, mortified at having spoken out of turn.

This felt like a trap. Lizzy tread carefully. "I don't know. I mean, I always eat my Wheaties...?"

Alas, de Bourgh did not crack even the smallest of smiles. "Tell us, Miss-Know-It-All-Bennet, what should the administration do, rather than—as you put it—cry over spilt milk?"

"Well, I guess I'd put my effort toward trying to find out whoever tied Wickham up in the first place."

Somehow, and Lizzy did not quite know how, she had stepped onto a hidden landmine—because suddenly, de Bourgh smiled. "Marvelous plan, don't you think, Mr. Collins?"

Even Mr. Collins seemed a bit taken aback by the abrupt shift in mood, double-checking his boss's expression before parroting, "Marvelous!"

"Great. I'm glad that's settled." Lizzy rose to her feet, hoping a hasty exit might save her from whatever unpleasantness was bound to follow.

President de Bourgh's voice reached her before she managed to make it out the door. "You'll let us know, won't you? As soon as you figure it out."

"As soon as *I* figure it out?" Lizzy was beginning to understand Mr. Collins's propensity for echoing.

President de Bourgh's smile was a full-on, cat-that-ate-the-canary grin now. "Very generous of you to volunteer to discover who tied George Wickham up in the campus square. Of course, as this is a time-sensitive issue, we'll need an answer by a week from today. Or we'll have to assume that you—as a person with decided interest in seeing Mr. Wickham publicly humiliated—are the culprit. And what do you think the punishment for such a crime should be, Mr. Collins?"

Collins looked thrilled at the sudden power that had been placed into his hands. "Suspension?"

"For an infraction this significant, Mr. Collins? I'd hate to think you'd gone soft."

He was practically quivering now with titillation. "Expulsion."

"Yes, Mr. Collins, I believe that would be the most fitting solution."

Lizzy kept her face composed, not wanting to give either the satisfaction of seeing her panic. And most certainly, it would be satisfaction that these two sadists would feel at the thought of seeing her squirm. "Then I will see you in a week…"

Δλε

It wasn't until she was safely in the windowless stairwell that Lizzy let herself collapse against the wall, sliding down to sit on one of the steps. "Well, shit."

Made in United States
North Haven, CT
13 March 2022

17092153R00143